COWBOY
Ever After

USA *TODAY* BESTSELLING AUTHOR

Jennie Marts

This book is dedicated to my family—
Todd, Nick, Tyler & Paige.
You're the ones who make me believe in real life happily
ever afters.

Thanks for always believing in me.

Chapter One

KAYLEE COLLINS NIBBLED A CRUNCHY cheese doodle and frowned at her laptop screen as she tried to ignore the pleading brown eyes of Gladys, her adorable corgi and self-proclaimed assistant. She never let herself use, or even consider, the words *writer's block*. She just couldn't figure out what was going to happen in the next scene.

In this chapter, she wanted the spitfire red-haired heroine, Sassy Scott, to convince the cute cowboy hero, Duke Ramsey, to do...something...she just couldn't figure out what. And to top it off, there were still a lot of scenes that had to happen between this one and *they lived happily ever after*.

"Any ideas on what the hero could do on a ranch that would show what a great guy he is?" she asked Gladys as she gave in and passed a cheese doodle to the corgi. Her six-year-old canine companion gobbled up the treat but didn't offer any suggestions. She had her head in Kaylee's lap in hopes of a chin scratch and catching any fallen chips. Kaylee pet the pudgy pup's side and chastised herself for not taking the dog for a walk—*again*.

Both of their waistlines could do with some exercise. And some fresh air. She squinted at the date on her laptop. *Ugh.* Apparently, she hadn't left the house in four days. She peered down at her favorite comfy yoga pants and poked an errant brown curl back into her messy bun. Was the stain on her shirt from her coffee this morning, or the spoonful of chocolate ice cream she'd snuck in the middle of the night? At least the characters in her books had active lives, doing…whatever ranchers did all day.

Her cell phone rang as she was typing *common activities done on a ranch* into the search bar. She shivered with dread when she saw the caller's name on the screen.

"Hello," she said, cringing as the remains of the cheese doodle dried up in her mouth.

"Good, I'm glad I caught you. Kaylee, we need to talk," her editor, Faye Montgomery bellowed. Kaylee held the phone away from her ear. Faye spoke as fast as she walked, and she imagined her editor striding through Millennium Park, phone in one hand, takeout coffee—black with one sugar—in the other as her sensible heels beat a staccato rhythm along the sidewalk.

"We got another one," Faye continued, not even pausing to let Kaylee speak. "These bad reviews are killing us. You're a brilliant writer, darling, but you're writing Western romance when you've never even been on a ranch. And it's starting to show. You faked it with that first book or two, but that's not going to work again. You can't just Google 'what do ranchers do all day' and still hope to connect to your readers."

Kaylee snapped her laptop shut as if Faye could actually see her search bar. "I'm—"

"I know what you're going to say, and it's not enough. I'm serious here. Both our behinds are on the line. I'm trying to convince the publisher to sign your next four books, but that won't happen unless something changes. And you know I wouldn't go to bat for you if I didn't believe so much in your writing."

"I appreciate that. And I'm willing to do whatever it takes to improve these books." She meant it. She'd never been afraid of hard work.

"I'm going to hold you to that. Because I've come up with an idea. It's a little out there, but you've *got* to put yourself out there if we're going to save this deal."

"Great. Let's do it. I'm in." She *needed* this deal. Not just to bolster her writing career, but to pay off the credit card debt she'd amassed trying to survive between now and the last advance check she'd received. If she didn't get that contract soon, she'd have to consider moving to the cheaper suburbs. She would've moved already if she hadn't loved Chicago and her apartment so much. Just because she hadn't gone to any cute restaurants or coffee shops lately didn't mean that she didn't still love having the option. And being able to get amazing Thai food delivered at ten o'clock on a weeknight was a luxury she wasn't willing to lose.

"You promise?"

"Yes, of course. Faye. You know how hard I've worked trying to become a full-time author. A career in writing is what I've been working toward my entire life. I *promise* I will do whatever it takes to make this new book the best it can be to help secure another contract. Just tell me what I need to do."

"Great. First you're going to need to get out a suitcase."

Her heart leaped. "Are you sending me on a writing retreat?" She loved the idea of holing up all alone in a cozy cottage on the beach and focusing solely on her book. "What about Gladys? Can I bring her?"

Faye chuckled, sounding more like an evil villain than a guardian angel. "Sure, you can think of this as a writing retreat. I'm sending you to Montana to spend a week at my brother's ranch."

"Montana?" Definitely *not* a cottage on the beach. *And not alone.* "I didn't even know you had a brother."

"Well, I do. And he's agreed to let you stay at our family's ranch in Bartlett, Montana, home to one stoplight and lots of cows."

"Your family has a ranch? What kind of ranch?"

"The kind you've been writing about in your books. Horses, cows, pigs, tractors, hay bales—Dusty Acres has it all. All the stuff you put in your scenes that you've never actually experienced. You, *and* Gladys, are gonna love it."

Kaylee squirmed in her seat. She hadn't left the city in years, and she'd never been west of the Mississippi River. Just thinking about it made her break out in a sweat.

"A ranch in Montana? I don't know."

"I know this makes you uncomfortable, honey. But that's the point. You need to get *out* of your comfort zone. We were just talking last week about how great JD Hawk's books are selling. That guy spent two weeks alone camping out in the middle of grizzly bear country when he was working on *Mountain Justice.* And it showed."

"I do love those books. And of course, I want my books to be that successful." She chewed on her bottom lip. "But don't you have any ideas of how I can get out of my comfort zone and still stay in my apartment? Like maybe some YouTube videos to watch? Or send me a rope, and I'll try to learn how to lasso something."

Gladys whined. Kaylee shook her head and mouthed *not you* as she gave the dog a reassuring neck scratch.

"No. This is just the kind of thing I'm talking about. You're writing about small towns and ranch work, but you've never experienced that sense of community or the ache in your limbs after a hard day's work on the ranch. You need to get out in the country, feed some cows, and get your hands dirty."

Kaylee cringed as she gazed around her tidy apartment.

She was not a fan of getting dirty. She was a fan of being organized, neat, and controlling her surroundings. A cow did not sound like something she could control.

"You promised," Faye said, as if once again, she could read Kaylee's mind.

She let out a sigh. She *had* promised, had just said she'd do *anything* to salvage this book. And it was only for a week. So really, how bad could it be?

"Okay, when do I leave?"

Three days later, Kaylee squinted through the windshield searching for a sign for the town of Bartlett, her eyes itchy and tired from driving the last ten hours. She'd made the trip in two days, deciding to drive instead of fly, figuring the twenty-hour road trip would be easier on Gladys and might be fun. Road trips always looked so great in the movies.

The drive hadn't seemed so bad when she'd first looked at it: get on I-90 and stay there until she reached Montana. But she hadn't factored in the late summer heat, the monotony of the long stretch of highway, or the struggle to find rest stops and hotels that could accommodate both her and the dog's needs.

She blew her bangs out of her eyes, praying she wouldn't lose service *again* as she searched for the exit her navigation system was instructing her to take. She'd already taken two wrong turns as she'd tried to find the small town. The Montana sky was indeed big as it stretched bright and blue in front of her, the highway seeming to go on forever through acres of fields and farmland. But there wasn't a town in sight.

"Why am I doing this again?" she asked Gladys, whose

head was resting on the console between them, the rest of her pudgy body sprawled across the passenger seat. The dog groaned but didn't offer much more of an answer.

She picked up the coffee she'd grabbed at the last gas station and brought it to her lips. Her hand jerked as the car hit a bump in the road and the dark liquid splashed down the front of her new Western shirt. Shrieking at the hot liquid, she pulled to the side of the road as she grabbed a stack of napkins and dabbed at the pearly buttoned front.

She'd already been regretting the 'Western' outfit the salesgirl had talked her into at the only shop she'd found in Chicago that carried anything resembling Western wear. The girl had assured her this was what women wore in Montana. But the outfit was nothing like Kaylee's normal attire. She liked soft tones, pastel colors, and from the looks of her closet as she'd been packing, a lot of black and beige. The kind of colors that let a person blend into the background.

There was no blending in this outfit.

The hot pink shirt was too bright for her taste, the high-heeled, pointy-toed cowboy boots had been pinching her toes all day, and the sparkly rhinestone belt was sure to draw too much attention.

She held back tears as she dabbed at the front of her sticky shirt. Her back was damp with sweat, her feet hurt, her head ached, and she was exhausted after a restless night's sleep in an unfamiliar and uncomfortable motel bed.

"What am I doing here?" she asked the dog.

Gladys belly-crawled across the console and into her lap. She licked the coffee from Kaylee's chin and then rested her head on her human's chest. Kaylee dropped her chin, nuzzling her face into the dog's furry neck. The corgi might not have any answers, but she always knew how to make her feel better.

"It's not too late to turn around. Who would know?"

Her cell phone rang, and Kaylee let out a groan as she

saw Faye's name on the screen. Faye would know. She swallowed, trying to pull herself together as she remembered her promise and answered the phone.

"Have you made it to Bartlett yet?" Faye's voice blared through the speakers.

"Not yet. I think I'm lost. I've taken two wrong turns already. My navigation says my turn is right up ahead, but there's no town in sight. All I see is this giant circular thing that looks like it could contain a missile or something."

Faye chuckled. "That's not a missile site. It's a grain elevator. And if you can see that, then you're almost there. Your turnoff is right before it. You can't see the town because it's down in the valley along the river. Wait 'til you see it, though. It's gorgeous this time of year. Nothing beats summertime in Montana. You're going to love it."

"I'm not so sure about that."

"Uh-oh. What's wrong? Spill it, Kaylee."

She already had, right down the front of her shirt. "It's been a bit of a rough day. And this is all so new and different."

"And nothing like your perfectly controlled environment."

Kaylee sighed. "Yes, but it's not just that. It's having to make small talk and trying to hold interesting conversations with folks I've never met. And you know I'm not good with people."

"This isn't *people*. This is just my brother. And a bunch of animals, and they don't care if your conversation is interesting, as long as you feed them."

A semi truck sped by, too close for Kaylee's comfort, and she gripped the steering wheel tighter as her car rocked in its wake. "Are you sure there isn't another way?"

"I'm sure. Besides, you promised you'd give this a try. It amazes me how you're so apprehensive in real life, but you can write these bold characters like Sassy and Duke who are smart and brave and constantly throwing themselves into new adventures."

"Because those characters are *fictional*. They're how I *wish* I could be, but they're not me."

"They could be. Listen, I've got another idea."

She gulped as her stomach clenched. "Oh gosh, I'm still trying to get up the nerve to go through with your first idea."

Faye laughed again. "You'll like this one. Every time you start to retreat back into your shell or shy away from doing something, I want you to ask yourself, 'What would Sassy do?'"

What would Sassy do?

She thought back to the scene she'd written that morning where Sassy Scott strode confidently up to the dark-haired, steely-blue-eyed hero, Duke Ramsey, and gave him a piece of her mind.

Sassy wasn't intimidated by anyone. Not even the handsome Duke, whose muscled forearms stretched the sleeves of his faded blue T-shirt as he tipped the front of his black Stetson toward the feisty heroine. Duke was the epitome of every hot cowboy Kaylee could put together in her mind: tall, sandy brown hair worn just a little too long, strong jaw covered in just a shadow of whiskers, with a cowboy boot saunter and a flirty grin that could charm even the hardest of hearts.

But Sassy was immune to his charms, at least for the first third of the book. Kaylee often tried to imagine herself as the confident redheaded barrel-racer, envisioning herself doing the courageous acts she wrote for Sassy.

She groaned. "You know I'd love to be as brave and daring as Sassy. Too bad I'm afraid of horses and haven't done a courageous act since middle school when I decided to get bangs."

"You can do this," Faye told her, dismissing her concerns. "The town is right ahead of you—you're almost there. I believe in you. And just remember—whenever you start having doubts or feeling like you can't do this, I want you to channel your inner Sassy and do what she would do."

Kaylee took a deep breath and pushed her shoulders back. *What would Sassy do?* She sure wouldn't be sitting in her car pulled over on the side of the road trying not to cry over a spilled coffee or a new opportunity on a ranch. "Okay," she said, trying to keep the tremble out of her voice. "I'll do it."

"Thatta girl. Now I want you to lift your chin up and get back on the road. Oh, and I was going to tell you to stop at the grocery store on your way through town and grab yourself a snack and a twelve-pack of Diet Coke. I know how you love that stuff, and I doubt there'll be any on the ranch."

"Thanks, Faye." Kaylee took a deep breath and pulled back onto the highway. Other than the semi, not a single car had driven by her while she's been pulled over. She slowed as she got to the grain elevator, and sure enough, there *was* a turnoff. And Faye was right. The road led her down into a valley where a beautiful little town was nestled against the river.

Bartlett, Montana appeared to be five blocks wide and about fifteen blocks long. Kaylee could see a park in the middle of town and the steeples of at least three churches. The sun sparkled off the river as she drove down the main street marveling at the quaint storefronts, barrels of bright flowers spilling over their edges, and streetlights fashioned to resemble old-fashioned gas lamps. American flags waved proudly from their perches in front of the shops, and window fronts gleamed as they showed off their displays. It was as if Kaylee had driven into a charming slice of Americana. She just hoped the reality lived up to the illusion.

She found the grocery store and pulled into a spot, leaving the windows rolled down for Gladys. "I'll just be a minute," she told the corgi.

The heels of her fancy boots clacked against the tile floor as she headed to the soda aisle and grabbed a twelve-pack of Diet Coke. In the bakery section, she paused, thinking it might be good to show up with a dessert in hand. She peered over the array of glossy fruit pies and chocolate cakes. *Which one?* She chewed her lip, the weight of the decision bearing down on her shoulders.

Come on. This isn't rocket science. Just pick a dang cake.

A gorgeous carrot cake with swirls of whipped cream cheese frosting was sitting closest to her. It was already packaged in a box. Perfect. She tucked the soda carton under her arm, then grabbed the box and took it with her to the register.

After she set her items on the conveyor belt, she tossed a package of peanut butter cups down with them. She told herself the cake and some chocolate was enough, but her traitorous hand grabbed a Snickers and a bag of Cheetos and added them to the pile.

The cashier was a woman about her own age, but with sleek dark hair pulled up into a perfect ponytail. As she rang up the purchases, she said, "You must be the author."

Kaylee looked down at herself, as if her profession were showing like the hem of an untucked shirt. "How can you tell?"

The woman gestured to Kaylee's car. "Rental car with out-of-state plates. We don't get a lot of visitors around here. Especially famous ones."

Kaylee ducked her head. "I'm hardly famous."

"Sure you are. We carry your books in the store, and I've read every one. I love them. The whole town knows you're coming." She pointed to her name tag. "I'm Marnie, by the way. You just get here?"

Kaylee nodded. "Just pulled in. Nice to meet you. I'm Kaylee."

"I know." The cashier laughed, but Kaylee wasn't sure if

it was with her or at her. "You heading out to Dusty Acres now?"

She nodded again, her cheeks warming. This was just the kind of thing she'd been worried about—small talk with strangers. How much information was too much, and how much was not enough? She often used small town gossip as a plot device in her books, but she had no idea how often it really happened, if at all.

Marnie paused to holler toward the back of the store. "Hey Caleb, bring me a box of Lucky Charms, would you?" She turned back to Kaylee. "Luke's out of cereal. And Lucky Charms are his favorite."

"Oh, okay. Good to know."

Before she could think of anything else to say, a teenage stock boy ran out from one of the aisles and dropped a box of cereal on the conveyor belt. "Here you go, ma'am."

"Thanks," she mumbled as Marnie ran the box across the scanner and dropped it into her bag. She passed the cashier her debit card, her ears warm as she tried not to think about how the pretty cashier knew not only that her new host was out of breakfast cereal, but also what kind was his favorite.

"See you around," Marnie said as she passed her back the card with her receipt. "Tell Luke I said hey."

She stuttered another "thank you" as she grabbed the bags and the cake box and hurried out of the store.

A blond-haired girl of around nine or ten was standing next to her car, her hand outstretched as she scratched Gladys' neck. The corgi was leaning her head out the window, her eyes closed in doggy bliss as she extended her neck out to take full advantage of the girl's pets.

"I love your dog," the girl said, smiling openly at her. "She's so cute. What's her name?"

"Gladys."

The girl's smile widened. "I like that name. It's funny.

My name's Emma." She giggled as Gladys licked her cheek. "I think she likes me."

"I think so too." Kaylee couldn't help but smile back at the girl. Talking to kids had always been easier for her than conversing with adults. She peered around trying to figure out where the girl had come from. "Do you live around here, Emma?"

The girl tilted her head to the side. "No. We live on a farm outside of town. My dad's just picking up some grain." She nodded toward the feed store a few doors down from the grocery.

As if on cue, a tall, good-looking man carrying a large brown bag on his shoulder came out the doors. He wore cowboy boots, jeans, and a Western shirt, and his close-cropped beard matched the brown hair just visible under the rim of his Stetson.

Kaylee's pulse quickened. Her first sighting of a real cowboy.

The man dumped the bag into the back of a beat-up truck sitting a few spaces from Kaylee's car, then offered her an easy smile and a friendly wave. "Hope you don't mind my daughter petting your dog. She's never met a stranger. She seems to think everyone's her friend."

I could use a friend in this town.

Kaylee waved back. "Not at all. Gladys is loving the attention."

"Come on, squirt. We need to get home," he told the girl who gave the dog another neck cuddle.

"Bye Gladys," she said then waved before skipping around to the other side of the truck.

"Bye Emma," Kaylee called as she opened the back door and put her bounty on the seat. Gladys jumped into the back and sniffed the box, then lay down next to it as if she were guarding a priceless treasure. Either that, or she was hoping a piece might fall out on the drive to the ranch.

Five minutes later, the corgi might've gotten her wish, given the bumpiness of the last bit of dirt road leading up to the ranch. Kaylee's teeth jarred as she bounced over the ruts. Her cell service had gone out again, but she followed Faye's earlier directions of going over the bridge, then turning right at the big white barn with the American flag painted on its side. Kaylee was supposed to stay on that road for about a mile, then watch for the sign for the ranch. Faye had described the house as an old yellow farmhouse next to a big red barn and a pond.

Despite the rough road and vague directions, Kaylee couldn't help but be awed by the gorgeous landscape spread out in front of her. She was still in the valley, the lush green fields spreading for miles before butting up against a range of majestic mountains. Small farms dotted the countryside, some with shiny new farm equipment and sunlight glinting off the silver aluminum of Quonset huts, and some older and in slight disrepair.

Rolling down the window, she caught the scents of freshly mown grass and overturned earth. Wild sunflowers grew in the roadside ditches, their petals reaching for the sun like toddlers raising their arms to be held. Then Kaylee spotted the small sparkling pond spread out next to a large red barn and a two-story yellow farmhouse, all against the backdrop of the mountains. She gasped at the picture-perfect scene.

It was just as Faye described. Only better.

She slowed the car and drove under the large cedar arches proclaiming, *Dusty Acres Ranch*. She couldn't believe her editor, the woman who wore power suits and Louboutin heels, had grown up here.

Split-rail fencing lined the long driveway, and she passed several horses serenely munching grass. A wide front porch wrapped around the farmhouse, with a set of rocking chairs and a quilt-covered swing. Chickens roamed freely in front of a small fenced-in chicken coop and through her open window, she heard the low mournful bawl of a cow. The ranch was charming and full of character. As if she wasn't enchanted enough, seeing the cat sprawled lazily in a patch of sunlight on the front porch swing completely did her in.

She hadn't even opened her door, but she already loved everything about this place.

If only she didn't have to spend her time here with some strange guy she'd never met before.

That thought had her slumping in her seat as she let out a weary sigh. "We made it," she told Gladys as the corgi leaned forward and licked her ear.

They'd survived the twenty-hour road trip, the bad motel bed, the spotty navigation, and a somewhat nosy grocery clerk.

But now the real adventure was about to begin.

Chapter Two

*L*UKE MONTGOMERY POURED A SCOOP of grain into the empty trough, then slammed the stall door behind him. The horse inside stamped his foot and let out an insulted whinny.

"Sorry," Luke told Max, his black gelding. "I'm not mad at you. This whole situation just gets my goat."

A brown and white billy goat lifted his head from where he was stealing a mouthful of fresh hay from Max's stall.

"Not you, either." He shook his head as he tossed the scoop back into the grain bin. "Where does my sister get off saddling me with one of her problems? I've got enough problems of my own without taking on a city girl from Chicago who's probably expecting a luxury spa or dude ranch experience."

The horse whinnied again, as if in response.

"I know. I know. I owe Faye. Which is the only reason I agreed to this cockamamie idea in the first place."

He knew his sister, and how different things were for her in the city and the high-powered field of publishing. Hosting one of her authors sounded like a lot of work. And who knew what kind of expectations she would have? Last time Faye had been home, she'd been miffed she couldn't find some fancy multi-grain cereal at the local grocery store. Luke had offered to put some sticks and oats from the horse's feed into a bowl for her, but she hadn't appreciated his humor.

He lived a simple life and found peace in farming his land and taking care of his animals. He didn't care about lavish restaurants or complicated coffee drinks. It was easy for him to imagine a high-falutin' city girl who was used to all those things looking down her nose at his modest ranch.

His cell phone buzzed. He pulled it from his pocket and frowned as he tapped the screen and held the phone to his ear. "Hey Sis."

"Is she there yet?" His sister's voice boomed from the phone, direct and to the point.

"Not yet."

"I thought she'd be there by now. I gave her directions, but a couple of those turns are kind of tricky. Does that old white barn still have an American flag painted on its side?"

"Yep."

"Then I'm sure she'll find it. She's a little unsure of herself sometimes, but she's smart."

"If she doesn't show up in the next half hour, I'll go look for her."

"Thanks, Luke." His sister's voice softened. "You're a sweetheart."

He grunted. "Don't let it get around."

She laughed. "Text me when she gets there. Love you. Bye."

"Bye," he replied, but she'd already hung up.

The sound of a car drew his attention to the window of the barn. "She's here," he announced to the horse and the goat.

His phone buzzed again, and he rolled his eyes as he assumed his sister had forgotten to give him another piece of her sage advice. Instead, the Caller ID read *Dean Austin,* his best friend since grade school.

"Hey Dean," he said, peering through the window as the compact SUV pulled up in front of the house. "What's up?"

"Just checking to see if she got there yet? I think Emma and I might've just met her coming out of the grocery store."

Dang. The woman had only been in town a minute and this was the second call about her. "She just pulled up."

"What do you think?"

"I don't know. I haven't even seen her. Like I said, she *just* pulled up."

"I want a full report. She seemed nice. And I think having an author visit sounds interesting."

"You would."

"You're not gonna tell her about...?"

"No, of course not."

"Good. Just checking," Dean said.

"I gotta go. You still coming out in the morning to help me feed those cows in the south pasture?"

"I'll be there."

"See ya then," Luke said.

"See ya. Don't forget, I want a full report."

Luke shook his head, hoping there wouldn't be much to report on, as he ended the call and pushed the phone back into his pocket. He had work to do and would be happy if she spent the whole time sequestered in her room with her laptop.

He stayed where he was, observing the newcomer as she got out of the car and opened the back door. "Get a load of that outfit," he told the golden retriever who'd been stretched out asleep in a warm patch of sun, but was now up and wiggling at Luke's feet, anxious to run out and greet the new visitor. "Hold your horses," he told the dog. He wanted another minute to watch what she would do.

What in the world is she wearing?

That hot pink shirt was practically neon, and the sun glinted off all the sparkly rhinestones on the belt circling her waist. She reached into the back seat and pulled out a light pink cowboy hat. She put it on and regarded her reflection in the car window. Her shoulders slumped, and she took it off and started to put it back in the car. Her lips were moving, and she appeared to be holding a conversation with herself as she paused and pulled it out again then lifted her chin and pushed the hat firmly on her head.

She turned around, and Luke got his first good look at her as she peered around the ranch. Her brown hair was shoulder length and curly, the ends forming wings around the crown of the cowboy hat. The outfit screamed city slicker, but he caught himself admiring how well her jeans hugged her curvy figure. Her face seemed open and friendly and carried almost an expression of awe as she took in the barn and the farmhouse. Even with her small, upturned nose, she didn't actually look all that snooty. In fact, with her obviously new cowboy hat tilted jauntily on her head, she looked kind of cute.

Cute?

Yeah, cute. And a little bashful as she shifted from one foot to the other, looking nervously from the house to the barn. She rubbed her palms on the front of her jeans then snatched the cowboy hat off one more time.

"I can't watch this anymore," he told the dog and headed out the door.

Her back was to him as he came out of the barn. He grinned as he noticed the hat was back in place as she reached into the backseat and pulled out a white bakery box.

"Hey there," he called. The dog raced ahead of him then sat obediently at the newcomer's feet, his tail wagging furiously as he whined to be pet.

"Aren't you the sweetest?" the woman said, bending to give the dog's chin a scratch. Straightening, she turned to him, a smile already in place. "Your dog's adora—" She stopped midsentence, her chin dropping as her smile fell.

Her hands fumbled the cake box, then she gripped it tighter as she tilted her head and stared at him, her mouth open like a gaping fish. "Duke?" she asked, an incredulous tone to her voice.

Duke?

"Nope," he said shaking his head. Maybe she *was* more aloof than he'd thought if she hadn't even taken the time to learn his name. "Luke. Luke Montgomery. And you must be Kaylee."

She shook her head as if to clear it, and he could see her visibly trying to collect herself. "Of course. Luke, yes. Absolutely. I knew that." Her eyes narrowed as she studied him, and he wondered if he still had some leftover lunch on his face. "I'm sorry," she said, tilting her head the other direction. "You just look exactly like...well...like someone else I know."

With the way her face had paled, and the way she was eyeing him, he wondered if the person he reminded her of had maybe passed away. She sure looked like she'd seen a ghost.

"Well, it's good to meet ya," he said. "My sister speaks real highly of you."

"You too." She shifted to her other foot and gazed around the ranch as if searching for something to say. She held out the cake box towards him as if she just remembered she was holding it. "I brought you a cake."

"Great. I love cake. As long as it isn't carrot. Never understood why someone would think grating a vegetable into a dessert would be a good idea."

Pink tinged her cheeks as she peered down at the box.

Oh, dang. He had a feeling there was a vegetable cake inside it. They were off to a great start. He was acting like a dork. Why would he say that about the cake? *And* he'd already embarrassed her. Although it *was* kind of cute the way her cheeks flushed.

There he went again. What was with him and this *cute* nonsense? And why was she making him feel like he was in junior high again and unable to talk to a girl?

He was saved from saying anything else by a mother goose who walked out from behind the barn, her three goslings waddling along behind her. They headed toward Kaylee, but only because they had to pass behind her car on their way to the lake.

Kaylee's face lit with excitement. "Oh, how sweet," she cooed, taking a step toward the mother goose.

Luke held a warning hand out. "I wouldn't get too close to that..."

Too late. The mother goose already had her feathers ruffled as she sensed danger to her goslings. She opened her mouth wide and released a menacing hiss as she made a run at Kaylee.

Kaylee let out a terrified shriek and launched herself towards Luke, smashing the cake box between them as she flung herself into his arms.

His arms automatically wrapped around her waist, as if some primal instinct to protect her kicked in. *Yeah, real tough, protect the city girl from the big bad goose.* Although he was a grown man, and he still got the creeps when a dang goose hissed at him. Which must be why he kept one arm securely around Kaylee as he shooed the goose and her goslings towards the lake.

"You okay?" he asked, peering down at the woman. The cake had smashed through the corners of the box, and globs of white frosting smeared across the front of her shirt and into the ends of her hair.

"Oh my gosh," she said, her eyes wide and her hands still clutching the crumpled cake box as she took a step away. "I'm so sorry. I can't believe I did that." Thick splotches of frosting covered the front of his shirt as well, and she reached up to wipe at the blob he could feel clinging to his chin. Then she jerked her hand back as if his skin was on fire. "I'll buy you a new shirt."

He shook his head with a mild annoyance at city folks and their need to throw money at every problem. But she seemed genuinely upset. "Don't worry about it. This shirt has seen a lot worse than a little frosting." He brushed at the front of his faded blue T-shirt, then scooped the frosting from under his chin and flung it on the ground. The golden retriever raced to the spot and lapped at the white confection.

He licked the remaining bits from his fingers. "Not bad."

Her shoulders hunched as she tried to scrape the frosting from her shirt. She looked miserable. He wanted to tell her not to worry, it was just a little frosting, but his words didn't seem to be making much of an impression. He looked around, and this time it was his turn to be searching for what to say. She had a nice smile, but now she just looked sad and uncomfortable, and he found himself wanting to draw that smile out again.

He gestured towards the open back door of her car. "You might not want to leave your door open like that. You never know what kind of critter could climb in around here."

Ugh. What he thought was a joke fell flat as she looked even more embarrassed.

"As long as it isn't a goose," she said, pressing her hand to her stained chest. "That thing scared the heck out of me. I didn't even know they could do that. That hiss was like something between a snake and a dragon."

He chuckled. "Yeah, they are scary when they feel like their goslings are threatened." He held up his hand. "Not that you were threatening them. They just get that way." Why couldn't he seem to talk to this woman?

She flicked another glob of frosting to the ground as she

reached for the door. But instead of closing it, she opened it wider.

"What the heck is that?" He tilted his head as a funny-looking creature lumbered out of Kaylee's backseat and headed for the frosting.

"That's Gladys. My dog."

"What happened to the rest of her legs?" he asked as his golden raced toward the other dog. The two of them wiggled happily around each other, taking turns sniffing each other and licking at the remaining frosting on the ground.

She pushed her shoulders back, bristling at his comment. "Nothing *happened* to them. She's a corgi. They have short legs."

"Huh. I've heard of them, but I guess I've never seen one before." He squatted down and the dog loped toward him, licking first at his hand then at the splotches of frosting remaining on his shirt. *Off to a great start, dude.* First you insult the cake she brings, then you insult her dog. At least she now seemed more miffed than embarrassed. He ruffled the fur around the dog's neck, and she leaned into his hand. "You're a good girl, aren't ya?" He peered up at Kaylee. "Sorry about that. Didn't mean any offense. She seems like a real sweet dog."

"She's the best." A small smile of pride now tugged at the corner of her lips. "Yours seems sweet too. What's his name?"

"That doofus is Cooper." He laughed as the dog raced around his legs then lay on the ground next to the corgi, his tongue hanging out one side of his mouth. "He seems to be showing off for Gladys." At least the dogs were getting along, and Cooper didn't seem to care if he was making a fool of himself in front of the other dog. "You probably wanna get settled. Why don't I help you grab your stuff and show you your room?"

"That would be great. But I can get it." She opened the

back end of the compact SUV and reached for the suitcase.

"I got it," he said, taking the handle of the bag. "Faye would skin me alive if I let you carry in your own stuff."

She let out a small laugh, and the soft sound made his chest feel funny. "I wouldn't want to be responsible for that." She handed him a duffle bag then hoisted the backpack and a small tote bag on her shoulder. "I hope it's okay for Gladys to sleep in my room."

He shrugged as he closed the hatchback. "Doesn't bother me. You can have as many animals as you want in your room. We've got a bunch of barn cats around here you can bring in, and we've got a goat who I'm sure would love to cuddle up to you in bed. I won't even charge you extra. But I may draw the line at a cow. They snore too loud."

She laughed, the sound somewhere between a giggle and a snort. He liked it and found himself laughing with her before he could stop himself.

He didn't usually consider himself a funny guy. In fact, if truth be told, he was often a bit of a grouch. But something about this woman, with her adorable laugh and her funny-looking dog, and the endearing way she blushed, had him wracking his brain trying to come up with something else witty to say as he led her toward the house.

Kaylee followed Luke into the house, thankful she had a minute out of his line of sight to collect herself.

She'd spent the last several hours of her drive rehearsing what she would say upon meeting Faye's brother. How she would channel her inner Sassy and come off as calm, cool and collected. But of all the ways she'd imagined meeting her host, shrieking in terror and smashing a cake into his chest while trying to climb him like a tree had not been among them.

And that was just the start of the craziness. She was also mortified that she'd called him Duke. Although as she followed his broad shoulders into the farmhouse, she was still marveling at the striking resemblance Luke Montgomery had to her fictional hero, Duke Ramsey.

She'd almost fainted when he'd come out of the barn. He was the spitting image of Duke, as if her imagined hero had come to life. He had the same crystal blue eyes, the just too-long thick sandy brown hair, even down to the black cowboy hat and the charming grin he wore as he'd sauntered toward her in a pair of jeans and square-toed cowboy boots.

But he wasn't Duke. Because Duke wasn't real. He was the made-up man she'd created. A hodge-podge of all her favorite classic Western heroes and celebrity crushes: a dash of John Wayne, a little Robert Redford, some Sam Elliott, a bit of Kevin Costner and Cole Hauser, and a whole lot of Chris Hemsworth.

Luke was Faye's brother—her *brother*. Not some eye-candy cowboy for Kaylee to be drooling over and fantasizing about.

Wait. Who said anything about fantasizing about Luke?

Get it together, girl.

Kaylee's thoughts about Duke—er, Luke—were forgotten as she stepped into the old farmhouse. The inside must have been renovated at some point, because it now had an open concept, with a big kitchen on one side and a large family room on the other. A huge stone fireplace went up the far wall, flanked by shelves bursting with books. An overstuffed tan sofa and a couple of recliners circled a square coffee table and faced toward the fireplace.

The walls were painted a soft moss green, and the deco-rations were modern farmhouse mixed with log cabin. The kitchen held modern appliances, but the wide countertop of the center island seemed to be made from some type of reclaimed wood, its surface smooth from sanding. A sign proclaiming *Faith, Family, and Friends Welcome Here* hung above the archway leading down the hallway.

"Wow. I love your house," Kaylee said, following Luke into the kitchen and setting the mangled cake box on the counter. She nodded toward the sink. "May I?"

"Sure, cost you a quarter though," he said.

She pulled her hands back from reaching toward the faucet then laughed as she realized he was teasing her. Was he flirting with her? Or was she just so used to being alone in her house that she was misinterpreting the attention of the first man she'd spent any time with in months?

"I'm just kidding," he said, setting down her bag and holding out a towel.

She lifted the faucet with her arm then squirted a pump of soap into her palm. Rubbing her hands together under the water, she looked up and gasped at the amazing view of the mountains from the big window above the sink. In the forefront, the sun sparkled off the pond, and Kaylee could see wild roses climbing along the split-rail fence surrounding the backyard.

"It's so beautiful here. This view is incredible."

Luke stepped nearer, and her skin warmed at the closeness of him as he peered out the window. "Yeah, it is. I guess I spend so much time here, I sometimes forget to appreciate what a pretty sight it is."

"Oh gosh, I can't imagine ever taking this view for granted. I live in a third-floor apartment, and all I can see out my kitchen window is the red brick of the apartment building across the alley and maybe on a good day, I can catch a glimpse of the dumpster down there."

He laughed. "Well, at least for the next few days, you can look at something new. And no dumpsters in sight." He pointed outside. "You'll have this same view from your room. The windows in there face the same direction. You can wake up to see the mountains every morning you're here."

She let out a sigh as she dried her hands. "Amazing."

He picked up her bags again and led her down the hall and into the first room on the right. "I put you in here. This is Faye's old room."

Kaylee stepped inside. The walls were painted a light tranquil gray, and the furniture consisted of a dresser, an antique roll-top desk, and a bed with a thick padded headboard. A pink and white quilt covered the bed, its squares a burst of floral patterns, which somehow seemed to match the large print of a pink peony hanging above the headboard. A white milk glass vase filled with blue and purple wildflowers sat on the side table next to what looked like an original pink rotary dial phone. Gauzy lace curtains fluttered around a large picture window that boasted the view Luke had told her about.

She let out a sigh. "It's lovely."

"Thanks." Luke shrugged. "Pink's not really my thing, but my wife decorated it, and she wanted it to feel new yet still keep Faye's personality and some of her things, so she'll feel at home when she comes to visit."

Kaylee stilled.

His wife?

Chapter Three

O F COURSE HE HAD A wife.

I mean look at the guy.

Kaylee's heart pounded against her chest as she twisted the handle of her tote bag between her fingers. *Get over it.* Why should it matter to her? She wasn't here for romance. She was here to save her writing career.

She forced her lips into what she hoped was a pleasant smile. "I look forward to meeting her. Your wife, that is."

"Oh, no. I'm not married anymore. Well, I am, I guess. Technically. Just not...she's not here. I mean, she died."

Kaylee gasped as she covered her mouth with her hand. "Oh my gosh. I'm so sorry."

Luke shook his head. "I don't know why that was so hard to say. She's been gone five years now. She was in an accident." He shrugged again, but there was no mistaking the pain etched on his face. "I guess I thought Faye would have told you."

"No, she didn't." And she was going to hear about leaving that important detail out. It seemed like her editor was just tossing her into the deep end and letting her sink or swim.

Her gaze was still on Luke, and she held back another sigh.

She could think of worse ways to drown.

Heat warmed her cheeks again as she grasped for something to say, something that would wash that look of pain from his face. "It's hard. My mom died when I was a teenager, and I still miss her. Sometimes it feels like a long time ago, and other times it seems like she was just here yesterday."

Oh, geez. Was that the right thing to say? Comparing the loss of a parent to the loss of a spouse? She should just shut up now.

Stepping farther into the room, she set her backpack on the bed then leaned toward the dresser, where an array of photos of Faye were clustered. A much younger Faye.

There was one of her in a cheerleading uniform, one of her in pigtails and a cowboy hat sitting astride a horse, and one where she was grinning as she held up a fish with what looked like the pond next to the farmhouse in the background. There was one with her standing in between a younger version of Luke and another boy who looked like a combination of the two, goofing around in front of an old green tractor, their heads tipped together, laughing, with Faye's arms wrapped around each of their shoulders.

Kaylee shook her head. "It's so hard to imagine the formidable Faye Montgomery as a Montana farm girl."

Luke let out a soft chuckle. "Yeah, she was something back in the day. But we knew she'd never stay in Montana— she was always destined for something more. Our mom died too, when we were kids, and Faye took on the role of mother as well as big sister to our other brother and me. Which made it that much harder for her to leave, even though she'd been dreaming about it for years. I practically forced her to keep her plans for college, then our dad died, and I got married, and after that, there was no reason for her to come back to the ranch. I mean, she comes back to visit, sure, but Chicago suits her much better than this place ever did."

"She's an amazing woman," Kaylee said. "Ferocious in her role as editor, but kind too. She's always treated me well, and I have the utmost respect for your sister." She was seeing Faye in a whole new light. "I can see how she'd take on that extra role. She's a bit like a mom to me too—but not a cookie-baking mom. More like a stern, 'you're grounded if you don't meet your deadline' kind of mom."

A laugh burst from Luke, and the sound warmed Kaylee's insides. "Yeah, I can see that. I'm a grown man, and she's still mothering me. She pays a couple of local gals to come out here and clean the place twice a month, and she worked out a deal for the diner to drop off a meal a couple of times a week." He flashed her a grin. "She even texts me every night to make sure I've brushed my teeth before I go to bed."

Kaylee's eyes widened. "She does?"

Luke laughed again. "No, I'm just kidding about that. But she really does do the other stuff." He lifted the suitcase and set it on the bed next to her backpack. "Speaking of cleaning up, I ought to let you get settled and get back to work. Those stalls in the barn aren't going to clean themselves." He waved as he backed out the door. "Bathroom's across the hall."

"Thanks," she said, but he was already gone. She dropped her purse on the desk and headed for the bathroom to try to clean off her shirt. Gladys, who'd been sniffing out the perimeter of the bedroom followed her in and flopped on the floor.

She groaned as she caught sight of herself in the mirror. Her curls had gone nuts in the heat, and they looked like they were clinging to the pink hat like the tendrils of a vine. Her shirt was splotched and stained, and one side hung loose at her waist. It must have come untucked during her scare with the goose. She was a complete mess.

A stack of towels sat on the side of the sink, and she

used a washcloth to rinse her face and scrub the stains from her shirt. She took off the hat and finger-combed her hair.

A few minutes later she emerged from the bathroom and walked into the kitchen to find Luke eating a piece of the mangled cake. He'd scraped a chunk from the box into a bowl and was scooping up bites with a spoon.

"Oh gosh. Why are you eating that? I thought you hated *vegetable* cake."

"*Hate's* a bit of a strong word." He scooped another bite onto his spoon. "Besides, you went to all the effort to bring a dessert. I figured the least I could do was to have a piece. And vegetable or not, it's still cake."

"You make a valid point," she told him. "Any chance you've got another bowl?"

He chuckled as he opened the cupboard behind him and took down a bowl. "Spoon's in the drawer to your right." Using the side of a spatula, he scraped a mess of mangled cake and frosting into the bowl and passed it to her.

"This was *not* how I imagined this cake business would go," she said, taking a spoon from the drawer and easing onto a stool across the counter from him. "What a disaster."

She cringed as she thought about the box she'd squished between them and the frosting that had splattered all over him. She'd written plenty of scenes where the hero or heroine reaches up to brush a tiny smudge of flour or whipped cream from the other's face. It was always wildly romantic as their fingers brushed the other's cheek or came close to their parted lips. But it was always the barest trace.

Never in her novels had she written where the hero had close to a quarter cup of frosting blob clinging to his finely chiseled jaw.

Luke lifted one shoulder. "It all gets mixed up once it goes in your mouth anyway. This way, we're just saving a step." He offered her a sheepish grin. "You say disaster, I say efficient."

She laughed and reached to cover her mouth so she didn't spray him with cake crumbs. "I like the way you think."

He licked the last bit of frosting from his spoon and dumped it and his bowl in the sink. "I'd better leave you to get settled," he said, heading for the front door. "I'm sure you've got some unpacking and writing to do. Make yourself at home. I'll be back around six to put together something for dinner. Hope you're not expecting anything fancy. We've got beanies and weenies on the menu for tonight."

Beanies and weenies?

What the heck did that mean? But it was too late to ask. Luke had already slipped out the door. Kaylee scraped the last of the cream cheese frosting from her bowl—it really was a pretty good cake—and carried it to the sink.

She headed down the hall, the peace and solitude of the pretty pink bedroom drawing her forward like bees to nectar. All she wanted to do was kick off the painful boots and crawl under that wonderful thick comforter and take a nap. But she wasn't here to nap. Or to sit in her room. She was here to find out what life on a ranch was really like. So, as tempted as she was to retreat to her room—and she was *seriously* tempted; she could practically feel the weight of the comforter on her shoulders—she knew she couldn't succumb to the temptation. Instead, she channeled her inner Sassy and grabbed a notebook and pen from her backpack and marched after Luke.

She considered changing her shirt, but Faye had warned her that she needed to get her hands dirty. Why mess up another item of clothing?

The air was warm and dry, so different from the humidity-soaked air in Chicago, and she stopped at the bottom of the porch steps to breathe it in. She could hear noise coming from the barn, so she headed that direction, hoping to find Luke.

She paused again inside the barn door, flipping open her

notebook and scribbling down notes as she tried to capture the feel of the barn. It was cooler in here and smelled like hay and earth and old leather. Gladys ran in behind her, the dog's wide fanny wiggling with excitement as she raced from one delicious new scent to another.

Kaylee was sure the corgi was discovering a whole new array of scents other than the few she'd just written down. If only the dog could type.

She had to smile at her pudgy pet, though. She hadn't seen the dog this excited since she accidentally spilled a bowl of ice cream on the floor last summer. Seriously—she couldn't even remember the last time she'd seen the corgi *run* anywhere.

Luke was inside, a pitchfork in his hand as he scooped hay out of one of the horse stalls. Cooper ran out to greet Gladys, and the two dogs zipped around each other like they hadn't been together in weeks.

Although if she were being honest, her heart was racing at the sight of Luke, who'd stopped his work and was leaning casually on the end of the pitchfork, and she'd just seen him ten minutes ago, too. Back when he'd told her he had work to do and she should go to her room and get settled in, which sounded like a nice way of telling her to leave him alone and let him get his chores done.

"What are you doing out here?"

Did she detect a note of annoyance in his voice?

She took a step back. *This was stupid.* She'd gotten some good material already. She should just go back to her room and write.

Stop it. She'd only jotted down a few notes. Detailing the leather and hay-scented barn would hardly fill a chapter. She swallowed and forced her shoulders back then walked over to the stall. "I'm here to help."

Luke's brow furrowed. "Help with what?"

"With whatever you're doing."

He raised an eyebrow. "You want to help muck out stalls?"

"I'm not sure what that means, but if it's an authentic ranch activity, then yes, I'm all in."

"Look, I know you're here to help with your writing, so why don't you take a nice walk through the fields or sit on the porch swing." His gaze traveled up and down her outfit. "I don't think you want to ruin your fancy duds there. This is pretty messy work."

She bristled. "I'm not afraid to get my hands dirty. And this shirt is practically ruined anyway." She peered around at the work Luke had been doing in the stall and formed a pretty good idea about what "mucking" entailed, and she fought to keep from wincing at the job. That porch swing idea suddenly seemed a lot more appealing.

Would Sassy sit on the porch swing? No. She would roll up her sleeves and get messy.

"I told you. I'm here to have some authentic experiences, so put me to work."

He eyed her for a moment—just long enough for her palms to start to sweat—then lifted his shoulders in a shrug. "All right. Suit yourself." He held out the pitchfork. "I don't think it's much of a stretch to assume you've never cleaned out a stall before."

"No, but when I was in fourth grade, I got to bring the class guinea pig home for Christmas break, so I've got a general idea of what to do." She shoved her notebook and pen into her back pocket and took the pitchfork.

Luke chuckled. "This will be sort of like that, except the 'muck' you'll be shoveling out will be about the same size as that guinea pig."

Eww. She held back a grimace.

After showing her what to do, he stood back to watch as she slid the pitchfork in and lifted a pile of soiled hay. He flashed a grin at her wrinkled-up nose. "You said you wanted a real ranch experience. Not gonna get much more authentic than that."

Kaylee held back a groan as she hung up her pitchfork a few hours later. She'd asked to be put to work, and Luke had obliged her request. Now her back hurt, and so did her legs *and* her arms, and pretty much every other muscle she had. But she didn't want Luke to see her struggling.

She plastered on a smile as the cowboy came up behind her. "Anything else I can do to help?" she asked, hoping he would say no.

He narrowed his eyes as he studied her then shook his head. "I think you've put in a good day's work already."

"Thank goodness," she muttered, trying not to sag against the barn wall in relief. If her pinched toes and feet were killing her before, they were downright murderous now. She was pretty sure her left one had gone numb. Thoughts of Sassy crept into her mind. Her feisty heroine wouldn't let a little struggle like sore feet get her down. She straightened and pulled her shoulders back. "I mean, thank *you*."

He tilted his head. "What in the world are you thanking me for?" His gaze traveled over her rumpled clothes and dirt-smudged arms. "Between the back-breaking work of cleaning the stalls and then spilling that water trough and falling in the mucky mud, I figured you'd be cussing my name. I sure wasn't figuring to get an offering of gratitude."

"Oh, but I *am* grateful. Really. This is exactly the kind of stuff I want to learn. I won't ever mention a pitchfork or a horse's stall in one of my books again without remembering the feel of sore muscles or blistered hands." She swiped at the still damp traces of mud drying along the leg of her jeans. "Or the smell of old trough water."

Luke chuckled good-naturedly. "That might be one you'd be inclined to forget."

"There is nothing about this day I'll ever forget."

A curious look crossed Luke's face before he waved a hand toward the barn door. "Why don't you go on up to the house and get cleaned up. I'll be along in a few minutes to start working on supper."

"Sounds good," she said, taking a step forward, then tightening her face as she tried not to wince at the pain in her feet. She pressed a hand against the work bench to steady herself. "You go on back to whatever you were doing. I'll just wait for Gladys then head out." She called to the dog, hoping Luke would leave the barn and not have to witness her painful journey back to the house.

Of course the dog came bounding toward her, the ecstatic corgi ferociously wagging her tail. Gladys wiggled with joy at her feet then raced out of the barn, stopping at the door to look back to make sure Kaylee was following.

Thankfully, Luke had moved farther into the barn and had his back to her now as he hauled a bale of hay toward the stalls.

Forcing herself to put one foot in front of the other, she did her best to hide the pain as she half-walked, half-limped back to the house. The last few steps to her bed were torture, and she face-planted into her pillow as she collapsed on the mattress.

She could have fallen asleep and slept for hours but the throbbing of her feet had her rolling over and sitting up to reach for one of the agonizing boots. Grabbing the heel, she flinched in pain as she yanked and pulled at one then the other, but to no avail. The boots were stuck.

She was going to be forced to wear them for the rest of her life.

"Come on," she pleaded with the boots. "Release me, you

evil beasts." She leaned forward, trying a different angle, but couldn't keep her balance and toppled off the bed, sprawling on the floor in a puddle of anguish and exhaustion.

She let out a whimper that had Gladys racing to her side to lovingly cover her cheeks in doggy kisses. Kaylee didn't even have enough energy to stop her.

Luke had to give it to her, he thought as he walked into the farmhouse a few minutes later. The woman had stuck with it much longer than he'd imagined she would. They'd worked together for several hours, and Kaylee stayed at his side, doing her share of the dirty work. She wasn't as fast or as strong as he was, of course, but she was steady and consistent and did the work in an orderly and organized manner. And for the most part, kept a smile on her face. Even when he'd thrown her a curve ball and told her they also needed to scrub out the troughs and the water buckets in the stalls.

She'd said she wanted to know what normal ranch activities were. Most jobs, especially ones involving animals, were hard and messy. If she wanted to know what that was really like, he was going to show her.

He figured it wouldn't take much to convince her to pack up her SUV and drive back to the city, but she'd been a real trooper, even when he'd put her through the paces. When she'd spilled the trough water into her lap and fell into the mucky water, he'd felt so bad for her, he'd almost let her out of the job. But she'd been so insistent on doing some genuine ranch work.

He couldn't believe it when she actually *thanked* him for letting her help before calling her dog and heading out of the barn. She'd kept up a brave front, but he caught sight of her limping across the driveway and up the porch steps when he'd walked by the barn door a few minutes later.

He hung up his hat and went into the kitchen to wash his hands. He'd been annoyed when his sister had called him to tell him she was sending one of her writers out to the ranch for a week. *A week.* Seven whole days of having to put up with a total stranger, and a famous one at that. He'd argued but eventually given in, knowing he owed Faye, and he would do just about anything for his big sister. But he didn't have to like it. And he didn't have to make it pleasant.

He'd devised a strategy that if he didn't go out of his way to make the experience too pleasant, maybe the writer would decide on her own to cut her stay short. Hence the supper menu he'd planned of beanies and weenies. He'd also purchased some corned beef hash for the next night—only the hardiest could stomach his hash—and intended to offer her cold cereal for breakfast and cold bologna sandwiches for lunch.

Opening the cupboard to get down a can of beans, he paused as he heard what sounded like a groan coming from down the hall. He imagined Kaylee was probably sore from the back-breaking work she'd done.

Another sound, this one more of frustrated cry had him taking a step forward and cocking his head to listen. "You all right back there?" he hollered down the hallway.

A stifled whimper followed by a big thud and a sharp yip from the dog had him setting down the can of beans and heading toward her room. He was halfway there when he heard her strangled cry of "Help!"

Chapter Four

"**I**'M COMING," LUKE CALLED AS he ran the last few yards to Kaylee's room. He rounded the doorway then stopped in his tracks, not sure what to make of the woman sprawled across the floor of the room.

Her arms were spread out, and her face was pink and flushed. "I give up," she said. Cooper had followed Luke in, and he sniffed at her head then gave her cheek a careful lick. She didn't even flinch. "You're going to have to bury me like this."

"Bury you? What happened? Are you hurt?"

She held up her leg where her cowboy boot had been pulled halfway off her foot. "Yes. No. I mean, I do hurt, but I'm not hurt like you mean. And if I had even an ounce of energy left, I'd put the hurt on the woman who sold me these stupid boots. I've been trying to get them off for the last fifteen minutes."

He smiled as he held out his hand. "I'd be in line behind you on whoever sold you those ridiculous things. They might look pretty, but they aren't made for working. Let me help you. It's easier if I pull them off."

"I hate to trouble you, but I will offer you a dozen *non*-vegetable cakes if you would." She took his hand and let him haul her back up to the side of the bed. Cooper jumped up behind her and laid down next to her leg.

"I got you. No cake needed." Kneeling in front of her, he took the heel of the boot in his palm and tugged. And tugged. "Dang, that sucker really is stuck."

Kaylee winced and bit down on her bottom lip.

Gladys came over and plopped down next to Luke, resting her head against his thigh as she let out a whine. "I know, girl. We're gonna fix this." He gave another tug, and this time pulled the boot free. Her sock came off with it, and he tossed them both across the room.

He heard her soft intake of breath as he gingerly lifted her foot, grimacing at the raw red marks and the inflamed blister on her heel. He took extra care with the other boot, pulling it gently, but firmly over her heel. Her other foot was in almost as bad of shape, swollen and red, but it didn't have a visible blister.

His chest hurt at the thought that she'd been out in the barn with him slinging hay with this mess happening to her feet.

"Hang tight a second. I'll be right back with something to help." He carefully set her foot on the floor.

"I'm not going anywhere," she said with a sigh. "I'm just glad to get those off."

He hurried across the hall to the bathroom and filled a basin with warm water then dumped in a handful of Epsom salts. Grabbing a towel, gauze and some aloe ointment, he carried the basin back to the room and set it on the floor in front of Kaylee. "Here, this will help with the swelling." He lifted her feet gently and rubbed each one for a minute before setting them in the water.

"That is heavenly," Kaylee said, relaxing her shoulders. "Thank you."

"Don't thank me," he said, leaning back against the wall and stretching his legs out in front of him. "I feel bad I was making you work so hard in the barn this afternoon. Your feet must have been killing you."

"You weren't *making* me do anything. I wanted to help. And I was having fun."

"Fun?" He shook his head. "I hate to see what you consider work then."

"At least we were outside and doing something new and active. Work for me is forcing myself to sit at the computer staring at a blank screen for hours on end trying to come up with something clever to write. Something that's compelling and interesting *and* different than the last ten stories I wrote. It's coming up with new character motivations and figuring out internal and external goals and creating new ways to torture my characters and add more conflict to their fictional life."

"That does sound kind of awful. Especially that torture part."

"It is." She let out a sigh. "Especially when you, in fact, hate having conflict in your own life. It makes it even harder to come up with more for your characters."

He rubbed the chin of the corgi who had sprawled out next to him on the floor. "So why do you do it if it's so awful?"

A smile tugged at the corners of her lips. "Because it's also wonderful. And I love it. And I can't imagine *not* writing. Sure, it's hard, and there are days when I ask myself why I'm putting myself through it, but there are also days when I see the story so clearly in my head and can practically hear the voices of the characters talking to each other. And those are the days that the words flow out of me like water from a fountain. And then it's so much fun. The time passes, and I don't even realize it because the story is just pouring out of me."

Embarrassed, she stopped and looked down into her

lap. "Sorry, I don't know why I just told you all that. That was probably way too much information."

He wasn't sorry at all. He liked watching her talk, watching her eyes light up as she spoke about her characters. "Don't be sorry. I asked."

She picked at a loose thread on the quilt next to her leg. "I know. But that stuff about hearing my characters talk probably made me sound a little crazy. Just so you know, I might hear *them* talking, but it's not like I talk back to them." She tilted her head as one side of her lip quirked up. "Well, not much anyway."

He chuckled. "It's okay. I get it. I've been known to carry on an occasional conversation with my horse and several with my dog." He nodded to Cooper who had wrapped his body around Kaylee and put his head in her lap. "I'm sure it's just because I spend so much of my time alone."

She nodded. "Me too. But I'm surprised you can work this whole ranch by yourself. It seems like a lot."

"It is. I have a good friend who comes over and helps me out when I need him. But it's kind of like you were saying earlier for me, too. Ranching is hard, back-breaking work. You got a taste of that today. So much of its success is out of my control, so it doesn't matter how hard I work if the weather and the economy and the price of beef aren't in my favor. I'll admit there are times when I hate it and wonder why I'm still doing it. But it's in my blood, and there are plenty of days I love it. Sometimes it stinks to get up before the sun to feed my animals, but nothing beats coming out of the barn and seeing that big ol' orange ball come up over the horizon and fill the Montana sky with the prettiest blues and pinks and purples you've ever seen."

Her voice took on a wistful tone. "I'd like to see that."

"Daily showings at six a.m. and another spectacular display in the p.m. Set your alarm so you don't miss it." He scooted forward and gingerly lifted her feet from the water and then carefully dried them with a towel.

She didn't say anything, but he heard the soft click of her throat as she swallowed. It seemed simple, washing and caring for another's injured feet, but it was also an intimate act. He hadn't stopped to think when he saw the damage, he'd just gone into first-aid mode, but it was different now as his hands held and soothed her skin.

Taking out the tube of aloe, he squeezed a line of ointment on her heels and carefully smoothed it over her skin before wrapping her feet in gauze.

"Thank you," she whispered.

That soft, breathy whisper told him she realized the intimacy of the act as well. He sat back on his heels, suddenly unable to look her in the eye as he collected the first aid items. Sneaking a glance at her, he saw her head was ducked, and she was avoiding his eyes as well.

He needed to get out of there. Something was happening inside his chest—a stirring in his heart that he hadn't felt in a long time. The kind of stirring he had shut down and promised he wouldn't let himself ever feel again.

He cleared his throat as he picked up the basin and stood. "Well, I'll leave you to finish up what you were doing. Dinner's in ten. If you're up for it."

"I'm starving. Anything I can do to help?"

He shook his head. "I've got it." There wasn't much to do beyond pouring a can of beans into a pan and chopping up some hot dogs into it.

Ten minutes later, he was considering if he should pour the mixture into a bowl to serve or just set the pan on a trivet on the table like he usually did. Now that she'd been hurt, he felt a little guilty for serving her such a lame supper.

Guilt was only one of the feelings he'd been having the last ten minutes. He was still thinking about that stirring inside him. It had been a long time since he'd let himself feel anything for a woman, yet one afternoon with the quirky romance writer had his chest coiling tight and attraction and desire fluttering around his stomach like fireflies on a warm summer night.

He didn't usually notice the color of a woman's eyes or think about the way she smiled, but he knew Kaylee's eyes were the same greenish-blue as the pond outside and that the sides of her lips did this funny little lift when she found something he said amusing.

And as much as he was trying not to admit it, he liked telling her things that made that little lift of a smile occur.

"Smells good," the woman he'd been thinking about said as she walked into the kitchen. She'd changed into a pair of flannel pajama pants, pink fuzzy slippers, and a faded t-shirt that read, *I'm silently correcting your grammar.* Her curly hair had been pulled into a messy knot on top of her head, and he had to tear his gaze away from the wispy tendrils that fell on her neck.

"Nice shirt," he told her, motioning for her to take a seat at the table.

She looked down at herself and chuckled. "Thanks. Your sister bought it for me."

"Is it true? Are you silently correcting my grammar?"

There went that little smile. "Sadly, yes. You might not realize it, but having good grammar skills is both a blessing and a curse."

He laughed. Then, fighting the notion of impressing her, he nixed the serving bowl and plunked the pan down on the trivet between them and dropped into the chair across from her.

It had been a while since he'd set the table, and he hadn't done much beyond setting out bowls, silverware, and glasses of water. But she didn't seem to care as she picked up the paper napkin and spread it across her lap.

Even though it had been part of his grand scheme to serve her an unimpressive meal, he now found himself a little embarrassed at the offering of canned baked beans and cheap hot dogs. He could have at least set out bread and butter. "Sorry for the skimpy supper."

"It's fine," she said, scooping a few spoonfuls into her bowl. "I'm kind of excited to try it. It feels like a real cowboy meal. Like maybe something you'd make over the fire out on a cattle drive."

He marveled at her enthusiasm. "You're right. A can of beans or two is usually tucked into a rucksack if we have to do an overnight drive."

"That sounds exciting. An overnight cattle drive, I mean. Not the two cans of beans."

He chuckled. This woman had made him laugh more in one afternoon than he'd done in the last month. "It isn't. It's usually cold and uncomfortable. The ground is hard, and I inevitably always tend to spread my sleeping bag out on a spot with a rock that sticks up somewhere in the middle of my back. Although it doesn't usually make itself known until halfway through the night."

"You're right. That doesn't sound great. In fact, nothing about that whole scenario, from the beans to the cold ground, sounds appealing to me in any way." Her shoulders drooped. "I'm afraid I'm not very adventurous."

"Have you ever been camping before?"

"No. But I did make a fort out of blankets and sleep on the floor once when I was a kid."

"I'll admit, it sounds awful, and most of it probably is, but there's also something pretty great about crawling out of the tent and greeting the mountains in the morning. You're usually freezing, but that makes that first scalding sip of Cowboy Coffee all the better."

"What's Cowboy Coffee?"

"That's the kind you make over an open fire. It tastes terrible, and you usually have to chew it due to all the loose grounds floating in it, but it's hot and strong enough to put hair on your chest."

She wrinkled her pert nose. "Sounds delicious. You're really selling this camping and cattle drive excursion idea."

He flashed her a grin. "All in a day's work for a cowboy."

"Speaking of work, what's on deck for tomorrow?"

The vision of her battered feet came into his head. "Nothin' much. It'll be a slow day. Why don't you just hang out in here? You can rest up and take care of your sore feet."

He swore he saw a look of relief wash over her face. But then it was gone as she lifted her chin. "I didn't come here to rest. I came to participate in a normal day on a ranch. So, I'll ask again, what are we doing tomorrow?"

His plan had been to show her the worst parts of ranching so she'd skedaddle back to the city. But she'd barely flinched at shoveling manure. And he did feel bad about those blisters. So maybe he needed to show her the monotonous part of his daily routine. Maybe he could *bore* her back to the city. "I'm afraid my morning is nothing to get excited about. I'm planning to spend most of the morning running fence."

Her brow furrowed for just a moment then she forced a smile. "Sounds great. What time do we start?"

Kaylee stifled a yawn the next morning as she took another sip of coffee and tried to force back the feelings of dread worming their way through her stomach. Her body was sore. She'd used muscles the day before she didn't even know she had.

She'd spent an hour soaking in the big claw foot tub the night before and had planned to jot down some notes about her experiences that day, but instead, had fallen into bed after her bath and gone to sleep the second her head hit the pillow.

She'd slept hard, her dreams full of scattered images of the handsome cowboy, cream cheese frosting, shoveling muck, and crunchy coffee. She woke, bleary-eyed and achy, and every part of her fought to stay curled under the cozy down comforter with Gladys cuddled at her side.

But Sassy didn't sleep in or hide from her responsibilities. Sassy was a take-charge woman. She'd probably even be excited about spending the morning running along some fences. Although for the life of her, Kaylee couldn't figure out why Luke would want to do that. Was it some kind of cowboy calisthenics?

There was so much she had to learn about what really happened on a ranch. Maybe Faye's idea hadn't been the worst one, she begrudgingly thought as she lifted her arms in a stretch. She bent forward then to the side, stretching her sore muscles in preparation for the run.

Ugh. She hadn't run in years. Why was she doing this again? At least her feet felt better this morning, especially since she'd shucked the stupid boots and opted for comfy sneakers.

She turned at the sound of thundering hooves and stopped mid-stretch to gawk at the cowboy galloping toward her on a large black horse.

Close your mouth. A bug might fly in.

Her grandmother's old admonishment came back to her. But holy cow, or holy cow*boy* in this instance, she couldn't help it. She could barely breathe from the way her stomach had just gone aflutter. Luke Montgomery, with his black hat pushed low over his intense eyes and commanding the imposing horse, was a sight to see. He looked like something out of a movie.

He pulled the horse to a stop in front of her. "Mornin'."

"G-g-ood morning," she stammered, her mouth dry as

she peered up at him. And she did have to look up, the horse was even bigger up close.

"I saw you from across the pasture. What are you doing? Some kind of weird yoga or that chai tea stuff?"

She shook her head. He'd seen her? From across the pasture? The thought had heat darting up her spine. *Calm down*, she told herself. She pulled at her t-shirt, yanking it down to make sure her waist was covered. "It's called tai chi. Chai tea is a beverage. And no, that wasn't what I was doing anyway. I was just stretching. Getting ready for our run."

He furrowed his brow. "What run?"

"Oh, um..." She pulled at her shirt again. "I thought you said you were going to take a run by your fences this morning." She gestured to his cowboy boots. "Although I can't imagine how you're planning to run in those boots."

He chuckled. "You do amuse me, Kaylee Collins." He swung down from the saddle and tipped his hat back. "I said I was going to run fence, not *go for a run*. Running fence just means you ride along it and check it for damage. I usually take the ATV or ride my horse."

"Oh." She looked down at her hands as she twisted them together. How embarrassing. As a Western romance writer, she should know a lot more about this ranching business. Faye was proven right again. "Sure, that makes sense."

He smiled. "Although I can see how you would mix that up if you weren't used to the term."

Now he just felt sorry for her for being such a dope. *Thanks for throwing me a bone, dude.*

"So, do you want to take the horses or the ATV?" he asked. "Do you ride?"

She took a frightened step back as the big horse stomped his foot and let out a huff. "No. And to be quite honest, they kind of terrify me."

"Terrify you?"

Why did she admit that? Sassy would never admit such

a lame weakness. But she'd already said it, so there was no taking it back now. "They're just so big. And unpredictable. And they seem hard to control."

"You seem like the kind of woman who likes to be in control."

It almost sounded like that statement might have had a little flirty undertone. But Kaylee took this subject seriously. And maybe a little too defensively, she thought as she lifted her chin. "There's nothing wrong with a little order and organization." Or *a lot* of order and organization, if she had her way.

"Have you ever ridden one?"

"No," she answered a little too loudly, fighting back the panic that accompanied the memories of the time she had tried.

Chapter Five

KAYLEE TWISTED THE HEM OF her shirt between her hands, not sure how much of the story she should tell Luke. She could already feel the heat warming her body as the shame of that day returned.

"I had a chance to ride a horse once," she told him, keeping her eyes trained on a small reddish rock next to his boot. "We were on vacation in Wyoming, and my stepdad took my younger sister and me out to a dude ranch. You know, one of those pay-for-an-hour horseback rides?"

"Sure. The horses have usually done the trails so many times they just follow in a line. Not much of an "authentic" experience."

"No," she said again, shaking her head. "But it was a memorable one. They assigned me this horse named Thunder. They said he was a little *spirited*, and I don't know, something about that word just freaked me out. When it was my turn, I kind of panicked and was afraid to get on. So, my little sister..." Half-sister, to be exact; a *perfect* half-sister who must have inherited all the good stuff from their mother, while Kaylee had only inherited the bad. "Well, she wasn't afraid of anything. So, she offered to switch horses with me and jumped right on Thunder like it was no big deal. But then something must have spooked him because he reared up then took off, racing across the field. One of the ranch guys had to go racing after her, and she ended up falling off and breaking her arm."

"Wow. That *is* a traumatic way to be introduced to horseback riding."

"Or horseback *watching* in my case. We ended up leaving the dude ranch and heading straight to the emergency room. Juliette, my sister, wasn't mad at me, but I always blamed myself for her getting hurt."

"So it was your fault the horse just happened to get spooked, and then you made your sister fall off in just the certain way that would break her arm?"

"Well, no, of course not. But if I would have just gotten on the horse...if I wouldn't have been so afraid..."

"Then you might have been the one who ended up with the broken arm?"

She finally looked up at him. "Exactly."

"And that would have been better?"

She nodded. "Oh yes, so much better. Because of the fracture, my sister couldn't finish her last few softball games that summer, and her team went to the finals. She was their star pitcher, but without her, they lost."

"And that was your fault too?"

"Of course. I spent most of my summer with my nose in a book. A broken arm wouldn't have effected anything if it had happened to me."

"That's a lot of liability to take on for a kid. How old were you?"

She let out a sigh. It had been the summer before she'd lost her mom. "Fifteen or sixteen. Too old to be afraid of a dumb horse." The big horse huffed again, and Kaylee held up her hand. "No offense intended. I don't mean you."

"I'm truly sorry that happened to you. But it sounds like an isolated incident. Like you said, something must have spooked him. Most trail horses are pretty docile." Luke patted the horse's neck. "But they're just like people. They have their own personalities, and every one of them is different. And just like people, they can be sweet or cantankerous, but most of them *are* good. This horse here is probably the best friend I have. I can't imagine my life without him."

"But that's just it. You've spent your whole life around horses. You're used to them."

"True. But still, a lot of them are very gentle. I've got a couple of really sweet mares that you could easily ride. I'd be happy to teach you if you want to try again. We could saddle one up right now."

She chewed on her bottom lip as indecision roiled through her belly. She wanted to be brave, to channel Sassy, who would never back down from a scary situation, but...she just couldn't. The fear of horses was just too deep in Kaylee, and she couldn't make herself get on one.

"Not this time."

He shrugged. "Suit yourself."

She wiped her sweaty palms on the sides of her legs, thankful he hadn't pushed her harder. "How about those fences?"

"Sure. Let me put Max up and then we can go. Will you be okay on the back of the four-wheeler?"

She swallowed, just now realizing she'd be riding the ATV *with* Luke. "Yes, I'll be fine." She wasn't fine. Just the thought of being so close to the good-looking cowboy was sending her pulse racing, but she'd already flaked out on horseback riding. She wasn't a total wimp. Well, she was. But he didn't need to know that.

"Back in a few," he called over his shoulder as he led the horse into the barn.

She sank onto the porch step and was flanked by the eager Gladys and Cooper. Scratching the dog's necks, she tried to put the memories of her sister out of her mind. There was enough to focus on today.

Ten minutes later, Luke had the horse put up and his tools assembled and placed in the corner of the steel mesh box on the back of the ATV. He patted the seat. "Climb on."

Kaylee eyed the four-wheeler. "Are you sure it's safe?"

"Oh sure. We're just riding out to the east pasture. It's pretty flat out that way."

She took a step forward then hesitated again and looked down at the corgi. "What about Gladys?"

"What about her? She can either come along or stay in the house. Cooper usually just runs along beside the ATV. No offense, but it doesn't appear that Gladys does a lot of running."

Kaylee bristled, then dropped her shoulders. "Ah, who am I kidding? Neither Gladys *nor* I do a lot of running. Unless you count running for the bus or the fridge... But I hate to leave her behind at the house."

"You don't have to." He tapped the steel contraption on the back of the vehicle. "This is a dog box. It's made for dogs so they can ride with you. Cooper likes to run, but once he gets tired, he'll ride in the box." He hefted the corgi into his arms and placed her inside the frame. He patted the spot next to her, and Cooper jumped onto the seat then into the box to sit next to the other dog. "See? They're good. And we can let them down to run around if we stop to fix a section of fence."

He climbed on and slapped the seat behind him again.

"Your turn."

Her cheeks went that adorable pink color as she approached the ATV and tried to figure out how to climb on without actually touching him. He pressed his lips together to keep from smiling as she tentatively rested her hand on his shoulder, lifted it, and then set it back down. She finally managed to swing her leg over and settle onto the seat.

Even though she was sitting right behind him, she'd left plenty of space between them. Her hands rested gently on his shoulders. "What exactly are we looking for?"

"Any place where the fence might need repair. We had a pretty big thunderstorm last week, so we're watching for spots where the ground may have washed out or where any downed trees or broken limbs may have fallen on it. If we see anything, we'll stop and fix it."

"Sounds easy enough."

"Basically, you're looking for any damaged places that a critter could slip through."

"Got it."

He settled back in the seat, his heart doing this funny racing thing from having Kaylee so close to him. Heat warmed every spot where her body was touching his. It had been so long since he'd had butterflies in his stomach over a woman, but the little devils were there now, swooping and swirling and banging into the walls of his gut. Hyper-aware of each place she was touching him, he tried to ignore the yearning that wanted more, that reveled in the delicious feel of her next to him.

Get ahold of yourself. She was a city girl celebrity who would only be around for a few days. No point in getting worked up over something—or someone—that didn't have a chance to begin with. So why was he thinking about her timid smile and noticing how amazing her perfume smelled—something light and floral that had him wanting to bury his head in her neck and inhale her.

Snap out of it. He was thinking like a teenage boy. Planting his feet on the sideboards, he started the engine and headed toward the pasture, trying to focus on the task ahead. He spotted a bumpy place in the path. "Better hold on," he told his passenger.

He probably could have gone around the rutted spot, but the teenager in him took over and instead, he gave the gas a little goose and went right through. The ATV bounced and Kaylee pressed closer to him and wrapped her arms securely around his waist.

It was probably good she couldn't see the grin that broke across his face.

Luke was still smiling twenty minutes later. They'd been riding along the fence in silence, but it was a comfortable silence and even though she kept her arms around him, he felt her stiffness ease as she settled into the ride.

They turned into one of the smaller pastures. It was closer to the mountains and the cows seemed to like this one. Forty or fifty head of cattle milled around the field, and a few looked up when they heard the ATV. Most barely moved. They were used to Luke bringing out salt cubes and bags of feed. Although his job was much easier in the summer, and he hadn't been out here as much since they had all this great grass to graze on.

Kaylee tapped him on the shoulder and pointed to a spot on the fence where a large branch had fallen and was weighing down a section of fencing.

"Good eye," he told her, pulling up to the damaged area and cutting the engine. Cooper whined but waited for Kaylee to climb off before he jumped down from the box and ran along the fence, his nose to the ground as he sniffed out all the exciting new scents. Luke turned to help Gladys, but the corgi had followed Cooper's lead and jumped down herself.

"You bored yet?" he asked Kaylee as he climbed off the four-wheeler and stretched his arms out.

"Not at all. This is fun."

"*Fun*? We haven't done anything or seen anything other than big green fields. I wouldn't call this fun. I'd call it monotonous."

She shrugged and smiled. "Maybe that's what I like about it. You don't have to think, you just get to enjoy the scenery. And one person's monotony is another person's fun."

"If you say so." He pulled the small chainsaw from the box and headed toward the fence.

Kaylee trailed along behind him. "Anything I can do to help?"

"Ever used a chainsaw?"

"Yes. Tons of times."

He turned back to her, trying not to look too surprised. "Really?"

She laughed, and the sound rippled over him like water flowing over stones in a babbling brook. "No, not really. I'm teasing you. Has anything in our limited time together led you to think I may have loads of experience using a chainsaw?"

He chuckled with her. "I was trying to give you the benefit of the doubt."

"Thanks. I appreciate it." She grinned at him. "I can slash paragraphs and prune bad prose, and I've even been known to hack out a flat character. But the closest I've come to operating a chainsaw would probably be the electric knife I've used occasionally at holidays to slice a ham."

"Hacked out a flat character?"

She lifted one shoulder as her smile turned mischievous. "Writer humor. We love clever word play."

He shook his head. This woman did amuse him. "This doesn't look too bad. I should be able to cut it out pretty easily."

"What's that?" She shielded her eyes as she pointed across the field.

He followed her gaze to a large red and white object stuck in the fence. "It looks like an empty feed bag. Must have blown off one time when I was out here feeding the cows."

"Why don't I make myself useful and go grab it while you work on this branch?"

"Sure, that would be great. And the dogs would love the run."

She whistled for the pups and started across the field. "Be back in a minute."

"Watch out for cow pies," he called.

"What's a cow pie?"

"You'll see." He turned back to the branch, then chuckled to himself as he heard her groan of discovery.

"Never mind. I figured it out," she called back to him.

He was still smiling a few minutes later as he finished cutting the broken branch from the fence and turned to check on her progress.

Oh no! His smile turned into laughter as he watched Kaylee make her way back across the field, the feed bag securely clutched in her hand.

He *had* to tell her.

But he knew she wasn't going to be laughing when she turned around and saw the parade of cows trotting after her hoping she had feed in that bag.

Chapter Six

KAYLEE GRIPPED THE FEED BAG, her concentration fixed on the ground as she surveyed the field in front of her and tried to plot out a safe path across without ruts or manure.

The dogs had run ahead. She finally looked up when she no longer heard the buzz of Luke's chainsaw. Her brow furrowed as she saw Luke watching her, an expression of amusement creasing his face.

What was so funny? She must have been walking goofy as she tried to avoid stepping in a cow pie.

"I don't want to alarm you," he called. "But you might not want to look behind you."

She froze. How was that warning *not* supposed to alarm her? She slowly turned her head, fearing a snake or maybe a bear, but never expecting a long row of cows to be running toward her.

She let out a shriek and took off running across the field, heedless of where her feet fell. Whipping her head back, she saw the cows were now chasing her, running faster as they tried to catch her.

"Help! The cows are attacking me!" she shouted to Luke, who was now bent forward, his hands on his knees as his shoulders shook with laughter. "Stop laughing and help me!"

She zigged and zagged across the field. The dogs raced back and ran along next to her, Gladys yipping at the cows picking up speed behind her. A couple of the cows mooed loudly as they loped toward her. "I thought cows were herbivores," she yelled.

"Drop the feed bag," Luke finally managed to holler in between gales of laughter.

She dropped the bag and sprinted toward him, launching herself into his arms once again.

He wrapped her in his arms, lifting her off her feet as he swung her around putting himself between her and her pursuers. "Oh my gosh," he said, trying to catch his breath. "That was one of the funniest things I've ever seen. They were really chasing you."

"I know," she said, peering around his shoulder. The cows had stopped when she'd dropped the bag and were milling around it, a few sniffing at the abandoned sack. "Why does everything around here want to kill me?"

"They don't want to kill you," Luke said, still laughing. "Or eat you. They wanted to eat what they thought was in that bag. They saw you carrying it across the field and must have thought you were going to feed them."

She tipped her head down and pressed her forehead into his chest. "That about scared the life out of me." Pulling in a breath, she peered up at him and then swatted him playfully on the arm. "And you just stood here laughing while I was about to be mauled by a herd of mean cows."

He jostled her against him. "Sorry. But that was funny. And those cows weren't mean, they were just hungry." His face took on a more serious expression as he brushed a lock of her hair back that had blown across her cheek. "Don't worry, Kaylee. I won't let anything happen to you out here. I would have stepped in and saved you if it would have really come to that."

She swallowed, suddenly unable to speak, to even think. All she could focus on was the way his fingers had felt as they brushed her cheek and the crystal blue shade of his eyes as he peered down at her. She was caught in his gaze, powerless to move as she drowned in their depths.

He leaned closer, just the slightest bit, and his gaze dropped to her mouth.

Every one of her nerves tingled and her lips parted, as if anticipating his kiss.

Was he really going to kiss her?

Her knees threatened to buckle at the idea. Things like this didn't happen to her. Ruggedly handsome men didn't take her into their arms and kiss her.

Although he hadn't taken her into his arms. She had hurled herself at him, practically knocking him over as she did. Oh, gosh. What if *he* thought *she* was making a pass at *him*?

She had flung herself into his arms. And hadn't let go yet. But that didn't mean she wanted him to kiss her. Although it didn't mean that she *didn't* want him to kiss her.

But that hadn't been her intent. *Had it?* Had she subconsciously found another way to end up in his embrace? Had she given him the idea she was interested in him? Been overly flirty?

She scoffed at the idea. She didn't even know *how* to flirt. She'd spent the majority of the last five years in her apartment creating fictional romantic experiences, not *having* any of them herself.

But just because she normally only wrote about the kissing scenes of her characters didn't mean she couldn't have an actual kissing scene of her own.

So why was she picking apart every second of this moment? She should be enjoying it, reveling in the delicious feelings of desire racing through her blood.

Luke leaned closer. She could smell the woodsy scent of his aftershave and the spearmint flavor of his gum.

Closer still.

This was it. She could almost feel the soft brush of his lips against hers.

Then the sound of a cow bawling behind Luke had a small cry issue from her expectant lips....and the moment was lost.

Luke blinked—almost as if waking from a trance—and pulled away, dropping his arms from around her and taking a step back as he turned around.

A calf was standing behind them, his neck outstretched as he let out another loud bawl.

"Sorry, pal," Luke told him, laughter back in his voice. "I got nothin' for you. She's the one who was carrying that bag."

Kaylee's hand fluttered to her mouth, her lips still tingling at the hope of being kissed.

Had Luke really been about to kiss her? Or had she just imagined that? And was she imagining the fact that he couldn't seem to look at her now?

A couple of other cows wandered closer to them, and she shrank back against the ATV.

"Hey now," Luke said, reaching out to touch the side of her arm. "Don't be scared. They're big. But they aren't going to hurt you."

"I've never been this close to a cow before."

He walked to the calf and scratched it behind its ears like it was a dog. The calf leaned into his hand and butted his head into his palm. "Maybe you should come over and see this one then. He's only about half a cow."

She hesitated, her heart pounding in her chest. Sure, the calf wasn't that big, but the cows standing behind him sure were. She peered around at them. "Where's his mom?

Won't she get mad? Try to fight us to protect him?"

Luke grinned. "Cows aren't really big into fighting. Granted, there are some bulls that can get pretty ornery, but these cows are fairly mellow."

She took a deep breath, stood a little taller, and forced her feet to move toward Luke and the calf.

"See? They aren't so scary," he said, as she stuck her hand out and gingerly touched the cow's forehead.

"No, this one is even kind of cute." She gestured to the other cows in the field. "Are all these cows yours?"

He nodded.

"Wow. What are their names?"

"Their names?" He scratched his head then pointed to several of the cows. "Well, let's see. That one over there is called Ribeye, and that one by the tree, his name is Filet Mignon. The one you're trying to pet is named Ground Beef, but we all just call him Chuck for short."

Kaylee's eyes widened in horror.

"I'm just kidding. I don't *name* any of them, unless you count me calling them The One over There by the Tree or That One with the White Spot on His Shoulder."

"Well those names are better than Ribeye and Chuck."

He shook his head. "Sorry, City Girl. But that's what they are. These cows are how I make my living. I can't think of them as pets." He rubbed his hands together. "Speaking of making a living, I'd better get back to the fence. I can see another spot across the pasture where it looks like a tree fell." He pointed to the ATV. "Why don't you get back on the four-wheeler, and I'll take care of that feedbag?"

She called for the dogs and had them all settled on the ATV by the time Luke grabbed the abandoned sack. He made a show of emptying any leftover crumbs out onto the ground then crumpled up the bag before returning to the four-wheeler and cramming it into the corner of the dog box.

A few cows followed him over, but most had realized

there was no food and lost interest. Luke climbed onto the ATV and drove them around the perimeter of the pasture. Kaylee watched for other damage but didn't see any until they got to the spot Luke had pointed out on the other side of the field.

A tree was lying across the top of the fence and had knocked the fence post sideways.

"Dang," Luke said, cutting the engine and climbing off the quad to examine the damage. "This was a pretty nice tree. Too bad. Looks like it's going to be firewood now." He grabbed the chainsaw and held it out toward Kaylee. "It's a little bigger than an electric knife, but I think you can manage it."

"Me?" Kaylee took a step back. "You want *me* to use the chainsaw?"

"Sure. Why not?" He pulled a pair of gloves from his back pocket and handed them to her. "I'll show you how."

She slowly pulled on the gloves, coming up with a million excuses in her mind as to why this was a terrible idea. But one small voice kept telling her she should go for it. *Sassy's voice*. She swallowed then nodded her head. "Let's do it."

He took a pair of plastic glasses from his pocket and passed them to her. "Safety first."

Safety maybe. But certainly not fashion. She did believe in a safe work environment though, so she pushed aside her qualms of looking like the nerdy girl in chemistry class and put the safety goggles on.

Luke nodded then pushed the starter and the chainsaw roared to life. Kaylee was glad it was loud—hopefully the sound of it drowned out the small squeak of terror she let out when the thing started.

That terror was nothing compared to the fear that grabbed her as Luke handed her the chainsaw then stepped behind her and put his arms around her. Her heart was pounding so hard, he could probably feel it the way his chest was pressed so tightly against her back.

Resting his hands on top of hers, he guided the chain-saw toward the tree. "See that juncture where the branch is coming out of the tree? That's where we're going to cut. We need to break this tree up first before I cut it off the fence." He spoke loudly in her ear, and the deep timbre of it sent shivers down her spine. "We want to keep far enough away that you don't hit that fencing with the blade."

Thoughts of the chainsaw sparking against the steel sent the other thoughts from her head, and she narrowed her focus to the task at hand.

Taking strength from Luke's sure hands and his solid arms around her, she pushed the chainsaw against the branch, digging the blade into the flesh of the tree. Frag-ments of wood flew through the air around the cut, and she was thankful for the safety goggles. She kept the pres-sure on, then suddenly the branch gave way and fell to the ground as the blade made it all the way through.

Luke cut the power on the tool, and Kaylee practically jumped up and down beside him. "Did you see that? I did it! I cut that branch off. With a freaking chainsaw."

"You sure did."

"That was awesome. I'm totally using this in a book." She turned her head to look at him, a grin pulling at her lips. "Can I do it again?"

He laughed, and she felt the sound of it echo through her body. She liked his laugh. And she liked making him laugh. She didn't normally think of herself as a funny person. She could come up with witty banter for her characters, but she could never think of those clever things when she was holding conversations with actual people.

Yet, Luke seemed to find her amusing. He was always laughing around her. Although now that she thought about it, most of that laughter seemed to happen when she was channeling her inner Sassy, so maybe it was her character who he thought was funny, not her.

That thought sobered her a little, but she pushed it back, determined to enjoy the moment of doing something so completely out of her comfort zone. She never would have imagined when she woke up that morning that she would be using a chainsaw that day. Or any day.

She couldn't wait to tell Faye.

Luke leaned back in his chair and patted his stomach. "Not the fanciest of lunches," he told Kaylee who was sitting across from him. "But it tasted good and was filling."

"I can honestly say this is the first time I've ever had, or even heard of, a fried bologna sandwich."

"And what's the verdict?" He waited for her to say it was terrible or that it didn't compare to the kind of things she ate in fancy Chicago restaurants.

"I thought it was delicious." She tipped up her empty plate and offered him a sheepish grin. "Obviously."

Well dang. She surprised him again. Just like she'd been doing ever since she got here.

He kept expecting her to react one way, and she kept throwing him curve balls and defying his expectations. At times, he could see the hesitation in her, the slight pause where it almost looked like she was having some kind of internal debate with herself, like this morning with the calf. He could tell she was nervous and scared, but after that first few seconds of uncertainty, she squared her shoulders and walked right up to the cow. Granted, it was a baby cow, but it still seemed like it took a lot of courage for her to take that first step.

And the way she'd taken on that chainsaw. He was sure

she'd balk at it—he could feel her hands trembling when she took the machine—but she still did it. Then asked to do it again.

It surprised him how much he'd enjoyed hanging out with her this morning. He'd laughed out loud as he'd recanted their morning adventures to Faye, telling her about the cows chasing Kaylee and her wanting to know what all their names were.

His sister had called when he was putting the ATV away and Kaylee had already gone up to the house to wash up. They hadn't talked long, but he realized after they'd hung up that he had done most of the talking, and it had been a long time since that had happened. He just hadn't had a lot to talk about. Apparently, it took a quirky author with a sweet smile showing up and spending time with him to make him realize how lonely he'd been. He had Dean and Emma, of course, but this felt different.

He'd had fun with Kaylee. She'd made him laugh. It was only when she mentioned using their experience in her next book that he remembered why she was here and spending time with him. And it didn't have anything to do with *him*.

It was all about her books. And her fancy writer career.

That's why she was here. He'd known that since the beginning. So why was that bothering him now?

Good question. And one he wasn't too interested in figuring out an answer to.

Time to change the subject.

"I like your shirt," he told her. "I've been listening to Chase Dalton for years now. I've even seen him in concert a couple of times. And I think one of them was that same tour." Back when Beth was alive, and he used to actually do things—when he used to participate in the world. But those days were gone.

Just like her.

He felt the familiar stab of hurt in his chest. But he

pushed it away, just like he tried to do every time memories of her poked too hard at that ache.

Kaylee looked down at herself as if just noticing the shirt she had on. It was a faded blue concert T-shirt with the white outline of a cowboy hat on the front and the name of one of the country singer's road tours from several years ago on the back. "Oh, I've never actually been to a Chase Dalton concert. But my sister has. She's been to a million concerts, and she almost always brings me back a shirt. It's just a thing she does."

"Like my family went on a cool vacation and all they brought me back was this crummy T-shirt?" Luke asked, his lips curving into a smirk.

"Something like that." She stared down at the table as she ran the tip of her finger over an old scratch in the top. "My sister, Juliette, she's the adventurous one. She's got this great zest for life. If she hears of something fun or cool to do, she just throws some stuff in a bag and hops in the car or on a plane and off she goes. I swear an idea can hit her and she can be packed and out the door in thirty minutes."

"And you can't?"

"Oh, gosh no. Packing for me takes *hours*. It took me two trips to the store, four checklists, and three days to pack just to come here."

He pulled his head back. "You're kidding. Checklists? I think the last time I went anywhere, I was packed in about three minutes. All I need is a couple of fresh shirts, my toothbrush, and a stick of deodorant. What takes you so long?"

She rubbed at the scratch on the table as if she might be able to buff it away. "Because I like to be prepared. And I want to make sure I have on hand everything I might need."

"Yeah, but it seems to me that if you forget something, you can always buy it when you get there. Don't they have stores where you go on vacation?"

She huffed out a laugh. "I wouldn't know. I don't really

ever *go* on vacation. In fact, this is the closest thing I've had to one in years."

Dang. *This* was her vacation. Now he really felt guilty for making her muck out stalls and eat fried bologna for lunch.

He raised an eyebrow. "Does my sister work you that hard?"

That got a smile out of her.

"No, not at all. She's always telling me I need to take 'self-care' breaks."

"Sounds like Faye."

"She's hard to argue with, though. The last vacation I took was at her insistence. Your sister made me take two entire weeks off."

"Cool. Where did you go?" He tried to picture if she was more of a beach person or a cabin in the mountains type. He figured the cabin. He could just imagine her showing up with four suitcases and a first aid kit.

"Go? I didn't *go* anywhere." She tilted her head. "Wait, I did take Gladys for a couple of walks in the park, and I went to the market a few times."

"That doesn't sound like much of a vacation."

"It was to me. It was just more of a *stay*cation. I spent the whole two weeks deep cleaning my apartment and purging my closet. And I took a couple of days where I stayed in my pajamas all day and binged on junk food while watching every season of *Downton Abbey* and having a *Harry Potter* movie marathon."

"Ugh. Now that sounds like torture to me. Not the pajamas and junk food, but spending two weeks cleaning doesn't seem like much of a vacation. Didn't you have any adventures that you wanted to take?"

"Not really. Don't get me wrong, I love the idea of adventures. I just like to enjoy other people's from the safety of my living room on the television screen or in the pages of a book."

He nodded. He hadn't been very adventurous since he'd lost Beth.

She looked sad. Her words said that she enjoyed adventures on the pages of a book, but the wistful look in her eyes made him feel like maybe sometimes she longed for a little bit more.

He shook his head. When did he get so philosophical? "Well, speaking of going to the market, I never got a chance to thank you for bringing me a box of Lucky Charms. How did you know I was out of cereal?"

"Marnie told me. The woman at the grocery store where I stopped to get the cake. She said you were out and that it was your favorite." Her cheeks flushed, and she couldn't seem to look at him again.

What was that about? Why would a box of cereal make her embarrassed?

"Ah. She must've noticed when she was here the other day."

"She seems nice."

"She is. We've known each other a long time. We went to school together."

"So…" she paused, as if on the verge of asking him something else about Marnie or the cereal, then looked as if she changed her mind and forced a smile. "So, what's on the schedule for this afternoon?"

Schedule? The word rankled him, like he was supposed to entertain her or something. "Nothing. I've got some errands to run so I was going to go into town this afternoon. I need to stop at the feed store and grab a couple of things at Milligan's."

"What's Milligan's?"

"Milligan's Mercantile. It's like a general store. The owners, Bud and Pearl Milligan have been running it forever. Faye and I both spent a couple of summers working there. It's one of those stores that has just about anything you could need—from a fly rod and a new pair of waders to first aid to cowboy hats and boots. I need a couple pairs of work gloves and some duct tape."

"Would you like some company?"

"Nah. I'm good. You can stick around here. I'm sure you've got some writerly stuff to do."

"I *always* have writerly stuff to do. But if it's okay, I'd really like to tag along."

A spark of gladness lit in him that she wanted to hang out with him.

"I'd like to see more of the town," she continued. "For my research. Besides stopping at the grocery store, I really just drove through. But going with you might give me a chance to see the true inner workings of the community."

"Oh yeah. Sure." Of course it was about the book. Not about *him. Which is how it should be,* his rational brain tried to tell him. This was her job. So what was going on with him that he was even thinking it shouldn't be?

"What about the dogs?" She glanced down to where both dogs were sprawled out, sound asleep on the floor.

"I think we'll leave them home this time. They both look beat. Did you know your dog snores like a lumberjack?"

"Yes. But it's unladylike to point it out." She picked up her plate. "Can I help you put these in the dishwasher?"

"That would be great. If I had a dishwasher."

"You don't have a dishwasher?"

"Hard to believe, huh? We only just got indoor plumbing a few years ago."

Her eyes widened then her lips curved into a smile. "Very funny."

"Don't worry about it. We can leave them in the sink, and I'll wash them up with the supper dishes."

"Okay." She put her plate to the sink then washed her hands and dried them on the towel. "I'll be ready to go in ten."

"It's a ways into town. You sure that'll give you enough

time to pack for the trip?"

"Smart aleck," she said, tossing the towel at him.

Chapter Seven

*A*N HOUR LATER, THEY PULLED into a spot in front of Milligan's Mercantile. Kaylee leaned forward to peer through the windshield. The store was huge. It covered half the city block and had a life size replica of a palomino horse on the roof gazing out onto the street.

If the shop windows were any indication, Luke was right about the place having a little bit of everything. One display boasted a summer scene with a trio of bicycles surrounded by fishing and gardening equipment and supplies while the other featured Western apparel—which looked nothing like the outfit the salesgirl in Chicago had talked her into buying.

She and Luke had already picked up salt cubes and dog chow from the feed store, dropped off a deposit at the bank, and mailed a package. Milligan's was their last stop. But Kaylee had spied a cute coffee shop a few doors down, and she was hoping to convince Luke to let her buy him a latte when they were finished. There was a little chance that Luke was a latte kind of guy, but hey, she'd just eaten a fried bologna sandwich, so maybe she could convince him to try a little steamed milk in his cup of joe.

"I just need a couple of things in here, but I thought you might want to look at cowboy boots," he told her as they got out of the truck.

She winced.

"Not like those silly ones you wore here. You need a good pair of Ropers."

"Ropers?"

"That's the brand. Justin Ropers. They're good boots, rugged, but also made for comfort. The toebox is wider so it won't mash up your toes, and you can get a pair that only go up to your midcalf, so they're easier to get on and off." He nudged her playfully with his elbow. "Just in case you don't have me around to help you."

The thought of shoving her feet into another pair of cowboy boots made her toes curl, and not in the normal romance author sense—after a great kiss. She swallowed, not sure why she was thinking about a great kiss, or *any* kiss. It might have something to do with the warm spot on her shoulder Luke had just nudged. "I don't know. I guess it can't hurt to take a look."

She stopped in front of the store as he reached to open the door for her, and her eye caught on the colorful poster stapled to the bulletin board outside the shop. "What's a Summer Celebration?"

"It's a big event the town throws every summer. They close off Main Street and set up craft booths and have a rodeo and all sorts of stuff. It kicks off with a pancake breakfast and a parade on Friday and ends with a concert and fireworks at the street dance on Saturday night."

"How fun." She let out a gasp as she peered closer at the poster. "Did you see who's playing on Saturday night?"

He leaned closer to read the name then gave her a grin. "Looks like your sister isn't going to be the only one who's seen Chase Dalton in concert."

"I can't believe he's going to be here."

"Apparently he's from a small town and still plays occasional festivals like this one. I haven't paid much attention to this year's event. I forgot it was even this weekend."

She chewed on her bottom lip. "Should we....I mean, would you like to go...together? With me, I mean?"

"To the concert or the Summer Celebration?"

She lifted her shoulders. "All of it, I guess. I've never been to a rodeo *or* a pancake breakfast."

"Okay, sure. We can go. Although I wouldn't get your hopes up too much. The pancakes are lukewarm at best, and the parade is a few floats and a bunch of little kids on their bikes and a few 'big kids' on riding lawnmowers. And by big kids, I mean grown men who have too much time on their hands."

"Riding lawnmowers? In the parade? This I have to see." She nudged his arm as she walked past him into the store. "I know you're trying to make it sound less appealing, but you're making me want to go even more."

She stopped inside the door, pausing to take in the shop. "I swear it smells like new leather and root beer in here."

"Yeah, isn't it great? Bud put in an old-fashioned sarsaparilla station last year. It dispenses three different flavors of root beer and cream soda. You'll have to try a cup."

A sarsaparilla station? She felt like she'd just stepped back into the 1950s.

A woman walked out from a back room muttering to herself as she stared at the clipboard in her hand. She raised her head but seemed to look right through them.

"Pearl?" Luke said, his voice soft as he approached the woman. "You okay?"

Kaylee followed and as she got closer, she could see the redness of the woman's nose and puffiness around her eyes. She was dressed in jeans, moccasins, and a blue and white Western top. The lapels of the shirt didn't exactly align, like the buttons were off by one, and she had a pencil and two pairs of reading glasses amidst the fluffy silver curls of her hair.

She waved a hand at Luke. "I'm fine. But did you hear that dang fool, Bud, went and fell off the roof yesterday and broke his leg? He's laid up in the hospital, and I swear I didn't get but two or three hours of sleep last night for worrying about him." She fussed with the clipboard. "I don't think we've spent but a few nights apart in all our forty-five years of marriage."

"If you're worried about him, why don't you go over and see him?"

"Because I've got too much to do here."

"Where's your shop girls?" Luke scanned the store for them. "I'm sure they can handle things."

"They could, if I wouldn't have made the mistake of giving them both the last few days off. I didn't know they were cousins when I hired them, and it hasn't mattered until they both needed time off for their family reunion."

"Then just put a note on the door and lock up for the day," he suggested. "I'm sure folks would understand."

She shook her head. "I can't. Not with Summer Celebration happening this weekend. Besides the extra snack inventory I need to put out, I've also got a huge shipment of event T-shirts arriving this afternoon that I need to be here to sign for. Half the town has already pre-ordered theirs." She pointed to a stack of colorful cardboard pieces on the floor. "Then I've got to put that display together and get all the shirts folded and priced and ready to sell. Not to mention, the new boots we just got in that need to be unpacked and stocked, and Bud ordered a bunch of dang nails that need to be sorted and dumped in the bins." Her voice rose as she reeled off each new task.

"Hey now. Everything's going to be okay." Luke eased the clipboard from her hand. "Why don't you let me help? I can stay here and take care of the T-shirts and the display and stocking the new inventory. You know I helped Bud put those nail bins in. I know how to fill them. You go on home, get something to eat, maybe take a nap, then go be with Bud. We can stay till five then lock up and drop the keys off to you over at the hospital."

She rested her hand on Luke's arm and closed her eyes as she leaned into him. "You are an angel, Luke Montgomery."

He wrapped an arm around the woman's shoulders and spoke softly into her hair. "Don't let it get around. Now, you go on home."

She peered up at him. "I surely can't go home and take a nap. I'm too worried. But I will promise to get something to eat at the hospital cafeteria, and I'll close my eyes for a bit once I'm settled into the chair next to Bud's hospital bed."

"Deal."

"You sure?"

"Course I'm sure. I can handle all that stuff, no problem. And I'm sure I can talk Kaylee into helping me."

Pearl turned to Kaylee as if noticing her for the first time. "Oh my heavens, you're Kaylee Collins. I love your books."

Kaylee ducked her head, surprised that the woman would recognize her *and* know her work. "Nice to meet you. I'm so sorry to hear about your husband."

"Our book club just read your newest release. We loved it."

"Thank you." Kaylee never knew what to say when readers talked about enjoying her books. She loved the praise of her words but didn't know how to accept the admiration of her. "That's so nice that your club chose my book."

"Oh, we read all of Faye's authors. At least once. She usually sends us advance copies. But we really love your books and JD Hawk's thrillers. Although that last one practically gave me nightmares. But goodness, I still couldn't put it down." She gestured to a display shelf of books for sale. A placard next to the top shelf read, *Faye's Finds.*

Kaylee recognized several of her titles as well as many of JD Hawk's. She was honored and thrilled, but still felt unworthy at sharing the same shelf space as the famous author. "That's very kind of you. And I've read every one of his books too."

"All right now," Luke said, almost as if he could feel her unease. "You get along now. And give Bud our best."

Kaylee liked how Luke said *our* best. Almost as if they were a couple. She swallowed. But that was silly. She'd only known the man for a few days. *And* he was Faye's sibling. She was quite sure her editor had not sent her to Montana to get involved with her brother.

The next few hours flew by. Three boxes of T-shirts were delivered within ten minutes of Pearl leaving, and Kaylee unpacked and folded them while Luke put together the display. Then they filled it together. Several people had already come in to buy them or pick up their preordered shirts. Luke was familiar with the store, and following his directions, they'd priced and stocked the new boots and snacks and filled the nail bins.

During a slow point, he convinced Kaylee to at least try on a couple of pairs of cowboy boots, and she'd found two pairs of Ropers that fit and that she kind of liked. She put one of each pair on and tried to decide between them.

"Cute boots," a voice said from behind her.

Kaylee turned and was delighted to see the young girl from the grocery store the day before. "Hi, Emma." She turned to show off both styles. "I can't decide. What do you think?"

"Easy. The pink ones."

The boots weren't really pink. They were brown leather but had a mauveish-pink overlay and pink stitching. The other ones were plain black. "You sure? I was kind of leaning toward the black. I think the pink ones might be too showy?"

Emma wrinkled her brow as she studied the boots. "No way. The black are boring. And we all need a little more pink in our lives."

"Let the woman make up her own mind, Em," the girl's father said coming around the corner of the shoe section. "Sorry about that," he told Kaylee. "My girl has never had an opinion she didn't feel inclined to share."

"It's okay," Kaylee said. "I was looking for an opinion." She sat down to pull the boots off and put them back into their boxes. Emma put the box of black boots back on the shelf.

"I guess I'm taking the pink ones then," she said, a grin on her face.

Emma shrugged. "You know you wanted them. You just needed a nudge."

She *had* wanted them. They were definitely a Sassy choice, and she normally would have taken the boring black, but the pink felt right.

"Did you bring Gladys with you?" Emma asked.

"No Gladys today."

"She and Cooper were zonked out on the floor when we left for town," Luke said, coming from the same direction Emma's father just had. "We had a pretty busy morning." He ruffled the girl's hair. "What are you guys up to?"

"We came in to get our shirts for Summer Celebration," Emma said. "I'm supposed to wear mine for the parade. Are they here yet?"

"Just arrived an hour ago." Luke gestured to Emma's dad. "Kaylee, this is Dean Austin, he's been my best friend since the second grade when his family bought the farm down the road from ours. And it looks like you already met his daughter, Emma."

Kaylee smiled. "Oh yeah. We go wayyy back too." She patted the box with the pink boots inside. "And she just helped me pick out a new pair of cowboy boots."

"Let me know if you need help with any other odd jobs," the girl said. "I've already been doing tons of babysitting, lawn mowing, and dog-walking. I'm trying to make enough money to buy a new bike." She pointed to the front of the store. "It's the purple one in the front window. I've been saving up for it all summer."

"Good for you. How close are you?"

"About halfway. It's a *really* nice bike." She leaned closer to Kaylee. "So if you think of anything you'd like to pay a ten-year-old to do, be sure to call me. Luke has my number."

"I'll keep that in mind," Kaylee said, already racking her brain for a job to give her. She tapped her finger to her chin then grinned at Emma. "You know, Gladys really does need an extra walk, and my car got awful dusty driving here and could use a vacuum." She looked up at Dean. "If it's all right with your dad, I'm sure I could find some things for you to do."

Dean grinned and nodded. "Just name the time, and I'll drop her off."

Emma clapped her hands together as the door of the shop opened, and two women around Pearl's age walked in, their arms laden with books.

"There she is," one of the women said as they headed toward Kaylee.

"Yoo hoo!" the shorter of the two called, juggling the books into one arm so she could wave with the other. "We're so excited to meet you, Kaylee. We were wondering if you wouldn't mind signing our books."

Kaylee looked from the women to Luke, as if unsure if she was the one they were asking. Obviously they were. She could see copies of her books in their hands, but she wasn't used to being recognized. She had met readers at signings before, but she wasn't often approached in public. "Um, yes, sure. Of course."

"We saw Pearl at the hospital, and she told us you were helping out over here," the taller woman said, dropping the books into the chair next to Kaylee. "I'm Rita Mullins, and this is Carol Carson. We're in Pearl's book club."

"Nice to meet you."

"That's so nice of you," Carol said, handing Kaylee one of her books and a marker. "Helping out here and all."

"Hey, what about me?" Luke said, offering the woman a teasing grin. "Don't I get any credit for helping out? I'm the one who just carried in all those boxes and put that T-shirt display together?"

Rita patted his arm. "I'm sure your cardboard assembling skills are excellent, dear, but you're not a famous author. Or the writer who has taken us on wild adventures and made us swoon over our favorite hunky hero, Duke Ramsey."

Luke shook his head. "I should hope not." He gestured to Dean and Emma. "Come on, you two. I'll help you get those shirts while we leave the famous writer to her adoring fans."

Had Kaylee caught a hint of derision in Luke's voice? She never thought of herself as a famous author. Just the opposite, in fact. She lived in fear that at any moment someone would figure out she had no idea what she was doing and had just gotten away with writing the last sixteen books.

"I also brought you some of my famous strawberry jam," Carol said, ignoring Luke as she pulled a small Mason jar from her purse. The jar had a cheery pink ribbon tied around the top with a tag hanging from it that claimed, *Carol Carson's Award-Winning Strawberry Jam.*

"Wow. Award-winning, huh?"

"Oh for heaven's sake," Rita said. "She took first place at the county fair."

Carol lifted her chin with a huff. "Three years in a row."

"Oh, alert the media. Somebody better call Betty Crocker to warn her she's in danger of losing her apron."

"You're just jealous because my jam beat yours."

"I can't wait to try it. I'm sure it will be delicious," Kaylee said, not sure how to diffuse the argument. Then she held up the book she was holding. "Who should I make this out to?"

Chapter Eight

"**W**HAT A FUN AFTERNOON," KAYLEE told Luke later that night as they pulled up in front of the hospital. "Those ladies with the books were a crack-up. You're going to have to help me eat all this stuff."

He didn't respond. She looked over, and his face had gone pale as he stared through the windshield.

Kaylee's tone softened as she reached out to touch Luke's arm. "Hey, are you okay?"

He inhaled a deep breath. "I haven't been here since the accident. This is where my wife…"

A stab of pain shot through Kaylee's chest. "Oh no. I'm so sorry."

"I wasn't thinking when I said we'd drop the keys off." His voice was quiet, barely above a whisper.

"I can take the keys in," she offered. "You said you needed to fill up anyway. Why don't you go get gas while I run in and drop them off?"

He slowly shook his head. "No, I should be able to do this."

"But you don't have to." She knew what it was like to

not be ready to face something. She held out her hand for the keys. "Really. I'm glad to run them in."

He pulled the keys from his pocket and set them in her hand, closing his fingers around hers for just a moment. "You're right. It makes more sense for me to go fill up the truck. Two birds with one stone and all."

She squeezed his hand then took the keys. Pushing open the truck door, she nodded to the park across the street from the hospital. "I'll be right back out. And I'll meet you in the park. Over there by the playground." She didn't want him to have to drive into the hospital parking lot again.

"Sure, okay. By the playground." He was staring at the center of the steering wheel.

She pushed the door closed, and he shot out of the parking lot, his tires practically spinning as he tore off. Kaylee pressed her hand to her chest, aching for his pain, then she turned and hurried into the hospital.

The door to Bud's room was open. Pearl had called the store earlier to check on them and given them the number, and Kaylee knocked softly on the jamb.

Pearl was in the chair next to the bed, and she looked up from the book she was reading. "Come on in, honey. I want to introduce you to the only old coot ornery enough to put up with me all these years."

Kaylee laughed as she entered the room.

The man in the bed was around the same age as Pearl, but he had a lot less of the soft silver hair than she did. His leg was wrapped in gauze and propped up on the bed. He had a lean, wiry frame and a friendly face as he smiled at Kaylee. "Don't let her fool you. She's just as ornery." He held up a bandaged hand. "I'd shake your hand but this one is temporarily indisposed."

"Oh no," Kaylee said. "Pearl told us about your leg, but I didn't know you hurt your hand too."

He shrugged. "It's nothing. Just scraped it up when I fell."

"How are you feeling?"

"Better since Pearl showed up." He shot a quick smile at his bride. "We can't thank you enough for helping out at the store today. Hope it wasn't too much trouble."

"Not at all. It was fun." She passed the keys to Pearl. "And Luke made sure to tell everyone why we were there. He said the 'guilt factor' would get them to buy more, and he must have been right. According to him, we had a banner day." It hadn't hurt that she had bought the pair of cowboy boots, a better fitting pair of jeans, a dress, a jean jacket, and several cute western shirts—all of which Emma had helped her pick out.

Pearl hung her head. "I heard you had a few visitors today. Sorry about that. I didn't realize they'd all run over there with books for you to sign."

Bud grinned. "In this town, there's three ways to get information out—telephone, television, and tell-a-Rita."

Kaylee laughed. Three other women had stopped into the store with books for her to sign. "It was fine. I had fun meeting them. And I ended up getting a loaf of banana bread, a chocolate cake, and some prize-winning jam out of the deal. So I'd say I came out ahead."

"I like this one." Bud nodded to his wife. "And don't let her fool you. She's one of your biggest fans. She was just too star-struck to tell you when she met you earlier today."

"*Star-struck*?" Heat warmed her cheeks. "Oh gosh. Not for me."

"Of course for you," Bud confirmed. "She's read every single one of your books. I've even read a few."

"You?"

"Oh sure. I may look tough on the outside," he said, giving her a wink. "But I like a good romance just as much as the next guy."

She laughed.

"Although I have to tell you, there were a few parts that

gave away your city-girl status. Like when you had the heroine, who was supposed to be an experienced rider, get on her horse from the wrong side."

"I know," she said with a groan. "That's why Faye sent me here. To get some hands-on ranching experience."

"And how's it going?" Pearl asked.

"Good, I think. So far, I've mucked out stalls, been chased by some cows, used a chain saw, and sampled some authentic ranch fare." She grinned and held out her palm. "And I've got the blisters and the indigestion to prove it."

Bud chuckled but Pearl narrowed her eyes. "What's Luke been feeding you?"

"So far, I've tried fried bologna and beanies and weenies."

"Beanies and weenies?" she repeated with a horrified look on her face. "Tell that boy I'll be bringing out some homemade fried chicken and mashed potatoes and gravy."

Kaylee shook her head. "Oh no, you don't have to do that. You've already got your hands full."

"Nonsense. It's the least I can do after you watched the store for me today."

"No sense arguing with her," Bud said. "I learned that a long time ago. Best just to say 'yes ma'am'."

Kaylee liked these people. She smiled at Pearl. "Yes, ma'am."

Luke leaned his chin on the steering wheel as he watched Kaylee hurry across the park toward the playground where he was parked.

He hadn't known driving into the hospital parking lot would affect him so much. The tall building was like a stark reminder of all he'd lost. And a warning of why he should shut down the feelings he'd been having for Kaylee.

She had only been kind earlier when she realized what was going on and hadn't judged his reaction. He'd seen right through her ploy to have them meet in the park instead of making him drive up to the hospital again, but he appreciated the gesture. He'd barely been able to breathe for what felt like a hundred-pound weight sitting heavy on his chest. And he hoped she couldn't see the way his hands were shaking. He couldn't get out of there fast enough.

Having something to do, even if it was just the mundane task of filling up his gas tank, helped to focus his mind and take it off all the memories surrounding the loss of his wife.

Even though it was close to six, it was still warm outside, and Kaylee's cheeks were flushed as she pulled open the door and climbed into the truck. Her scent—something soft and floral—filled the cab. And something in his heart.

"Everything go okay?" he asked as he leaned back in the seat.

"Yes, great. I really like Bud."

Luke smiled. "Yeah, everybody does. He's a good man."

Kaylee turned to him, capturing his gaze with her gorgeous blue eyes. Her voice was soft but firm with resolve. "So are you, Luke."

He swallowed, unable to respond, her words touching a space inside him, some deep part that had been closed off for years. Not that the door of that part had flung open, but he may have felt it crack.

It had been so long since he'd had the fluttery feelings in his stomach that being around the writer brought on. But the last time he gave in to those feelings had led to pain and a heartache unlike anything he'd ever known.

Losing Beth had almost destroyed him. He'd vowed never to let himself fall in love like that again. Not that he was falling in love with Kaylee—that would be nuts. He'd only known her a few days. But the dang fluttery feelings, and the sweaty palms and the goofy smile his lips were always forming when she was around, were real.

And she was the first woman in five years who'd even made him question that vow.

He pushed the feelings down. He had to. She was only here for a few days, *and* she was one of his sister's writers. Everything about this spelled disaster. *Focus on the situation,* he told himself. Not the smell of her hair or the adorable crinkle around her eyes when she smiled.

"You hungry?" he finally managed to ask.

"Starving."

He'd planned to make her chipped beef on toast for supper—another one of his not-so-delectable culinary delights—but she'd worked hard today and kept a great attitude, and he didn't have the heart. He put the truck in gear and pulled out of the park. "Great. Let's go find a cheeseburger."

Thoughts of his vow to stay focused kept him up later that night as he tossed and turned in bed. They'd driven through and grabbed fast food to eat back at the ranch. The dogs were thrilled to see them and most of their supper conversation had been about them. He'd eaten quickly and told Kaylee he was tired and planned to get his chores done and turn in early.

He was jumpy and needed to get out of the house. And away from her. He was too hyper-aware of everything about her, and of all the feelings stirring inside him when she was around. Stirrings that felt like desire and want and need. He'd tossed his trash and headed outside to do his chores and burn off that energy.

When he came back inside, he saw she'd done the dishes from earlier in the day and was already in her room with the door closed.

Good. He was glad he hadn't had to face her, to make conversation. So why had he paused in the hallway and stood outside her door for close to a minute listening to her movements inside and contemplating knocking, just to check on her?

He'd finally dragged himself to bed where he'd tried to put thoughts of the writer down the hall out of his mind.

What was she doing in her room?

It was late, but he'd noticed the light was still visible under her door when he'd gotten up and gone into the kitchen to rummage for a snack. He wasn't hungry. Not for anything he could find in the cupboards of his kitchen, anyway.

His eye caught on the bologna in the fridge, and he had to smile at his failed attempt to scare Kaylee away with mundane chores and Western grub. The woman seemed to jump into all his schemes with both feet and a smile on her face.

Maybe he needed to change his tactics. Instead of trying to shoo her off the ranch with unpleasant things, maybe he needed to give her what she wanted. If he showed her *more* ranch stuff, she'd get the research information she needed and be able to leave sooner. Maybe if he introduced her to a few more animals and got her on a horse, she'd be satisfied and not feel like she had to stay the whole week.

Yes, this could work, he thought as he headed back to bed and tried to ignore the stone that just settled in his stomach at the idea of her leaving at all.

The next morning Kaylee was bleary-eyed as she crawled out of bed. She'd been up too late working on her manuscript. Ideas for several new scenes with Sassy and Duke had struck her the night before and the words had flown from her fingertips.

It had felt different, though. She could already tell the contrast in her writing as she set the scene, layering in the warm dry scents of earth and hay in the barn, the soft swirl of hair on a calf's forehead, and the far-off sound of a tractor in the background. But it wasn't just the new added textures of the ranch life. She'd also written a kissing scene the night before that crackled with tension and had her opening a window in her bedroom to let in the night air to cool her heated skin.

She couldn't remember the last time she'd written with such passion—with both the quickness of her thoughts, and the subject on the page. Her characters came alive in her imagination, as if she really were Sassy Scott. And it wasn't hard to imagine who she was thinking of as the handsome Duke Ramsey. Her own heart raced as she filled the pages with her thoughts and feelings...er...Sassy's thoughts and feelings.

Although it was easy to get caught up in the fantasy. The soft whisper of denim as Luke...dang it... *Duke's* hand reached for Sassy's. The tentative touches and stolen glances. The rush of desire when the hero's lips finally found the heroine's.

It was no wonder that when she finally fell into bed, her dreams were filled with images of her and Luke playing out the same scenes.

But those dreams were pushed aside the next morning as a stream of sunlight covered her bed, and the only kisses she was getting were slobbery ones from Gladys.

She quickly took a shower, then dressed in jeans, one of the short-sleeved shirts she'd bought, and her new boots. Trying to convince herself she was ready for whatever Luke threw at her today, she strode down the hall to the kitchen in search of caffeine and the cowboy.

But instead of finding Luke, she found a note on the

counter stating he'd be back soon and that he'd left a pan of scrambled eggs and sausage warming in the oven for her.

Just as well. Her mind was still racing, as it often did in the morning with thoughts for the new book, and she wanted to get some of it down while it was still fresh. She grabbed a notebook and pen then filled a plate and poured a cup of coffee for herself and took them out to the front porch.

Inhaling a deep breath, she took in the view of the mountains and the still soft sounds of the morning on the ranch. The faint clucking of the chickens, the gentle lap of the pond, and the low whinny of a horse from the pasture. It was beautiful.

The air felt different here. And so did she. Something about being on the ranch was filling an empty place inside her. Maybe a place she didn't even know was there. Not until she got here and found the missing pieces to fill it with.

She opened her notebook, and her pen flew. She absently shoveled scrambled eggs into her mouth as she tried to capture the thoughts and feelings of waking up to a morning on the ranch.

She'd filled several pages and had just popped the last link of sausage into her mouth when she heard the sound of Luke's truck and looked up to see him coming down the driveway. He was pulling a small white trailer behind the truck.

Taking her dishes into the sink, she snuck one more bite of scrambled eggs and a quick glance at herself in the mirror before heading back out to meet Luke. "What's in the trailer?" she asked as she approached the truck.

A mischievous grin beamed from his face as he led her toward the doors of the trailer. "I got to thinking about you last night and your fear of horses, and I came up with an idea."

"Oh," was all she could say, still stuck on the part where he said he'd been thinking about her the night before.

He'd seemed a little cool after they'd left the hospital the night before, and they hadn't shared their usual easy conversation at supper. She'd figured it had to do with the memories being at the hospital dragged up, and hoped it wasn't her that had made him broody and sullen as he'd headed out for his nightly chores.

His mood obviously hadn't dampened her writing or her thoughts about him sleeping just down the hall from her, but the notion that he had been thinking about her sent little tingles of nerves shooting across her skin. That and the roguish grin he was flashing her way.

"You know how they say you have to take small steps before you can run?" He opened the back end of the trailer with a flourish. "Well, I figured you could start with a small horse then graduate to a bigger one."

She gasped as she peered into the trailer at the cutest little horse she'd ever seen. It had a brown coat, a thick tawny-colored mane, and a hot pink daisy tucked jauntily behind its ear. "Oh my gosh. It's adorable."

"Her name is Marigold. And she's a mini horse. She belongs to Rita Mullins, one of the women you met yesterday who brought in all the books to sign."

She nodded, her focus still enraptured by the charming creature. "Yes, I remember who Rita is."

"She lives up the way and when I called her this morning, she was thrilled to loan us Marigold for the day. She said to tell you, no pressure, but she thinks she'd be a perfect addition to one of your books. She even sent along a pan of her famous cream puff dessert and a baked ziti to sweeten the deal."

"A baked ziti? When did she have the time?"

He shrugged. "I don't know, but I think she was trying to outdo Carol's prize-winning jam."

"All this competition is gonna make me as round as Gladys." Kaylee giggled as the mini horse sniffed her hand.

Gladys, who had been hanging behind her, slowly moved closer to check out the new arrival. The two animals sniffed each other's noses then Gladys rubbed her ear along the horse's cheek.

"Speaking of food," Luke said, pulling a baggie from his front pocket. "Rita also sent along a few treats. She said the carrots are Marigold's favorite. You want to give her one?"

Kaylee nodded. "I'm a little nervous, but I'm trying to think of her as a big dog instead of as a little horse."

"Smart. Except giving a horse a treat is much different than the way you hold one out for a dog." He held his arm out straight, his palm up. "Hold out your hand like this, keep it flat so she doesn't accidentally nibble on your fingers."

Kaylee held out her hand, mimicking what Luke was doing.

He set a small chunk of carrot in her palm. "Now keep your hand flat. Let *her* take it from you."

Kaylee held her breath as the little horse snuffled her fingers then delicately took the carrot in her teeth. "I did it."

Luke chuckled. "You sure did. Here's another one." He tossed a piece of carrot to Gladys and one to Cooper, who had jumped out of the truck earlier and just finished his rounds of sniffing all around the ranch and returned to Luke's side.

Kaylee fed the horse another carrot then reached up to gently pet her nose. "She's so soft. Her skin around her mouth and nose are like velvet."

"See? Not scary at all." Luke stood next to the horse and scratched her ears. "I thought we could take her into the barn, and you could brush her."

"Yes, I'd like that." Summoning her courage, Kaylee reached out and put her hand on top of Luke's. "Thank you. For doing this for me. And for not making me feel like an idiot about being afraid of horses." She couldn't believe he'd gone to all this trouble. For *her*.

"Lots of people share that fear," he said quietly, not moving his hand from under hers. "You helped me yesterday, so I wanted to do something for you today. And I knew you couldn't help but fall in love."

She sucked in a quick breath. *Fall in love?*

"With Marigold, I mean," he said, pulling his hand away and stuffing it into his pocket. "She's such a cute little thing. You can't help it."

He was pretty cute, too. The way he suddenly seemed almost shy and like he wasn't sure where to look.

He picked up Marigold's halter and led her toward the barn. Kaylee followed, pretty sure the mini horse wasn't the only one she was falling for.

Chapter Nine

"**I**T'S OKAY," LUKE SAID LATER that afternoon as he stepped in behind Kaylee. "Just think of her as a bigger Marigold."

"That's easy for you to say," Kaylee said, trying to calm her shaky nerves. Brushing the mini horse was easy. She was so cute and seemed to enjoy it. But switching to the full-size horse was much scarier. It was one thing to be outside the gate petting their noses, it was another to be *in* the stall standing next to them.

And the fact that Luke was standing behind her and less than a foot away only amped up the already nerve-wracking situation.

It was mid-afternoon, and the barn was warm. Cooper and Gladys were sprawled out in a patch of sunlight in front of the door. This should have felt perfect. Instead, Kaylee's heart was racing and her palms were so sweaty, she could barely hold onto the brush as she raised it to the horse's side.

The morning had flown by. She'd had a great time brushing and playing with Marigold. The little horse had so much personality. And things had felt back to normal—whatever normal was—with Luke as they'd made sandwiches in the kitchen together.

It had been her idea to eat lunch out on the front porch, and maybe it was the fact that they were sitting side-by-side instead of facing each other that helped to smooth their conversation back into the easy dialogue they'd shared the day before.

Which was maybe why Luke had asked her if she wanted to go for a walk after lunch. They'd strolled through the pastures, the dog's running ahead then racing back to check on them. She'd never seen Gladys so active, but the corgi seemed to be having the time of her life.

And so was she.

She was enamored by the vast green fields leading up to the base of a purple snow-capped mountain range. And she loved hearing Luke talk about ranching and the land. As an introvert, she was skilled in the art of asking questions to avoid having to talk about herself, but in this case, she was truly interested in the answers as she peppered Luke with questions about the animals and the price of beef and how the fall harvest worked. She only wished she'd brought her notebook. It would be full by now. Instead, she took mental notes and felt excited about incorporating it all into her books.

If she were honest, at times when Luke was talking, she forgot all about her books and her research and just fell into the easy rhythm of listening to his voice as she kept pace next to him. He spoke with a passion and fervor for the subject of the ranch, but also shared stories of his childhood and what it was like to grow up there with Faye and their other brother.

Those were the stories she liked the best—the ones that caused him to softly chuckle or belt out an occasional laugh. She sometimes forgot he was talking about her workaholic boss as he shared tales of horseback rides and county fairs and sibling pranks.

They'd walked for over an hour before making it back to the barn. Kaylee had enjoyed it so much, she could have walked across Montana with him. She didn't want it to end. Especially not with her shaking and trembling as she tried to muster the courage to face her fear of horses.

Luke had been patient and kind as he introduced her to Scarlett, a huge mare with a silky brown coat and big gorgeous hazel eyes. "She's a sweet old gal," he'd said. "Probably close to twenty now. She was Faye's horse, so we've had her forever. She got her name from my sister's favorite book at the time. She went through such a *Gone With the Wind* phase."

"I couldn't help but notice a bit of a literary theme as you introduced me to Mr. Darcy and Atticus."

"And don't forget Anne," he'd said.

"Of Green Gables?" she guessed.

"You got it."

"Did you and your brother get to pick any of your horse's names?"

He gave her a sideways look. "We got to name our own. But otherwise, have you met my sister?"

"Yes," she said with a chuckle. "Believe me, yes, I have."

Her chuckle died on her lips though as he opened the stall and ushered her inside. And now her bangs stuck to her damp forehead, and her knuckles were white as she clutched the brush in her hand.

"You've got this," Luke said, his deep voice calm and soothing. "And I'm right here."

He *was* right there. She could practically feel his breath on her neck. "I know this has to seem irrational to you. I'm not even trying to ride her. I'm just standing next to her. Why am I so scared?"

He rested a hand on her shoulder and gently massaged the tense muscle. "It's okay, Kaylee. It doesn't have to make sense to me. And just because the fear seems irrational or whatever, doesn't make it any less real."

She nodded, trying to focus on her breathing instead of the warm pressure of his hand on her shoulder.

"Let's try something else," he offered, prying the brush from her hand and setting it on the side of the stall gate. "Don't worry about brushing her for now. How about you just focus on getting to know her." He took her hand and rested it gently on the side of the horse's neck. "Kaylee, this is Scarlett. She likes long walks in the moonlight, galloping, and butterscotch candies."

"Butterscotch candies?"

"Oh yeah, she loves them. You can give her one in a bit, but for now I just want you to focus on stroking her neck and getting to know her." His hand stayed on top of hers as she drew her palm across the horse's soft coat. "It's your turn now. Tell her about yourself."

She turned her head toward him, but with one finger on her chin, he directed it back toward Scarlett. "Don't tell *me*. Tell *her*."

"Talk to the horse, you mean?"

"Sure. Don't you talk to Gladys?"

"All the time. But I'm not usually sharing what sounds like my dating profile. I've never told Gladys that I like taking walks in the rain or searching for constellations in the summer sky."

"Do you?" He tilted his head. "Like walking in the rain and looking at the stars?"

She slightly lifted one shoulder. "Yes, but not usually at the same time."

He chuckled, and she could feel the movement along her back and shoulder where his body touched hers. She wanted to lean back into him, to tuck herself into his solid embrace.

But he wasn't embracing her. He was trying to help her

overcome one of her deepest fears, which made her feel weak and scared and even more timid than she normally found herself to be.

Had she really just told him that she liked walking in the rain and searching the night sky for constellations? Who even talks like that?

She knew, of course. Her characters did. But they were fictional. Of course they said things that sounded somewhat sappy and wildly romantic. But that probably wasn't how most humans spoke to each other in the real world.

Ugh. Which was another reason she liked living in books and her imagination.

Focus, she told herself, just as Luke said the same word, almost as if her were in her head.

"Focus. If it helps, don't think of her as a horse. Just imagine Scarlett as another version of Gladys."

"But with bigger teeth," she said.

"And longer legs."

She heard the mirth in his voice but swiveled her head to level him with a stare. "Hey, don't make fun of my dog's short legs."

"I'm just kidding," he said then mumbled under his breath, "Sort of." He laughed as she bumped his chest with her shoulder. "Stay focused on the horse," he told her with a flash of a grin.

How could she even remember a horse was standing there after seeing that grin? And that playful teasing glint in his eyes? It was enough to make a grown woman swoon.

She swallowed as the front of his thigh pressed into the back of hers, nudging her closer to the horse. Taking a shaky breath, she leaned closer to the horse's head.

"Hi, Scarlett. I'm Kaylee. I'm from Chicago, and I make up stories for a living. I've written quite a few stories with horses in them, but I haven't been this close to one in a long time. I'm trying not to be scared of you, because you seem perfectly nice and have the most gorgeous brown eyes."

The horse nodded her head as if she were listening and agreed with the assessment.

"I know your master, or owner, or whatever you call her. I know Faye. And Luke, of course. Maybe he's your 'whatever' now, since he feeds you." She took another deep breath and tried to think of something else to talk about. "This would be much easier if I could just ask you questions and let you talk."

"Like you've been doing with me the last few hours," Luke said quietly behind her. "Don't think I didn't catch on to what you were doing."

"I hear you like butterscotch candy," she said, smiling as she deftly ignored Luke's comment.

Scarlett drew her head back at the mention of butterscotch and nodded again before letting out a low whinny.

"She knows the word," Luke told her as he pulled an orange candy from his pocket with his free hand. He forced the candy from the wrapper and dropped it into Kaylee's open palm. "Keep your hand flat, just like you did with Marigold." He pulled out another candy and popped it into his mouth. "I've got one more if you want it."

"No thanks. I'm more concerned about her gobbling up my entire hand right now." She nudged her hand forward, still very aware of the pressure of Luke's other hand where it rested on top of hers.

Scarlett sniffed at her fingers then very delicately nibbled the candy from her palm.

"She didn't bite me," Kaylee whispered as she turned her body towards Luke. Her breath caught in her throat as she saw Luke's gaze drop to her mouth, as if *he* were considering taking a bite of her. He was so close, their faces less than a foot apart.

She looked up at him from under her lashes, her pulse racing as he drew his gaze back to hers. She could smell the sweet sugary butterscotch on his breath mingled with the masculine scent of his cologne.

The fingers of his hand, the one still on top of hers, moved just the slightest, shifting to between hers, entwining their fingers as he closed his hand over the back of hers. It was such an intimate gesture, holding her hand that way, the way a lover might, but against the side of a horse instead of tangled between cotton sheets.

Her back was basically still to him, but her body had shifted enough when she'd turned that the back of her shoulder was now in the front crook of his arm. If this were a scene in her book, Duke would cup Sassy's cheek and draw her to him, slanting his lips across hers in a fevered kiss.

But this wasn't Duke, and no matter how hard she'd been trying, she wasn't Sassy. Kaylee had dated a few guys but none of them had been anywhere near as devastatingly handsome as Luke. And she'd never had one ever cup her cheek or experienced a fevered kiss.

But she'd sure like to experience one now.

With everything in her, she yearned for Luke to pull her into his arms and kiss her senseless.

It didn't matter that he was Faye's brother or that this was a terrible idea. All that mattered was the feel of his arms around her and the desperate desire for his lips to press against hers.

Her heart pounded so hard, thumping almost painfully against her chest, and she felt dizzy and light-headed.

Luke's grip on her hand tightened, and he dipped his head, so close to her lips, she could almost feel their soft graze.

"Woof!"

One of the dogs let out a loud bark, and they both tore out of the barn. Luke jerked back and dropped her hand, and the horse behind them stamped her foot and shifted her weight.

He must have recognized the sound of the engine pulling into the driveway. "That's Dean's truck," he said, his voice a little breathless.

He took another step back and smoothed his shirt, leaving Kaylee feeling unsteady. She leaned back against the solid side of the horse. With all the other emotions swirling through her from the almost kiss, she forgot to be afraid.

"Luke! Kaylee!" Emma's voice called to them from the driveway. "Where are you guys?"

"We're in here," Luke called back after clearing his throat. He opened the stall door and stood back for Kaylee to walk past him. She felt foolish now, like maybe she'd misread the situation, and awkwardly rushed past him, trying not to stumble on her own feet.

She was sure he'd been about to kiss her. He was holding her hand, for goodness sakes. But he hadn't. And the moment had been lost.

"Hey guys, there you are," Emma said, bursting into the barn, the two dogs on her heels. "Sorry we're late."

"Late?" Luke asked.

"Yeah, don't you remember? We have Dine for a Dime tonight. We brought over all the stuff, but Dad said if we don't get started, we'll never make it to the church by five-thirty."

"Oh shoot. I forgot that was tonight," Luke said as he closed the stall door then hurried from the barn. "What are we making again?"

"Taco salads."

"Oh dang. We do have some work to do, then."

"What's Dine for a Dime?" Kaylee asked following Luke and Emma toward the house.

"It's a thing our church does every Thursday night. It's a way to give back to the community. Different groups or families take turns providing a meal and anyone can come in for supper." Emma opened the front door as if she lived there, and they traipsed into the kitchen where her dad was unloading several bags of groceries. "It's supposed to cost a dime to eat, but people can drop whatever they feel like in the can when they leave. And no one really has to pay."

"We never know how many people will show up. It could be two or it could be twenty."

"Remember that one night we had almost a hundred?"

Luke nodded. "I do. We'd had a tragedy in our church, and I think people just wanted to be together," he explained to Kaylee. "That's what's kind of neat about it. It's more than a meal. People come to eat, but they also come for the company. And no matter how many people show up, we always seem to have enough food and the can always seems to hold enough to cover the cost of that night's ingredients."

"Wow. That sounds amazing."

"It is," Emma said. "And it's fun 'cause it's different every time. Dad and Luke and I are in charge of the second Thursday of every month."

"Hey Kaylee," Dean said then changed his focus to Luke. "I thought you would've already started."

"He forgot," Emma told him.

"You forgot?" Dean asked as he pulled a stockpot from one of the cupboards. "How could you forget? I put it on your calendar for the next six months." His gaze jumped to Kaylee as he grinned at his friend. "Huh. It's almost like you have something else taking up space in your head."

"You let me worry about what's taking up space in my head and just focus on getting that hamburger started," Luke grumbled at the other man. "We've got plenty to do without you worrying about what I'm thinking. Although right now I'm thinking we have a lot to do in a short amount of time."

"I'd be glad to help," Kaylee offered. "Just tell me what to do and put me to work."

"You don't have to," Luke said at the same time Dean was handing her a cutting board and a head of lettuce.

"That'd be great," Dean said. "We've got to shred this

and chop up tomatoes and onions."

"I'll start grating the cheese," Emma said, as if this were her normal task. She found a grater and bowl in the cupboard then climbed onto one of the stools next to the counter. Both she and her dad moved easily around the kitchen, grabbing things from cupboards and drawers with the familiarity earned from spending a lot of time there.

She patted the stool next to her. "You can sit next to me, Kaylee."

"Okay." She set the cutting board on the counter then waded into the kitchen, squeezing between the two men to wash her hands and the head of lettuce. Gladys was usually the only other one in the kitchen with her when she occasionally cooked, and she shrunk her shoulders in, trying not to bump into Luke or Dean.

Luke leaned in next to her, using the stream of water from the faucet to rinse a couple of tomatoes. "You don't have to do this. We can handle it if you want to go write or something."

"No, I said I want to help, and I meant it." She tried not to start every time the back of his hand brushed against hers.

Even though there was a part of her that wanted to retreat to her bedroom and hide away, there was another part, the newer Sassy-inspired part that wanted to be part of the group and to help prepare the meal.

This was another thing she wrote about in her books but didn't really have any experience with. Her hand itched to take notes as her mind went crazy with phrases and thoughts about the bump of elbows, the passing of tools and ingredients, and the feel of the jostling of positions as several people tried to work in the kitchen together. It wasn't just the choreography of the people; it was also the sound of meat sizzling and the scent of garlic and chili powder hanging in the air.

The radio in the kitchen had been playing softly, and Emma bounced in her chair as a new song started. "Oh, I love this song. Turn it up, Dad."

Dean and Luke groaned together as if this were a familiar ritual.

"Come on," Emma told them. "You know this one too."

Kaylee recognized the upbeat lyrics and Pink's distinct voice and offered a sideways glance at Luke. "You know this song?"

He shrugged, but she caught the slight redness that bloomed on his neck. "Not really."

"Yes you do," Emma said. "We all sang it last week in the truck when we were taking that load of hay out to the pasture."

"Fine," he grumbled and quietly sang along with the next few lines.

"Come on, Luke," Emma urged. "You know this part."

"Yeah, Luke," Dean said, nudging his buddy in the ribs. "Don't make me show you up on the chorus." He and his daughter joined voices and belted out the lead up to the chorus.

Kaylee pressed her lips together to keep from laughing. She was dying to see if Luke, the brooding cowboy she'd spent the last few days with, would actually join in on the catchy song.

He raised an eyebrow at her, almost as if she were daring him and he was debating taking the bait, then he opened his mouth and in perfect harmony, crooned the entire chorus with Dean and Emma.

Kaylee's mouth curved into a broad smile as her foot tapped and her hips came dangerously close to swaying. She loved this song and knew every word. She cracked up as Dean completely flubbed the next line, mixing up the words and purposely going off-key.

Emma had jumped off the stool and was using the cheese grater as a microphone. She raced to Kaylee's side and held the grater up to her mouth. Kaylee drew back, vigorously shaking her head. "No, not me."

"Come on, you know this part," Emma said. "I know you do. *Everyone* knows this song."

The past few days Kaylee had been stepping outside her comfort zone, pushing the boundaries of her comfortable box. But singing *out loud* with what were essentially strangers was more than she could manage.

What would Sassy do?

Dang it. Sassy would jump on the counter and do an air guitar solo.

The lyrics were building to the next chorus. Kaylee knew the next part...but she couldn't seem to open her mouth.

What's the worst that could happen? Sassy's voice resonated inside her head. *So what if you make a fool of yourself? You're leaving in a few days, and you'll never see these people again.*

Emma held the cheese grater higher, a smile beaming across her sweet face. Kaylee took a breath and forced her mouth to open. Her voice was soft on the first line, but Emma leaned her head in to sing into the pseudo-microphone with her, and Kaylee's voice rose as she belted out the spirited lyrics.

On the other side of the counter, Dean used the wooden spoon in his hands as a mock-guitar, and he and Luke put their heads together and warbled the last few lines.

The song ended with all of them cracking up. Kaylee held her side, bending forward with laughter. She couldn't believe she'd sang with them.

"Okay, okay," Luke said, waving his hands above his head. "Dusty Acres Karaoke night is officially over. We need to get down to business or we'll never get over to the church on time."

"Yes, sir," Emma said, tucking in her chin in mock obedience as she climbed back on to the stool and grabbed the block of cheese.

Kaylee followed Emma's example and got to work chopping the lettuce, but first she snuck a grin at the girl and the two of them dissolved into laughter again.

As they spent the next thirty minutes chopping and grating, Emma filled her in on the latest gossip in town and kept her laughing with silly stories and impressions. She did a pretty accurate one of Luke. By the time they'd finished preparing and packing up the food, Kaylee's cheeks hurt from smiling.

But all the laughter sure felt good.

She rode into town with Luke, a dog on either side of her and a crockpot of taco meat cradled in her lap. On the short ride to the church, he explained how the evening would work. They would have just enough time to get tables and chairs set out and then the four of them plus a few other volunteers would serve the meal.

"Rita and Carol, the two gals you met yesterday, already made cakes and pies for dessert," he told her as she followed him into the church and down the stairs into the large basement. She was surprised when he told her that both dogs would be welcome, but no one seemed to bat an eye as the corgi and the golden trotted into the building after them.

He pointed toward a partitioned counter at the back of the room then nodded his head to the left and then the right. "Kitchen's at the back. Sunday School classes on that side and choir rooms on the other."

"Have you gone here all your life?"

"Yep. Faye and our brother too. Pearl Milligan was our Sunday school teacher for most of elementary."

Kaylee marveled at the lifelong relationships Luke and Faye had with so many of the townspeople. She and her family had moved so many times growing up, there was no one she knew as an adult, other than her relatives, who had known her as a child.

She followed Luke into the kitchen where two women

were wiping down counters and setting up plates.

"It's about time you got here," one of the women said.

Kaylee recognized her as Marnie, the checker from the grocery store, but tonight she had her long hair down and it curled in perfect waves around her shoulders. She wore Ropers in a type similar to Kaylee's, but hers were faded from wear, and the frayed cuffs of her bootcut jeans indicated this was her usual style. Her T-shirt and jeans showed off her cute figure, and her lips curved into a gorgeous smile as she came around the counter toward Luke.

Kaylee clutched the box of food she was holding, her skin heating as she felt like an outsider—the dumpy writer who was masquerading as a cowgirl, in her too-shiny boots and a pink plaid shirt unlike anything in her closet at home.

Her stomach churned as she felt the venomous green tendrils of envy snake through her, threatening to choke her as she fought to swallow.

"Hey darlin'," Luke said as Marnie threw her arms around him and planted a kiss on the side of his cheek.

Chapter Ten

*D*ARLIN'?

The word sent a sharp knife slicing through Kaylee's gut.

Her earlier assumptions must have been correct. That kiss and the familiarity between Luke and Marnie certainly suggested why the woman might have intimate knowledge of the man's favorite breakfast cereal.

He turned to her, his arm still around the other woman. "Kaylee, you remember Marnie? I think you all met at the grocery store the other day."

Kaylee nodded, unable to find her voice. Her throat felt thick, and she swallowed at the bile rising there.

"Nice to see you again," Marnie said, her friendly smile turning to one of concern. "Here, let me take that for you." She reached for the box she was holding, but Kaylee took a step back, her hands gripping the corners so tightly the cardboard was crinkling.

"Hey, are you okay?" Luke took a step toward her. "You look a little pale."

She shook her head. "Um...yes...no...I'm...is there a

bathroom?"

Luke pointed to a door behind her.

She pushed the box onto the empty counter and fled through the door. A hallway lay on the other side, and she hurried down it, Gladys trotting along at her heels. Her cheeks were burning, and she couldn't seem to catch her breath. She needed to splash her face with water. Or maybe dunk her whole head. She'd made a fool of herself, standing there stammering like an idiot when Luke introduced her to the woman who must be his girlfriend.

She racked her brain trying to remember what he'd said when she'd asked him about Marnie. It seemed like his answers were vague. All she remembered was him saying they'd known each other a long time. But she hadn't specifically asked him if he was involved with anyone.

A water fountain stood against the wall. She stopped to take a drink and greedily gulped at the cool liquid. It felt wonderful on her parched throat. Wetting her hand, she pressed it to her heated forehead as she pushed through the door at the end of the hall.

Except it wasn't a bathroom. It was some sort of pantry or stockroom. The walls on one side were filled with shelves of canned and dry goods and the shelves on the other side held paper products like plates and paper towels.

Oh geez. She couldn't even do that right. How hard was it to find the bathroom? She balled her hands into fists and pressed them to her mouth. Squeezing her eyes against the tears that threatened, she held back a scream of frustration.

What was wrong with her? She felt like such an idiot. Had it been so long since she'd been out among people that she completely mistook Luke's attention and somehow turned it into something romantic? Just because she *wrote* romance didn't mean that it was in the cards for her.

And just because a handsome guy was nice to her didn't mean he had romantic feelings for her. What was she thinking? Of course Luke had a girlfriend. Why wouldn't he? Look at the guy. He was so dang good-looking it almost hurt to look at him.

Sure, he was kind of broody, but he was also funny and sweet and nice to old ladies. There had to be a long line of women scrambling for Luke's attention.

Why would a guy like that ever be interested in someone like her? She may have been pretending to be more outgoing than she really was the past few days, but no amount of cheerful conversation could disguise the awkward nerdy woman with frizzy hair and the evidence of too many M&M's and too many hours sitting at a desk on her ample hips.

How had she let herself get caught up in the idea that he *liked* her? Even desired her? She was so angry with herself, she wanted to stomp her feet and kick and scream and throw things. The shelf next to her held several rows of paper towels, and she grabbed a roll and hurled it at the wall behind her. It hit a patch of wall next to the door and fell harmlessly to the ground, but the act of throwing it had felt amazing.

She grabbed another roll and chucked it at the wall. Gladys let out a little yip and raced to the fallen roll to retrieve it. The dog ran around it, opening and closing her mouth as she tried to get her jaw around the large roll.

Kaylee wasn't finished. She grabbed two more rolls, one in each hand and heaved them toward the wall.

Just as the rolls left her hands, the door swung open, and Luke walked in. He deftly caught the first roll, but the second hit him square in the chest, and he let out an *oof* as the roll dropped to the floor.

Kaylee's hands fluttered to her mouth. "Oh my gosh, I'm so sorry." Luke must have followed her in. Her chin dropped to her chest. Could this night get any more embarrassing?

"No worries," he said, rubbing his chest where the launched paper goods had nailed him. "I'm okay, but I wasn't sure if you were. I thought I'd better check on you. But you weren't in the bathroom. Are you all right?"

"I'm fine," she snapped, her harsh tone more out of embarrassment than anger.

"You sure?" He peered around at the paper towels on the floor. "Because from the looks of things, it seems you're either upset about something or you came in here and had to fend off an attack from the Brawny man or the quicker picker-upper." He leaned down to pick up a few of the scattered rolls then crossed to where she stood and placed them back on the shelves.

Warmth spread up her neck and heated her cheeks. Why did he have to follow her?

"I told you, I'm fine. Really." She stared down at her hands where she had them clasped together in front of her stomach. "You don't have to worry about me. You can go back to your *girlfriend.*"

"My *girlfriend*?" He furrowed his brow then shook his head. "You mean *Marnie*? She's not my girlfriend."

Kaylee let out a huff. "Are you sure? She seemed awful friendly. Plus, I heard you call her darlin'."

He turned around and leaned back against the shelf. "So?" He shrugged his shoulders as if that were no big thing. "I call lots of women darlin'. Plenty of horses too."

"You've never called me that," she mumbled not quite under her breath.

Luke narrowed his eyes at her then a coy grin curved his lips. He sidled a little closer to her. "Kaylee?"

She crossed her arms around her stomach but forced her chin up as she stared at him. "What?"

He arched an eyebrow. "Would you like me to call you darlin'..." he paused and lowered his voice just a tad deeper, "*Darlin'*?"

Oh. Her throat tried to swallow but seemed to have forgotten how to manage the act as her mouth went dry.

Was it warm in here? *Who turned on the heat?*

The door of the stockroom swung open, and Rita Mullins strolled in. She jumped and let out a little shriek when she saw them. "Lord have mercy, you scared me to death. I might have just wet myself." She pressed a hand to her chest. "What in the devil are you two doing in here?" Her inquiring expression changed to one of speculation and she let out a knowing, "Ahh."

"We were just looking for some paper towels," Luke said, grabbing one of the rolls he'd just returned to the shelf.

She planted a hand on her hip and leveled Luke with a knowing stare. "Uh-huh."

Gladys, who had still been wrestling with one of the rolls finally got her teeth chomped through the plastic and let out a victorious yip as she held the roll aloft.

"Good dog," Kaylee said, scooting around Rita and hurrying down the hallway. She didn't realize Luke was right behind her until she stopped at the door of the kitchen to compose herself.

He put one hand on the center of her back and leaned close to her ear. "I want to show you something," he said, pushing the door partway open and nodding to where Dean and Marnie were standing by the counter setting up the food.

Kaylee couldn't hear their conversation, but Marnie was laughing and looking up at Dean as if he had just hung the moon. She was standing close to him and had her hand on his arm as she gave him every ounce of her attention like it was a gift lovingly wrapped and presented.

"She's been in love with the guy since we were in high school," Luke said.

Kaylee sighed, once again feeling embarrassed at her lack of people-reading skills. "Is she Emma's mother?"

"No, but she'd like to be. He was dating someone else back then, and they got married right out of high school. She'd acted like all she'd wanted was a family, and they had

Emma that first year, but the *idea* of a baby and actually *having* a baby proved to be two different things in her mind, and she split to California and left them before Emma even turned two. They hardly ever hear from her."

"Oh no, poor Emma. So, is Dean with Marnie now?"

He shook his head. "No. He would be if Marnie had her way. And I think she'd be good for him. For *them*. But he's still pretty gun-shy when it comes to women, and she's been stuck in his 'friend-zone' for years."

"That's a bummer." Something was still niggling her. She'd already made so many wrong assumptions, she might as well ask him. "But if Marnie is so into Dean, how comes she knows what your favorite cereal is and that you were almost out of it?"

He chuckled. "Ah. So that's where this thing started. She knows that because she and her sister are the ones Faye hires to come out and clean my house every other week. And because Marnie works at the grocery store, I sometimes talk her into picking stuff up for me and bringing it out with her. I told you Faye had them out the day before you arrived to stock up the kitchen and make sure the house was extra spiffy."

"Oh." Well, that was a perfectly reasonable explanation.

He leaned a little closer to her ear and lowered his voice to that rich deep tone that had her toes curling in her new boots. "And for the record, I *don't* have a girlfriend." He slid around her and pushed through the door, leaving her with her mouth open and little sparks of heat shooting up her spine.

Letting out her breath, she followed him in and was immediately engulfed in the noise and hubbub of the busy kitchen.

Emma was dumping corn chips into a bowl, but she squealed when she saw Gladys at Kaylee's feet, the roll of paper towels still clutched in the corgi's mouth. "Oh my gosh, Gladys is so cute." She squatted in front of the dog. "You're such a good girl, aren't you?"

Gladys held her prize a little higher but didn't give it to the girl. Cooper was lying on a dog bed in the corner of the kitchen and lifted his head when he saw Gladys. The corgi trotted over and curled up beside him, finally releasing her grip on the paper towels. She let them drop in front of her but rested her chin on them as she surveyed the happenings of the kitchen.

Emma hugged her arms around herself. "Aww."

They were pretty dang cute.

"You two just gonna stand in the way?" Rita said, coming through the door behind them, her arms full of paper plates and plastic cups. "Or are you going to help me set up these plates?"

"Sorry," Kaylee said, reaching out to take a stack of plates. "I'm on it. Where do you want them?"

"You can put them at the end of that counter," Rita said, pointing a finger. "But you'd better be quick about it. The hungry hordes will be here any minute."

Rita wasn't kidding. Within the next ten minutes, the basement was filled with church members and people from the community as they lined up and filled their plates.

The next few hours flew by as Kaylee helped to serve food and fill glasses and pick up discarded plates. She loved the sound of laughter and spirited conversation that pervaded the room. She was surprised by how so many folks all seemed to know each other. Small towns were so different than big cities where anonymity was valued and even craved. No one in Bartlett would be able to get by with anything because no doubt someone in town would recognize them and probably spend three minutes in chatty conversation about how their family was doing.

Things eventually did start to wind down as more people finished eating and left. Kaylee wiped off an empty table then crossed back into the kitchen. "Looks like we haven't had anyone in line for a while now," she said to Luke and Emma, who were manning the food line. "Should we start putting the rest of the food away?"

"Not yet," Emma told her. "Bear hasn't arrived. He's usually the last one in."

"Who's Bear?"

"An old guy who lives west of town. I don't think he's missed a single meal since we started this thing," Luke said.

"Why do you call him Bear?"

"Because he's as mean and grouchy as a big ole bear," Emma whispered.

"Now Emma, be nice," Dean admonished, coming up behind his daughter.

"Well, he is," Emma said. "He's cranky and kinda weird. His house is so rundown, it's scary. And he's always walking around town pulling a wagon and digging through people's trash."

"That's no reason to be unkind," her dad told her.

She hung her small head. "Sorry."

"The guy's last name is Berenger, but most people only know him as Bear," Luke explained. "You'll see why. He didn't used to be quite so grumpy, but his wife died several years back and since then, he's kept more to himself and kind of stopped caring what people think of him. He's an ornery old coot, but he's harmless. His bark is much worse than his bite."

Dean cleared his throat and nodded to the large man who walked into the back of the room and there was no doubt he was the man in question. He was tall and barrel-chested with a full bushy beard shot with gray and thick eyebrows just visible under a worn gray felt cowboy hat. He looked like he could be Hagrid's grandpa.

The few people who called out greetings to him were met with a scowl as he made his way to the counter and picked up a plate.

The man was even more imposing up close. He was well over six feet tall, and his hands were almost as big as the plate he was holding. But Kaylee knew what it was like to want to be left alone and to have a need for solitude be misunderstood as weird or odd.

She smiled at him as she held out the bag of corn chips. "Hi there. We're serving tacos tonight. Would you like some corn chips?"

He winced as if her cheery voice hurt his ears. "Who are you? And what are you so goll-danged cheerful about?"

"Hey Bear," Luke said, holding out a scoop of taco meat. "This is Kaylee Collins. She's my guest at the ranch this week."

Bear held out his plate for Luke to fill as he eyed Kaylee. "Since when do you have *guests* at the ranch?"

"Since Faye called and told me she was sending me one."

The large man answered with a knowing grunt then moved down the line. With his plate full, he picked up a glass of iced tea and shuffled to an empty table. He kept his head down as he ate, his body language giving off a definite *stay away, I want to be alone* vibe.

Now that Bear had arrived, the rest of the group commenced cleaning up. Kaylee was happy to wash dishes in the kitchen, but Rita handed her a pitcher of tea and instructed her to go offer refills. Even in the short time she'd known her, Kaylee knew Rita wasn't someone to be argued with. Maybe Rita and Faye were long-lost sisters or cousins.

Most people were finishing up and clearing out as Kaylee made the rounds and eventually ended up in front of Bear. "Could I refill that for you, Mr. B—" She caught herself before calling him Mr. Bear like he was a character in a fairy tale.

He studied her as he pushed his empty cup across the table. "You can just call me Bear."

"Could I get you a piece of pie?"

"No," he answered gruffly then narrowed his eyes as he peered toward the kitchen. "But I wouldn't say no to some of that cake."

She found the largest slice of cake left on the counter and picked it up. It was chocolate cake with cream cheese frosting—one of her favorites—and on a whim, she grabbed a second piece for herself and brought them both back to the table. "Mind if I join you?"

He shrugged. "Suit yourself."

She wasn't sure what made her sit down with him. Maybe the feeling of recognizing a kindred spirit. She'd found that as an introvert, she could often sit quietly with another introvert and neither would feel the need to come up with awkward small talk.

Bear stabbed the cake with the fork as if it were a piece of beef. "You're the writer," he said as more of a statement than a question.

"I am."

"I've read some of your books."

She studied his face. "You have?"

"Sure. I like to read, and they have several of them at the library." He offered her a small smile, but she still caught the amusement in it. "I can't remember the title, but I just read that one where Duke and Sassy had to fend off the cattle rustlers. Even though I prefer cake, that part where Duke tried to bake her a pie was one of my favorite scenes. And I really like the parts with the goat. They always make me laugh."

Kaylee tried to imagine this man laughing while reading a scene in one of her books. It was hard enough picturing him reading one at all, let alone cracking up at the goat. "Those are some of my favorite scenes too."

He leaned back and narrowed his eyes at her. "You remind me of her, ya know?"

"Who, the goat? Thanks a lot."

He made a noise that sounded almost like a chuckle. "No, not the goat. Sassy. The heroine."

Kaylee waved her hand at him. "You're kidding."

"Do I look like I do a lot of kidding?"

"Well, no, maybe not. But I'm nothing like her."

"She came out of *your* imagination. I'll bet you're probably more like her than you think."

Kaylee shook her head. "No way. I'm nervous and skittish. Sassy is confident and bold. She's brave and not afraid of anything. And I'm scared of everything."

"Not everything. You just plopped yourself down in front of the meanest old cuss in town."

"You don't seem that mean."

"You don't seem that scared."

She leaned closer and lowered her voice. "It's all an act. Faye sent me here to experience life on a ranch so I could make my books more authentic but the whole idea of leaving my apartment and Chicago and coming to Montana to stay with a stranger terrified me. The only way I've gotten through it is to try to channel Sassy. Every time I find myself in a new scary situation, I try to ask myself what Sassy would do and then I pretend I'm her."

"Seems to be working. I never would have pegged you as skittish. It appears to me you fit in around here and have already made some friends." He glanced toward the kitchen where Luke was standing at the counter watching them. "Maybe even more than a friend."

"Oh gosh," Kaylee said, ducking her head as she floundered for a way to change the subject. "I like your watch," she said, nodding to the fancy silver band.

"Thanks. I just found it last week. You'd be amazed at what perfectly good things people throw away these days. They say one man's trash is another man's treasure. I find all sorts of things that just take a little fixin' up then I sell them to the consignment store." He held up his wrist. "All this took was a little tinkering, and now it works good as new."

"Not everyone has the skill for tinkering. I wouldn't have any idea how to fix a watch."

He leaned forward and lowered his voice. "To tell you the truth. All this really took was a new battery. I feel kind of bad for keeping it. I've been tempted to knock on the feller's door and give it back to him."

Kaylee laughed. "I'd bet he'd be surprised." This man might have been as big as a bear, but he wasn't mean or grouchy at all. Okay, maybe a little grouchy, but underneath that gruff exterior, he seemed more like a teddy bear than a grizzly.

He narrowed his eyes at her as he pushed up from the table. "You know, people are sometimes like that too. They think they're broken or used up or not worth much, but sometimes all it takes is a little tinkering or for someone to replace the part that's missing, and they can feel good as new too."

She nodded, trying to hear his meaning with her heart as well as her ears. "Thanks, Bear," she said, her voice coming out closer to a whisper.

"Take care, Ms. Collins. And keep writing." He tipped his hat then picked up their empty plates and dumped them in the trash. He stopped on his way to the door, and Kaylee smiled as she saw him drop a twenty-dollar bill into the donation bucket.

No, not a mean old bear at all.

Luke watched Kaylee with the old man. His eyes widened as he caught Bear actually chuckling with her. He didn't think that man smiled at anyone anymore, let alone offered them a laugh.

What were the two of them talking about?

It must be something funny the way they were both smiling at each other. Not many people had the guts to sit down across from Bear. And not many could coax a smile or a laugh out of him.

But Kaylee wasn't just anyone. He was realizing that more and more. She was different. Special. She saw things in a unique way. And for someone who claimed to spend all her time alone, she really cared about people.

"Thanks for letting me tag along tonight," Kaylee told Luke as they pulled up in front of the house later that night.

"I should be thanking you. You were a lot of help. It was a good night." He lifted the grocery tote from the seat between them then opened the truck door. "And we came away with just enough leftovers to cover us for lunch tomorrow."

The sound of crickets filled the warm summer air, and the back of Luke's hand brushed hers, not once, but twice as they walked from the truck to the house. Both times had sent butterflies spinning and tumbling through Kaylee's stomach.

But her butterfly-filled stomach pitched as they walked up the steps of the porch and saw Luke's front door standing ajar.

"What the devil?" His voice was low as he moved to position himself between Kaylee and the door.

Cooper and Gladys had been walking beside them. The hair on the back of Kaylee's neck raised as both dogs froze, their bodies alert.

Cooper let out a low growl.

Without thinking, Kaylee grabbed Luke's hand and gripped it tightly. She let out a tiny yelp as the sound of a crash came from inside.

Chapter Eleven

"**S**TAY HERE," LUKE TOLD KAYLEE, his body as tense as the dog's as they approached the front door.

"No way," she whispered, clutching his hand. "What if it's an axe murderer?"

He stopped and swiveled his head to look at her. "An axe murderer? I was thinking more like a neighbor who came over to borrow something or the less likely idea that I'm being robbed. But I hadn't even considered an axe murderer."

She shrugged. "I'm a writer. I have a vivid imagination."

"Okay, but why would anyone want to murder me? With an axe, no less."

"Axe murderers aren't always logical."

"All the more reason for you to wait out here."

"By myself?" Her voice squeaked.

His lips twitched up in a grin. "All right, we can face the axe murderer together. But at least stay behind me, okay?"

"Deal." She pressed closer as she followed him up the stairs. He set the bag of leftovers in one of the rocking chairs and let go of her hand as he picked up the broom that had been left there from when he'd swept the mud off the porch earlier that day.

"A broom's not gonna do much against an axe," she whispered.

He turned his head back toward her. "You sure you don't want to wait out here?" he whispered back.

"Sorry. I'm sure that broom will work great."

He nodded as he turned back. Holding the broom out in front of him, he carefully pushed open the door with the end of the handle.

Kaylee had hold of the back of his shirt as she followed right behind him. She gasped as she peered around his shoulder.

The living room had the pillows from the sofa knocked to the floor, but the kitchen was the real disaster. The pantry door was open, and canned and boxed goods had been pulled from the shelves and littered the floor. Pasta noodles lay scattered amongst cans of green beans, and the air held a mix of garlic and tomato scents from the jar of pizza sauce that had broken, the contents from which were now splattered across the lower cabinets.

A bag of flour had burst open when it fell, and the dust had exploded across the hard wood. Tiny floury footprints crisscrossed over the kitchen floor then up a cabinet and across the counter, leading to the masked bandit.

But their intruder wasn't holding an ax. Instead, he gripped a red box of Cheez-Its in his furry paws.

A large raccoon sat on the kitchen counter, calmly nibbling a cracker from the package as he peered at them across the wreckage.

For one moment, they all just stared at each other, then all heck broke loose as the dog's raced toward the kitchen, barking and growling at the masked trespasser.

The raccoon took off across the counter, knocking off the bowl Emma had been grating cheese into as it ran, but still keeping hold of the box of crackers. The bowl hit the hard wood, spilling the leftover cheese onto the floor, but not shattering the glass.

Cooper barked again, but Gladys stopped to gobble up the orange cheese shreds then licked at the pizza sauce on the cabinets.

"Get down from there," Luke yelled, waving the broom toward the raccoon as he tried to get it off the counter.

Kaylee hopped from one foot to the other, not sure how to help, but unable to stand still. She pointed to the raccoon as it climbed on top of the pink pig-shaped cookie jar and leapt up to the top of the refrigerator, a cracker still clutched in its paw. "Get it, Luke. It's on top of the fridge."

"I can see where it is," he called back. "How do you expect me to get it? Hold out my arms and tell it to jump?"

"I don't know," she shrieked. "I've never had a raccoon in my house before."

"Well, I haven't either."

Kaylee let out another shriek as the thing leapt off the refrigerator.

It hit the floor with ease, but instead of running toward the door they'd left open, it scampered straight toward Kaylee.

She turned and sprinted into the living room, leaping onto the top of the coffee table. Gladys yelped and jumped up next to her, the pasta sauce forgotten.

The raccoon raced through the living room, jumping onto the fireplace hearth then into Luke's chair then back to the floor, leaving bits of flour and cracker crumbs in its wake.

"Git," Luke yelled, trying to shoo the animal out the door with the broom. He was nowhere near close enough to actually touch the raccoon with it, but either the motion must have startled it or the animal finally spotted the open door, because the raccoon gobbled the last bite of cracker then scampered to make its exit.

He stopped just inside the door and looked forlornly

back toward the kitchen as if contemplating going back for the box of crackers.

"Go on now," Luke ordered, and it turned and scurried off the porch, down the steps and across the driveway.

Luke set down the broom and leaned back against the messy counter, oblivious to the flour getting on his shirt. He let out a laugh as he peered over at Kaylee where she still stood on the coffee table. Gladys was pressed to the side of her leg, and Cooper had jumped up on the other side. "You know that critter jumped all the way up on the counter and then onto the fridge? That coffee table would be an easy leap for him."

She laughed with him, but more out of nerves than humor. "I didn't know what else to do. That thing was running right toward me." She wrapped her arms around her middle. "I've never seen a raccoon that close up before."

"Hopefully, you never will again. He was really coming after you." He was still chuckling as he crossed the room and held out his hand to help her down. But his laughter died as she put her hand in his and he must have felt their tremble. "Your hands are shaking." He put his arm around her waist to assist her then pulled her into a hug. "Hey, it's okay. He's gone now."

She pressed her cheek to his chest, hoping he couldn't feel how hard her heart was still pounding. "He scared me half to death."

He pulled her closer and spoke into her hair. "I was just kidding around about him coming after you. I don't think he was chasing you as much as trying to find a way out."

She let herself melt into his embrace, just for a moment then pulled away. "Sorry. You can probably tell I'm not very brave when it comes to wild animals." She smoothed the wrinkles from the front of his shirt then took an awkward step back. She rubbed her hands over her arms. "Actually, I'm not very brave when it comes to anything." Although she had braved a conversation with the town grouch earlier *and* faced down a miniature horse, so her courage seemed to be growing.

"That's not true. You followed me right into the house, even when you thought an axe-murderer might be inside."

She shook her head. "Only because I was more afraid of being left alone on the porch."

He furrowed his brow. "Seems to me, you're brave in a lot of ways. You've taken on a career that involves putting yourself out there all the time for people to reject you and yet, you excel at it. And I think it took a heck of a lot of guts to drive halfway across the country to stay on a ranch with some dude you didn't even know, just to make your writing better."

"Some would claim those things take more of a *lack* of intelligence and common sense than courage."

"They'd be wrong." Gladys stood next to him, still on the coffee table, and he stroked a hand down her neck. "And you're not afraid of all animals. You do great with Gladys. And with my goofy mutt, too."

She breathed out a soft laugh and reached out to scratch Cooper beneath his chin. "Neither of them are very scary." She let out a shudder. "Not like that raccoon."

Luke shook his head. "I wonder how the thing got in here." He crossed to the front door and examined the knob. "The latch sometimes sticks. Or maybe we didn't get it closed all the way when we left."

"We *were* in a bit of a rush."

He stepped onto the porch and peered around the ranch. "No sign of him now." He grabbed the bag he'd left in the rocking chair and grinned as he held it up toward Kaylee. "I'm just thankful it didn't grab our leftovers."

She laughed, this time a real laugh. Her pulse had returned to a reasonable rate, even after racing like crazy when Luke had hugged her. But he still had a way of calming her down. His soothing voice and relaxed composure seemed to settle her, even after being pursued by a wily critter and hugged by a handsome cowboy.

She loved that he'd said he thought she was brave. Whether it was Sassy's influence, or something she was truly finding in herself, she could feel just the smallest amount of courage starting to grow in her. She had shown bravery earlier tonight when she'd greeted and served the townsfolk their meals and when she'd followed Luke into the house to face the axe murderer. But the thing that was scaring her the most right now were the feelings she was having for the charming cowboy and how fast the time she was getting to spend with him was going.

She pushed down those fears as she peered around the kitchen and into the cabinets then pointed to the box of cereal on one of the higher shelves. "I'm thankful it didn't nab your Lucky Charms."

Luke chuckled. "That would have been a real catastrophe."

Kaylee picked her way into the kitchen and took hold of the broom. "Come on. I'll help you clean this place up."

"You don't have to. But I won't turn down the help." He set the bag on the counter. "You've got to be beat. This has been quite a day."

"Yeah, but in a good way." She swept the loose pasta and flour into a pile. "I had a lot of fun today. And especially tonight. That was a really neat event. Thanks for letting me be a part of it."

"Thank *you*. You were a huge help. And a total hit with the locals."

"I don't know about that."

"I do," Luke said, taking the leftovers from the bag then pulling out two copies of her books and setting them on the counter. "Janet Presley, the choir director, brought these into the kitchen tonight when you were out talking to Bear.

She said these are her favorites and was wondering if you'd be willing to sign them."

"Oh sure. Of course." She ducked her head and focused on sweeping the flour out of the pantry. It was such an odd feeling to have so many people here know who she was and to ask her to sign their books. "I'd be glad to."

"I figured you would."

"Why didn't she ask me herself?"

He shrugged. "I think she was a little intimidated. You being so famous and all."

She shook her head. "Oh, stop it. You know I'm not famous."

"I don't know that all. Faye makes you sound like a celebrity, and I've seen your books on the shelf at the grocery store. That seems pretty famous to me."

"I'm just a regular person trying to get through the day, same as anyone else." Except half the time she was terrified someone would find out she didn't really know what the heck she was doing. Although, if she were honest, that's kind of what led her to this ranch in Montana.

The thing she most feared, that readers would know she didn't know what she was talking about, had happened. And the world hadn't stopped spinning. Her career hadn't been ruined.

Her editor had just sent her out to get more experience.

Maybe she didn't have to be quite so scared, after all.

Kaylee noticed a light coming from the living room when she got up to go to bathroom later that night. It was close to midnight, and Luke had said he was going to bed hours ago.

It had taken them close to an hour to clean up the mess

from the raccoon then Luke had gone out to do his chores and she'd retreated to her room. Sitting on her bed, she'd chuckled to herself as she tapped at her keyboard, hammering out a new scene for her book where Sassy and Duke faced off against a raccoon.

She padded quietly down the hall. Luke was there, sitting in the recliner, Cooper snuggled against his leg. The golden retriever looked up, but Luke's attention was fixed on the book he was reading. *Her* book.

She couldn't believe it. Luke was sitting out here in the middle of the night reading *her* book.

She let out a tiny gasp, but it was loud enough for him to hear, and he peered at her over the top of the paperback. "You okay?"

She nodded, searching for her voice. "Are you?"

He let out a sigh. "Couldn't sleep."

"So you got up and decided to read my book?"

"Well, I got up to get something to eat, but I saw your books sitting there and thought I'd give one a try." He leaned forward and stretched out his arms. "It's pretty good."

"Oh gosh." She didn't know what else to say.

"I mean it." He held the book sideways, and she could see he was already half-way through. "I was just gonna read a couple of pages, but I couldn't put it down. You're a great writer, Kaylee."

"Thank you," she whispered. "That means a lot." His words touched something in her.

"I can see what Faye is talking about, though. There were a couple of places I noticed that made me think you hadn't actually been around many horses or cows before."

She lifted one shoulder. "Apparently there are some things you can't just Google."

"Apparently there are some you can. You get plenty of things right."

"Now that I've been around some horses, I feel like I'm

totally blowing it with the way I portray them. I'm really excited about going to the rodeo tomorrow night and getting to see some actual barrel racing in action. I may even take a few of my own videos instead of always trying to search for them on YouTube."

"That will be good. But we really need to get you up *on* a horse so you get the authentic experience of riding one."

She swallowed, her palms already going clammy at the thought. "I don't know."

"I do." He gave her a curt nod. "It's happening. Tomorrow. Be prepared."

She wrung her hands in front of her. "Now, I'll never be able to sleep tonight for worrying about it."

"You'll be fine." He waved the book toward the kitchen. "Now go back to bed and let me get back to my book. I'm just getting to a good part, and I want to read *one* more chapter before I turn in."

She tried to keep the smile from her face as she turned on her heel and headed back to her room. She would go back to bed, but there was no way she was falling asleep now.

Luke tried to focus on holding the saddle in place instead of on holding Kaylee's hand as he encouraged her to get on the horse. "You can do it. It's just like getting on a bicycle."

"Yeah, if I were riding a thousand-pound bicycle with scary teeth." She pressed her free hand to her mouth. "Oh sorry, Scarlett. I hope I didn't just imply that you're fat."

Luke chuckled. "In that respect, you probably just gave her a compliment. She's probably closer to fifteen hundred pounds. But she's not scary." He patted the horse's neck. "I told you, she's a real sweet old gal. And we're just going to ride around the corral. I won't even let go of the reins."

Kaylee let out a shuddered breath. "You promise?"

He gave her a solemn nod. "I promise." He could feel her hand shaking and gave it an encouraging squeeze. "Now come on. I know you can do this. Just start by putting your foot in the stirrup." He transferred her hand to the saddle horn and stepped around behind her. The bicycle analogy may not have been the best one, but it was better than the merry-go-round one he'd first thought of. "Imagine the stirrup is your pedal and you're swinging your leg over the seat."

She blew up her bangs and lifted her foot toward the stirrup. "Holy cow, the stirrup is so high. Are you sure you didn't set them for a taller person?"

He shook his head, doing his best not to take charge and just lift her up. He was pretty sure she wouldn't appreciate his effort. He held the stirrup in place. "You got this."

She leaned back into his chest as she raised her foot again, this time securing it in the stirrup. "I got it."

"Good job. Now push with your foot and pull yourself up with the saddle horn. Use those muscles. You can do it."

"You sound like the instructor in the spin class your sister dragged me to last year."

"Yeah? Did their encouragement work any better than mine?"

"No, I quit and never went back."

"Well, you're not quitting on this. You're almost there."

She set her shoulders and gripped the saddle horn tighter. Luke thought he heard her quietly mumble, "Come on, Sassy," then she pulled herself up, swung her leg around, and dropped into the saddle.

The mare stamped her foot once but otherwise seemed untroubled by the rider on her back.

Kaylee's bangs were stuck to her damp forehead, and she was breathing a little hard, but she wore the slightest look of pride on her face as well. "I did it. I'm in the saddle."

"You sure did. You ready to ride around the corral a little?"

She gripped the edge of the saddle. "No. This seems like a pretty big step for today. Can't I just get down and we can try the actual riding around part tomorrow?"

"No way. We're doing this. Trust the horse," he told her. He rested a hand on her leg and stared up at her. "And trust *me*. I won't let anything happen to you."

She nodded and lifted her chin a little. "Okay, let's do it."

"That's my girl." The words were out of his mouth before he had a chance to stop them. Turning his head, he focused on the horse and led her slowly out of the barn and into the sunshine of the corral. *That's my girl?* Where had that come from? Kaylee was *not* his girl. He didn't *have* a girl. Not anymore.

Hopefully she was preoccupied enough with trying to not fall off the horse that she hadn't heard him.

He led the horse slowly around the corral several times, and he could feel Kaylee starting to relax a little. She still stiffened at the slightest fuss of Scarlett, but after fifteen or twenty minutes of gentle walking, she was sitting easier in the saddle.

Scarlett plodded back into the corral and stood patiently by her stall as Luke helped Kaylee dismount.

"I did it," she beamed, obviously proud of herself.

"Good job. You both deserve a treat." He handed her a couple of orange cellophane-wrapped butterscotch candies. "Now are you ready to try something a little more challenging?"

She peered up at him as she unwrapped a candy. "More challenging than facing down one of my childhood fears?"

"Yes. But I promise it will be worth the effort."

She chewed on her bottom lip as she held the candy out for Scarlett. The horse nibbled it off her outstretched palm and crunched it between her teeth. Kaylee took a deep breath then turned back to him. "Okay. I'm in."

Chapter Twelve

THIRTY MINUTES LATER, KAYLEE WAS regretting her hasty acceptance of Luke's challenge as she took in the steep mountainside in front of her.

Luke had made a ride with him on his horse, Max, sound fun and easy. Until she was actually sitting atop the huge horse with Luke's strong arms wrapped around her as he loosely held the reins.

She sat in the saddle and he sat behind it, but he was still close enough that her back brushed against his chest as the horse plodded along the short path to the base of the mountain in back of the farmhouse.

"This is my favorite trail," Luke told her. "And it leads to one of my favorite places on earth. You're going to love it."

As thrilled as she was that Luke wanted to show her one of his favorite places, her nerves were jumping like crazy as she warily peered at the mountain in front of them. "What trail? I don't see a trail. All I see are trees and rocks."

He laughed, and she felt the rumble of it against her back. "That's what's so cool about it. It's like a hidden path. But don't worry, the horse knows the way. He and I have done this hundreds of times. I've been coming up here since I was a kid."

Her knuckles were white as she grasped the saddle horn with both hands. She let out a small squeak as the horse entered the shade of the trees and started up a rocky path.

"This used to be an old deer trail, but I've taken my horse up it so many times, it's become a regular trail now. It's a tough hike on foot, but Max can practically go up with his eyes closed."

"Does that mean it's okay for *me* to close my eyes while we go up it?"

He laughed again.

"I'm only half joking."

"You could close your eyes but then you'd miss this amazing view."

The trail leveled out as they got further into the trees and the hush of the forested woods fell around them. Gladys had decided to stay at the farmhouse and take a nap, but Cooper raced ahead of them, occasionally darting back to make sure they were following.

"It is gorgeous," she whispered as she relaxed a little into him. The scent of pine and moss perfumed the air around them. Birdsong and an occasional huff from Max were the only sounds. The branches of the pine trees reached out as if to grab them but didn't quite make it to the trail.

"You ain't seen nothin' yet."

Oh gosh. She wasn't sure if she should be scared or excited. Or both. But scared definitely took the lead as the horse wound its way around a large boulder in the hillside and started up another path. Kaylee flinched as rocks and sticks crunched under his hooves.

"Don't worry, the horse is more sure-footed than we are. And he doesn't want to fall either. Trust Max. He knows the way, and he knows what he's doing."

The path led through more trees and around an outcropping of rocks before they emerged into a small clearing that opened up on the side of the mountain.

Kaylee gasped as a huge expanse of cerulean blue sky filled the space in front of her. She could see for miles as the valley stretched out before her. Lush green fields laid out in rectangular patterns and were cut in two by the dark raging water of the Missouri River. A cluster of boulders jutted from the side of the mountain and tiny waterfalls trickled their way over the rock faces.

"It's beautiful," she whispered as Luke slid off the horse behind her.

"I told you," he said, holding out his hand to help her down.

She grasped his hand, holding it tightly as she climbed from the horse. Her legs were wobbly and shaky, and she reached for his arm to steady herself. But she didn't want his focus to be on her fear of riding, she wanted it to be on this place—*his* place. The one he chose to share with her.

Sucking in a deep breath, she straightened as she inhaled the clean freshness of the air. "I've never seen anything like this." She walked a few steps to stretch her legs. There wasn't far to walk. The clearing was small, and the grassy edge dropped off the side of the mountain.

Luke gestured toward the rocks as he tied Max's reins to a tree. "Have a seat." Cooper ran over and climbed onto what looked like a stone bench that had been naturally formed at the base of two of the boulders.

"How neat," she said, running her hands over the smooth granite before sitting down. The bench gave her a perfect bird's eye view of the valley. She shifted her boots on the loose bit of gravel in front of her. "I know my feet are on solid ground, but if I look straight out, it feels like I'm flying." She grinned at Luke as he settled in next to her.

His brow furrowed as he stared at her, a small smile barely on his lips. "That's how I've always felt, but no one else has ever said that before." He tilted his head. "Although to be fair, very few people have been up here before. It's kind of my secret place."

"I can see why. Did you make this bench?"

He shook his head. "Nope. God did. He and Mother Nature, I guess. The rocks have always been like this. The waterfalls are bigger during the spring snow run-off, and they're what's made the rock so smooth."

She looked around, the awesome beauty of it bringing tears to her eyes. She swallowed at the emotion in her throat. "It's amazing."

His eyes widened. "Hey, it's okay. I didn't mean to make you cry."

She smiled. "You didn't. I mean, I'm not crying. Not really. I'm just overwhelmed. At how beautiful it is. And at how thankful I am that you chose me to share your special place with."

He smiled back, but his smile had a touch of sadness to it. "I haven't been here in a while. I used to come up here all the time. Especially after Beth died. I call it my thinking spot, but Faye's always called it my 'really bench.'"

"Really bench?"

He shrugged. "Yeah, 'cause I come up here when I'm *really* sad or *really* mad or *really* need to think about something."

"What kind of things do you think about?" She didn't want to delve into questions about Beth's death, but she also wanted to leave it open in case he wanted to talk about it.

"Everything. The weather, the price of beef, when I should sell my cattle, what I want the ranch to be like in five years, in ten years, what sounds good for dinner. You know, just normal life stuff."

"I do know. I'm a thinker too. But I spend most of my time thinking about *other* people's lives."

"*Other* people?"

This time it was her turn to shrug. "Well, other *fictional* people. The majority of my headspace gets taken up with making up stories and adventures for my characters. If I'm not thinking through one of my character's back stories or pondering their inner motivations, I'm racking my brain to come up with a black moment and a grand gesture that seems new and unique and hasn't been done a million times before. And if I'm not working on my own character's stories, I'm making up a meet cute for the two people in line in front of me at the coffee shop or plotting a thriller novel from a piece of news story I've heard on the radio. My brain is always racing with stories."

"That sure makes my pondering of my supper menu seem dull in comparison."

She laughed. "But there's no pressure for you to come up with an amazing list of food options. You can throw together anything from the fridge or pantry and not have to present it to your editor or agent and hope they love it enough to offer you the money you need to pay your rent for the next several months."

"I think my rent would fall short if I offered them my specialty of beanies and weenies."

"I'm always worried my rent is in jeopardy."

"Why? You're a great writer."

Heat warmed her neck at his compliment, but she rolled her eyes as she shook her head.

"You are," he insisted. "You had me reading a romance at midnight last night, and I was so engrossed, I read another whole chapter before I went to bed."

"You did?"

"Heck yeah I did. I had to see if Duke showed up in time to save Sassy from those cattle rustlers. Although I loved it when she ended up saving herself *and* him after they caught him sneaking around the barn." He shook his head. "I could never do what you do. Make up stories like that then make sure they all fit together and make sense."

She let out a sigh. "Some days it's tough. There are a few times when the writing just flows and the words come faster than I can type. But most of the time, being a writer is like having really hard homework. Every. Single. Day. And now writers basically run their own businesses, so when I'm not writing books, I'm trying to come up with newsletter content, cover copy, doing edits, and trying to learn how to run ads on social media."

"Geez. That's a lot. Do you ever stop to have fun? Don't you go out with friends?"

She shook her head. "Not really. I don't have any close ones in the city. Faye drags me out to lunch once a month. But most of my social interactions are online, with readers and other writers who live all over the country."

He'd been worrying a small stone between his fingers, and he looked down at it as he nonchalantly asked, "What about going out on dates?"

She huffed out a laugh as her cheeks heated again. "I haven't been out on a date in a *long* time. I used to force myself to go out on at least one every six months. But the last one was such a disaster, it made me not want to even try again."

"Disaster? Uh oh." He grinned as he casually leaned back against the stone bench. "I've had one of those too. Want to bet on whose was worse?"

She covered her face with her hands. "No way. Then I would have to tell you about mine."

He laughed as he leaned forward and planted his elbows on his knees. "Come on. It can't be that bad."

"It is."

"Okay, here's the deal. Whoever has the worst date story has to buy dinner at the rodeo tonight."

"Wait. Then that will make me seem like a loser twice."

"Okay. Valid point. How about this? Whoever has the

worst date story gets *out* of buying dinner tonight."

"That's better. Then at least I'll get some kind of compensation for spilling this embarrassing story."

"Now you've got me really intrigued."

"You go first."

"Okay, mine's easy because I've only gone out on one date. It was last year and after months of one of the ladies at church trying to set me up with her granddaughter, I gave in and agreed to go to a movie with her. Which I thought would be an easy date, plus I really wanted to see the movie."

"This doesn't sound so bad."

"It was. The woman brought her three kids on the date because she wanted them to have a say in helping to pick their next daddy. Then she made me pay for all of them plus popcorn and snacks and the kids talked and fought through the whole movie then one of them barfed in the seat ten minutes before it was over."

"Okay, it's getting worse. But I'm still in the lead."

"I'm not done. At the end of the date, when I told her I didn't think we were going to work out, she told me that was fine because she'd thought she was going out with my brother anyway. Oh, and then she asked me for his number."

She let out a laugh. "That's pretty bad, but buckle up, Buttercup, because you're going down. My date also brought companions with him on our date, and I only wish they were his kids." She paused for effect. "My date, Stuart, told me he was so nervous about his date that he brought along his ventriloquist dummy, Mr. Jangles, to do his talking for him."

Luke narrowed his eyes. "You're making that up."

"I *wish* that I were. Because Stuart might have been nervous, but Mr. Jangles was a laugh a minute, cracking non-stop jokes and most of them were at my expense. I would have walked out, but he didn't bring the dummy out until after I'd ordered, and I was starving and just curious enough to want see what was going to happen."

Luke was holding his stomach from laughing so hard. He paused for a breath then held up his hand. "Wait. You said he brought *companions*, plural. Please tell me he brought more than one dummy."

She sighed. "If only. Apparently he'd picked a restaurant in the same block as his apartment building. I know this because his mom, who he *lived with*, showed up halfway through the date to check on him. Or to check me out. Still not sure exactly which. But she proceeded to pull up a chair and converse with me, Stuart, *and* Mr. Jangles. Then at the end of the meal, she asked if I was going to finish my chicken parm and when I said no, she took a folded-up piece of foil—from her purse—and wrapped up the rest of my meal in it to take with her."

Luke was bent double with laughter as he pulled his wallet from his back pocket and passed it to her. "Take my money. Just take all of it. You win."

She had to laugh with him. "I told you I would. And I didn't even tell you about the great date that I'd thought I'd had, until I discovered he stole my credit card and had already run up $1000 in online purchases by the time I'd got home."

He waved his hand in front of her. "Stop. I'm dying."

Even though it was brought on by her terrible date stories, she loved hearing his hearty laughter.

"Please tell me you're planning to use those in a book sometime." He leaned back against the rock to catch his breath. "Wow. I haven't laughed that hard in a long time."

She passed him back his wallet. "Me either."

"I'm sorry it was at your expense."

"It's okay. I knew you would either find that story humiliating or hilarious. I'm glad you went with the latter."

He shoved his wallet back in his pocket and wiped his eyes. "Regardless of a few terrible dates, and you were right, those *were* terrible, I still think your life in Chicago sounds more fun and exciting than mine here at the ranch."

"Exciting? Are you nuts? More like boring. I've done way more fun and exciting stuff in the short time I've been here than I've done the last year in Chicago. It seems like every day here has been filled with something new and different."

"That's only because it's different *to you*. To me, it's the same old stuff every day. Feeding animals, running fence, working on repairs to the ranch. I spend the majority of my time tinkering around and fixing stuff that breaks. Last week I spent two hours trying to repair my old toaster."

"A toaster? Don't those cost like twenty bucks to replace?"

His lips curved into a sheepish grin. "It's the principle of the thing. And tinkering around with stuff gives me more time to brood."

She grinned. "You'd better be careful, or you'll end up like Bear."

"I think I'm already on my way."

She leaned back against the bench and held her palms up. "So what are you going to do about it?"

He raised an eyebrow at her as he leaned back next to her. "I think I'm going to sit here and think on it a bit."

A laugh escaped her. "Good idea. I'll join you."

Their hands were next to each other's on the bench between them. Luke shifted, and the side of his hand brushed against hers.

He looked out over the valley and let out a small sigh. "You have a great laugh."

Kaylee swallowed, the compliment catching her off-guard. She expected him to say something about ranching or how pretty the view was. A quiet, "Thank you," was all she could muster in reply.

"It's been nice to have some laughter around. To hear it on the farm again. Not that Dean and I don't josh around and have a good time. We do. And Emma is adorable. But I guess, I mean, you know, a woman's laughter." He continued to stare out at the sky, but his pinkie looped over hers. "It's nice. I like it."

She didn't know what to say. Her brain couldn't function enough to produce words. All she could think about was the pressure of his finger as it rested over hers. It was the smallest movement, the slightest touch, but it was a huge action that spoke volumes.

Luke's voice had dropped to a whisper, but she heard his next words as if he'd shouted them through a megaphone. "I like you."

Terrified to move her hand, she didn't want to ruin this moment. It felt important. Like more important than anything that had happened to her in years.

This was the kind of massive romantic gesture she wrote about, but those things didn't happen to her. Sure she'd held a man's hand, but this one tiny touch felt like something so much more. Like it was a question or more like an offer. And she knew her response could make or break this one special instant of time.

What would Sassy do?

Okay, Sassy would probably grab Luke by the collar and plant a kiss on his gorgeous mouth. But no amount of channeling her heroine could make her do that. But maybe she could still do something. Something a little Sassy with a splash of Kaylee.

Her mind threw out a *here goes nothing*, but this wasn't nothing.

Here goes everything.

She curled her pinkie around his, locking their two fingers in something as close to an embrace as she could get. Then she forced her lips to move. "I like you too."

She hadn't realized how tense his shoulders were until they loosened as he relaxed against the bench.

They didn't say anything more, didn't even look at each other, just sat there, pinkies linked and looking out over the view of the valley.

She wasn't sure how long they sat like that, could have been five minutes, could have been ten. She would have stayed for hours, until her hand cramped and her arm fell asleep, but apparently Cooper had other ideas.

He'd been laying at Luke's feet until a ground squirrel poked its head out from between the rocks. The dog leapt up and chased the squirrel back into its hiding spot then trotted back to Luke and Kaylee. He jumped up onto the bench between them, breaking their connection, as he wiggled his butt and tried to lick Luke's face first then Kaylee's.

"Come on, buddy," Luke said, wrapping his arm around the dog. "Settle down."

Cooper wiggled and squirmed some more, squashing himself into a tight circle between them and laid his head on Kaylee's thigh. He peered up at her with big brown eyes that expressed how truly sorry he was.

"Aww, he's so cute," she said, ruffling the fur around his neck. "I'll forgive you anything, Cooper."

Luke gave the dog's head a scrub with his palm then pushed up from the bench. "We should probably head back. I need to get Max brushed and get cleaned up before we head into town for the rodeo."

"Yeah, sure." Kaylee stood and brushed the dust from her jeans. She could have sat there with Luke all day. Not just because she was loving his company, *and* almost holding his hand, but because she wasn't ready to face getting back on the horse again. Her heart thundered just thinking about it. The only good thing about it was having Luke's arms wrapped around her as he held the reins. That *almost* made up for the terror of getting back in the saddle.

The rodeo stands were starting to fill up later that night as Kaylee and Luke found an empty spot in the bleachers. Their hands were full of fry bread tacos and napkins, and they each had a bottle of pop tucked under their arm.

"I'm kind of glad I lost the bet so I got to choose where we ate. You're gonna love these things," Luke told her, taking her pop and setting both bottles on the concrete by their feet. "They're greasy and messy, but man are they delicious."

"Then it seems like I won all the way around." Kaylee peeled back the foil and inhaled the scent of chili powder and fried dough. She wasn't sure about them when Luke suggested the idea, but her mouth watered as she watched the guy ladle chili and cheese on the flat bread then fold it in half like a taco. Taking a tentative bite, she groaned at the burst of flavor.

"Told ya," Luke said, grinning around a mouth full of fry bread.

"I'm not sure you'll be able to talk me into that fried cheesecake you mentioned, but this is amazing."

She settled in next to him, aware of how close his shoulder was to hers as they watched the rodeo come to life in front of them. She'd just taken her last bite when the announcer's voice boomed through the loudspeaker welcoming them to the Bartlett Annual Rodeo.

They stood for the national anthem as riders galloped around the arena, the flags of both America and the state of Montana waving proudly from the poles secured next to their saddles.

Luke took off his hat and pressed it to his chest, raising his chin as he proudly sang the opening lines of the song. The sound of his deep bass voice filled Kaylee's chest, and she stood a little taller next to him, lifting her voice with his.

They'd announced the performer as this year's Girl of the West, and she sang in a loud clear tone. Tears pricked Kaylee's eyes as they often did when the vocalist belted out the line about the land of the free. A few cheers and hoots went up in the crowd as she held that last note, then the stands thundered with applause as she finished the song.

It was amazing—the sound of the people's voices lifted around them, all raised in patriotic pride.

Luke glanced down at her then offered her a wink and a grin. "Don't worry. It gets me choked up too."

She smiled back as they took their seats again. She really liked this man. Even though her body couldn't quite decide how to act around him. One minute she was totally calm and at ease, the next she was antsy and nervous and couldn't figure out where to put her hands. Not that she was hoping he'd try to hold her hand again. Except. Well. Okay, yeah, she was totally hoping for that.

"Hey guys," Emma called, waving to them from the aisle. "Can I sit with you?"

There wasn't much room, but Luke waved her in and Kaylee scooted closer to him, pressing her thigh and shoulder against his as Emma squeezed into the spot next to them.

"My dad is helping with the lights, and it was so boring. I saw you guys up here, and he said I could come sit with you."

"You're good," Luke said, reaching around Kaylee's shoulder to swipe a piece of blue cotton candy from the roll in Emma's hand.

Kaylee could barely breathe from the heat of his arm around her and the press of his leg next to hers.

The corners of Emma's lips were stained a sugary blue as she smiled sweetly at Luke. "Also, I came over here because I have a favor to ask."

"Uh oh," he said as he swiped another strand of cotton candy. "This is never good."

"Oh come on. It's easy," she said, but the way she was squirming around in her seat told a different story. "You know how I really, really, like *reallllly* want that bike at

Milligan's?"

"Yeah."

"And how I've been saving for months to buy it?"

"Yeahhh."

"Well, they're doing a competition tonight, and the prize is a *hundred-dollar* gift certificate to Milligan's. And I just know that if you did it with me, we could *for sure* win."

Luke glanced at Kaylee then back at Emma. "Just what kind of competition is it?"

"Wellll, it's more like a race than a competition." She held up her hand. "But we don't have to do the racing."

"I have a feeling I'm going to regret asking this, but who does the racing?"

"It's one of those chicken races where two teams have a bunch of chickens, and you and your partner have to shoo all your chickens across the finish line first. They're doing it in the middle of the arena between the bronc riding events and the mutton-busting."

Kaylee pressed her lips together to keep from laughing.

Luke let out a groan. "How about I just *give* you the hundred dollars."

Emma grinned. "I would totally take that, but you know my dad would never let me accept it. He thinks I have to work for the money. But this would count since we have to *work* together to win the race."

Kaylee nudged his arm. "You *absolutely* have to do this. A little girl's dream is at stake."

"Why don't you do it then," he mumbled.

"Because she asked you. And it seems like it would take a particular set of skills to race chickens that I would no doubt be lacking."

"Yeah, either that or you *are* a chicken."

She laughed. "Oh yes, definitely that too." She put an arm around Emma. "But I will be your biggest cheerleader. I'll clap so loud you'll be able to hear me all the way in the arena."

"Thanks," Emma said, then pressed her palms together as she peered at Luke. "So will you do it? I really need a partner. Please. Please."

"Fine, I'll do it," he grumbled.

The girl bounced up and down in her seat. "Yay. Thank you, Luke."

He gestured toward the arena. "Don't you need to go down there and get us signed up?"

She shrugged. "I already did. We have to report to the arena entrance in twenty minutes."

This time, Kaylee couldn't hold it in. She laughed out loud as Luke let out another groan.

Twenty minutes later, Luke, Kaylee, and Emma stood at the arena entrance. Luke grimaced as he watched a team set up the course for the chickens to complete.

"I can't believe I let you two talk me into this." At least he'd convinced Kaylee to come down with them. She was so keen to have him participate, so she wasn't getting out of being part of this whole crazy scheme. "We're gonna look like fools out there."

"But we'll be fools who will be able to buy a bicycle," Emma said.

"Oh come on." Kaylee ribbed him again. "It looks like fun."

A woman wearing a blue vest with the words 'Fairgrounds Staff' stamped on the back of it came up to them. She held up a clipboard and pointed her pen at Luke and Kaylee. "You two the team for the Dusty Acres Chicken Chasers?"

Emma lifted her shoulders as she grinned at Luke. "It was the best team name I could think of on the spot."

"Yeah, I guess that's us," he told the woman then pointed to Emma. "But she and I are the team."

The woman frowned at Emma. "Sorry. Competitors have to be eighteen and older."

The young girl's face fell. "Oh no. But we *have* to do it. I *have* to win that gift certificate. I'm trying to buy a bike."

"Your team is still signed up, so you can have your mom take your place," the woman said, nodding toward Kaylee.

Emma grabbed Kaylee's hand and squeezed. "Will you, please? You know how much I want that bike, *Mom*."

"Oh. Gosh. But I'm not. I can't," Kaylee stammered.

"Sure you can," Luke told her, wearing way too satisfied of a grin. He nudged her arm. "Weren't you just telling me how I *had* to do this? Remember? *Our* little girl's dream is at stake."

Chapter Thirteen

KAYLEE GROANED. WHY HADN'T SHE stayed in the stands? It'd been all fun and games when she was convincing Luke to do it. However, the amusement was lost now that she was being recruited to be a chicken chaser.

She looked from Emma's pleading face to Luke's amused one. She *had* faced one of her biggest fears earlier that day when she'd gotten on the horse. And taking that ride with Luke had had a major payoff. And she wasn't just thinking of the scenery.

She didn't know any of these people, she reasoned. And she'd be gone in a few days. And she couldn't destroy Emma's chance of getting that bicycle. So, what else could she do?

"Fine. I'll do it."

"Yay!" Emma jumped up and down then threw her arms around Kaylee. "Thank you."

The fairgrounds woman handed them each a clipboard and a pen. "You're gonna need to sign this waiver."

"What is it?" Kaylee said, scanning the page as Luke scribbled his name on his and passed it back to the woman.

"It basically states that you're an adult over the age of eighteen and that you won't sue us if any damages occur during the competition."

"Damages? Like what?" Her voice rose. "Are there hidden dangers in chicken racing?" She jumped as she heard the squawks of several chickens as they were brought out in two crates to the center of the arena.

"Lady, I don't know. I'm just a volunteer, but the event is getting ready to start," the woman told her as she held out her hand. "So you can either sign this, or I can go get the alternates."

Kaylee scribbled her name and passed the clipboard back.

Luke leaned in next to her and whispered, "Don't worry. It's not dangerous."

She nodded a thanks for his reassurance.

Then his lips curved into a grin. "Just don't trip and fall down or those chickens will attack and peck your eyes out."

Gah. She was the least coordinated person. *Of course* she would trip. Especially now that she was thinking about it.

Before she had time to grab the waiver form back, the volunteer handed them each a white vest covered in chicken feathers and a red felt cowboy hat with a plastic chicken attached to a spring on top of it. The chicken bounced on the spring and bobbled back-and-forth with the movement.

Luke held up his hands. "No way. I am *not* wearing that."

The woman cocked an eyebrow. "I thought you wanted to win."

"What does me wearing either of those ridiculous things have to do with winning the chicken race?"

She pointed to three people taking their seats at a table on the edge of the arena. "See those folks over there? They're the judges. This race isn't won just by getting your chickens across the line first. They also award points for style. So you've got to wear the hat *and* the vest *and* make 'em look good. And it *also* helps if you flap your arms around like chicken wings and holler 'bawk bawk' a lot. Like the more 'bawks' the better."

Luke's eyes widened as he stared first at the woman then at Kaylee.

"Don't look at me," Kaylee said, shrugging into the vest and nodding to Emma. "This was *her* idea."

Emma pressed her palms together again and gave Luke another pleading look. "Please *Dad*. I really want that bicycle. And it's just for a few minutes. Think of it like a shot, it will be over before you know it."

Kaylee could see him softening as he looked over to where the other couple, their competitors, we're getting ready and both of them had a chicken bouncing on their heads. He took off his cowboy hat and passed it to Emma then held out his hand. "Fine. Give me the stupid hat."

The fairgrounds woman passed him his props then pointed Emma toward the other side of the arena. "All right now honey. Your mom and dad need to get ready, so you go stand over there by that table," she told the girl. "You can cheer your folks on from there."

"All right, *folks*, you got this." Emma beamed, looking adorable with Luke's too-big hat sitting on her head as she held her hand up to high-five each of them then ran toward the designated spectator area.

"Just so you know," Kaylee told Luke as they walked toward the starting line. "Any hope we have of winning rests solely on your shoulders. I don't know a thing about chickens. Except that I prefer legs over thighs. I'll do what I can to help, but I just hope there's a good runner-up prize."

"I can handle the chickens. But I'm counting on you to do the majority of the bawk-bawking and arm-flapping."

"Oh thanks. I get the part that makes me look like an idiot."

He stopped and stared pointedly at her as he aimed a finger at the hat on his head.

She pressed her lips together to hold back a giggle. "Point taken."

They made it to the starting line, and Kaylee took his vest and held it out for him to stick his arms through. "Do you know those people?" she asked, nodding to their competitors.

"Yeah, sort of. They're Rod and Sandy Hooper. They run the Pizza Shack in the next town over. See their T-shirts? They're probably just doing this to get publicity for their restaurant."

The Hoopers looked to be in their mid-forties and both seemed to be having fun with the competition already. Sandy's chicken-bobbing hat kept falling forward on her head, and she was cracking up as she tried to get the feather-covered vest around Rod's stout arms. Her vest was stretched tightly across her ample figure. She had short legs, an apple-shaped body, and a big head of blonde hair.

Kaylee was trying to remember they were the competition and not get taken in by the couple's infectious laughter. "Well I don't care what they're doing this for. We're doing this for Emma." She plunked the chicken hat resolutely on her head. "Now, tell me how the heck to race chickens."

Luke chuckled. "It seems more of a chicken *chase* than a race." He pointed to the cages set at the starting lines. "I've never done one myself, but I've seen them, and I've certainly ran around trying to herd chickens back into their coop before."

"See? I told you. You've already got way more experience than me."

A tall man wearing a black cowboy hat stood up next to the judge's table and tapped a microphone. "Good evening, ladies and gentlemen. Welcome to the 9th Annual Bartlett Chicken Race competition. You all are in for some *egg-sellent* entertainment." I mean, we're about to have a real "egg-citing" race." He waved off the good-natured boos the audience threw his way. "Looks like we've got a real toss-up with tonight's competitors, and I can't wait to see who makes it to the top of the pecking order." He consulted his clipboard. "Racing for the red team, the Shack Attack, are Rod and Sandy." He paused as the Hoopers raised their arms and whooped and cheered. The audience ate up their antics and clapped and yelled for them.

Kaylee dreaded the announcer calling their names next. She had zero experience at this sort of thing and had no idea how to get the audience to cheer for them. Was it too late to back out of this whole silly idea? What had she been thinking when she'd agreed?

"And racing for the blue team, the Dusty Acres Chicken Chasers, are Luke and Kaylee." The announcer pointed their way.

Kaylee summoned every ounce of her Sassy spirit and took a step forward to wave to the audience. The front of her boot hit a plastic candy wrapper half-buried in the dirt, and her foot went sliding out in front of her. She pinwheeled her arms, trying to over-correct her body weight and not pitch forward, and instead fell backward. Right into Luke's outstretched arms. Her chicken hat fell forward on her face as her back landed hard against Luke's chest.

Without missing a beat, he popped her back on her feet and whispered close to her ear. "Take a bow and act like you meant to do that."

"What?" she stammered. Like she *meant* to make an even bigger fool of herself?

Luke waved and smiled at the audience. "*Style* points. Take a bow," he repeated through a fake smile.

She bent forward at the waist, and her cowboy hat fell off, the chicken landing in the dust. Scooping it up, she raised it in a wave, and the crowd went wild.

"Whoo hoo!" she could hear Emma's cheer from the judge's table as the girl jumped up and down and screamed for them at the top of her lungs. "You can do it Mom and Dad!"

Kaylee shoved her hair, and her pride, back and rammed the hat back on her head. "We've got to win this," she told Luke. "For Emma."

"Contestants, take your places," the announcer shouted into the microphone. "The winners will be determined by who gets their three chickens around the obstacles and across the "fowl" line first. Remember, you're not allowed to actually touch our feathered friends. No picking them up or any physical contact to "egg" them on. Use only your herding skills and your powers of persuasion. Ready? Set? GO!"

Wait? *Go?* She wasn't ready. She had no powers of persuasion or herding skills, especially not where chickens were involved.

But she did have heart. And she cared about Emma and didn't want to let her down. "What do I do?" she called to Luke as the cage door opened, and three chickens wearing bright blue ribbons around their necks waddled out.

"Stay over there, and don't let them get by you," he said, raising his arms out to the sides as he shooed the chickens toward the first obstacle. "And start bawking."

Arrggh. This was nuts. She folded her arms into wings but kept them close against her body. "Bawk," she squeaked, her voice barely above a whisper.

The crowd cheered as one of the chickens made a break for it and ran past her legs.

"Go get 'em, Kaylee," Luke yelled, still trying to corral the other two forward.

Go get 'em? How the heck was she supposed to do that?

She looked over at Rod and Sandy who were hopping around and clucking at their red-ribbon tied birds.

She had to do this. She was in it to win it.

Turning around, she chased after the chicken, her elbows

up as she flapped her arms and made loud bawking noises. "Here chicken, chicken," she called as she sprinted around and got in front of it. The bird didn't seem to be responding to her flapping, so she waved her arms in circles to try to shoo it back to toward Luke.

"It's working," she yelled. The chicken's tail feathers bounced as it let out a squawk and ran back toward its feathered friends.

"Hold the line," Luke called. His legs were bent in a squat as he scooted forward, keeping the birds from getting past him.

They circled the miniature barn obstacle and headed toward the finish...er, fowl line.

Kaylee glanced over at their competitors. One of their chickens had also gotten loose, and Sandy was chasing it around the back part of the arena. Bill was doubled forward, his hands on his knees, trying to control his gales of laughter at his wife's antics. "Get her, Sandy," he hooted then howled with another burst of laughter.

"We got this," she shouted to Luke over the noise of the boisterous crowd. "Don't let that one get by you."

He waved a hand at the escaping bird, trying to keep her from getting by him. The chicken turned back around and ran straight at Kaylee.

Memories of the attacking mama goose raced through her mind, but at least this chicken wasn't hissing at her. She stood her ground, raising up on her toes and squawking loudly at it. It worked. The chicken veered back toward the others.

They made it around the second obstacle and were in the home stretch now. Luke and Kaylee joined forces behind and to either side of the chickens and herded them forward. The crowd was cheering and laughing.

All they had to do was get their chickens across the line. Ten more feet, and they'd have it.

"We're going to win," Kaylee shouted, beaming at Luke.

Her smile fell as a chicken wearing a red ribbon around her neck went racing by them and crossed the finish line.

Luke shot a quick glance behind them. "That's only one. They still have to get the other two across. Come on." His face pinched into a grimace as he shook his head then he raised his arms into wings. "This is all for Emma," he yelled before letting out a loud, "Bawk Bawk."

Letting out a laugh, she joined in, flapping her "wings" and bawking their way toward the finish line. She could see Sandy and Rod coming up behind them, and she doubled her efforts, flapping harder and squawking louder.

They were neck and neck as two of each team's chickens had crossed the fowl line.

One chicken left.

The crowd was going crazy, clapping and cheering. It wasn't clear who they were cheering for, but they sounded like they were having fun.

"Go! Go! Go!" Kaylee yelled as their final chicken raced across the line inches ahead of the competitor.

"Yes!" Luke yelled, turning to her and holding out his arms.

The adrenaline must have taken over her body, because she didn't even think about it before leaping into his arms. "We did it. We won!" she cried, as he lifted her off her feet and spun her around.

Her boots had barely touched the grass when they were engulfed in a tackle hug from Emma. "I knew you could do it!" Luke let go of Kaylee and lifted Emma up as she hugged his neck.

"Let's go get your prize," he said, setting Emma down and grabbing Kaylee's hand to pull her toward the judge's table.

"Good job, Blue Team," the announcer said. "You're now the reigning Chicken Chasing Champions."

One of the judges handed them an envelope and a clip-board with a form attached. "I just need you to sign that you received the gift certificate."

Kaylee took the envelope while Luke scrawled his name on the form. She leaned forward, lowering her voice a little as she conspiratorially spoke to the judge. "We really worked it out there. Did we get extra for our style points?"

The judge stared blankly back at her. "*Style* points? What are those?"

Luke huffed as he shook his head. He yanked the feathered vest and hat off and tossed them onto the table. "That woman. She had us bawking and squawking like fools."

"Who cares?" Emma said, jumping up and down. "You won!"

"*You* won," Kaylee said, trying not to laugh at Luke as she passed Emma the envelope with the gift certificate.

The girl took it and pressed it to her chest. "I can't believe it. You guys are the best. I have to go tell my dad." She gave them each another hug before running toward the lighting booth.

Kaylee took off her props and set them on the table then beamed at Luke. She could feel the flush in her cheeks, and she was sure her hair was a tangled mess. But she didn't care. They had won. *And Luke had hugged her and held her hand.* "That felt amazing."

"It did," he agreed as he put his arm around her waist and led her toward the exit of the arena. "But I'm okay if I never do it again."

She giggled. Yes, *giggled.* Like a schoolgirl whose crush had his arm wrapped around her. "Agreed. But it *was* kinda fun. Who knew chicken racing was such an exciting event?"

Luke offered her a side-eye. "Don't you mean 'egg'-citing?"

She laughed again as she swatted playfully at his chest.

He dropped his arm when they got to the steps to the bleachers, holding the gate so she could go through first. They made their way back to their seats amidst hoots and hollers of congratulations and chicken jokes.

"I'm never going to live that down," Luke said, dropping onto the bleacher.

"But you'll be a legend among Bartlett's foremost chicken chasers." Kaylee teased as she settled next to him.

They made their way through two more sodas and a bucket of salty popcorn as they watched the rest of the rodeo. Kaylee was fascinated as she watched the barrel racing event, gripping Luke's arm as the women galloped their horses around the barrels then flew full speed past the finish line.

She tried to take in the sounds of the thundering hooves as they sped through the dirt, the thud of the cowgirl's heels against the horse's sides, the roar of the crowd, and the twang of the announcer as he broadcast the girl's names and the times of their rides.

In her mind, she tried to imagine how Sassy would feel as she anxiously waited for her turn then the rush of adrenaline as she spurred her horse into action and galloped into the ring.

She took pictures and shot some video so she could relive those few seconds of speed again as she wrote Sassy's next barrel-racing scene. Before they left, she sent Faye a quick text with a few pictures telling her how glad she was she'd forced her to come to Montana.

Faye had sent back a laughing emoji, and Kaylee could hear her editor's 'told you so' laughter in her head.

"Thank you," she told Luke later as they got out of the truck and headed up the porch steps. He'd given her his flannel shirt to wear earlier when she'd shivered, and the warm fabric kept out the cool of the evening air. "This night—this whole day—has just been amazing. I've had the best time." Before she could let herself think too much about it, she stepped forward and gave him a hug.

It was a quick one, but it was heartfelt, and had her pulse thrumming as she let him go and reached for the front door.

"Don't you want me to check for wild animals before you go in there?" Luke teased her as he reached around and pulled the door open for her.

She jerked back. "You don't think...?"

"I'm just teasing." He chuckled as they entered the house and were greeted enthusiastically by Gladys and Cooper. The two dogs ran around, their butts wiggling as they chased each other than raced back to get in a lick at Luke's or Kaylee's hands before running off again. Cooper unearthed an old tennis ball from under the sofa and dropped it at Kaylee's feet.

"Not tonight, buddy," Luke told the dog, ruffling his neck before opening the front door and letting the two dogs outside.

"It's so cute how they get along so well and play together."

"Yeah, Gladys has already claimed her favorite spot on the sofa." Almost as if they belonged here.

Both dogs finished their business and clamored back up the porch steps, whining to be let back in. Luke opened the door, and Gladys raced down the hall then stopped outside the bedroom door to wait for Kaylee.

"I guess someone's ready for bed."

Luke jerked a thumb toward the front door. "I'm gonna check on the animals before I turn in."

"Oh, you'll probably want this," she said, reaching for the lapels of the shirt. "Thanks for loaning it to me. I'm not used to the way it cools off at night here. Summer nights in Chicago stay hot and muggy." She started to pull her arm from the sleeve, but he waved her off.

"Keep it. It looks better on you anyway." He flashed her a grin that had butterflies taking off in her stomach, reeling and swirling as they crashed into each other. "Goodnight Kaylee."

"Goodnight Luke." She headed down the hall.

She didn't turn around, but a smile spread across her

face as she heard him say, "I had a really good time tonight too."

Chapter Fourteen

LUKE HEARD GLADYS SCRATCHING ON Kaylee's door as he walked by it the next morning. She'd told him it was okay to let the corgi out if he was up first.

He eased open the door, just enough to let the dog through. Gladys came flying out, racing around him and Cooper then popping to a sit in front of him. Holding her head up for a scratch, the corgi's hind end wiggled with excitement.

"You are a pretty cute little mutt," he said, giving her neck a brisk rub. The dog's eyes closed in bliss as she reveled in the attention, then she took off again, stopping to sniff her and Cooper's food bowls before she ran to the front door.

Even in the short time they'd been here, the dog had settled into a routine, making herself at home.

The dog wasn't the only one, he thought as he peered into the bedroom at the woman sleeping in his guest bed. She lay on her side and had her fist tucked under her chin. His throat caught at the flood of emotions that ran through him as he took in the serene expression on her face and the mass of wavy chestnut hair spread across the pillows.

She looked like an angel.

She slung one arm out as she rolled to her back, and he noticed she had on the flannel shirt he'd given her the night before. *Dang.* She'd worn his shirt to bed. That fact sent a slew of questions running through his head. Was she wearing it because she *liked* him? Or did she just pull it on in the night because she was cold?

Kaylee Collins had landed in his life, with her pudgy dog, hot pink cowgirl outfit and a smashed vegetable cake, and he hadn't been the same since. He'd expected her to be snooty or even a little stuck up, but instead she'd been sweet and charming and brought a breath of fresh air to his otherwise dull existence.

She made him see his life and his old farm in a new light, and he was finding that he liked it. Even when he'd thrown dull or grubby tasks at her, she'd attacked them with the kind of zest and excitement akin to if he'd offered her a job as a taste-tester in a cupcake shop. She seemed to make everything fun. Which was something he hadn't realized how much he was missing in his life.

He was actually looking forward to today's celebration, which he hadn't done in years. He'd often skipped it, entrenching himself in chores to have an excuse to stay home. Some years, Dean and Emma had dragged him out, but he hadn't stayed for the street dance in a long time.

He and Kaylee had talked about going together, but the fluttery feeling in his stomach he was getting from watching her sleep suddenly made him wonder about tonight. Was this a *date*? Would she think it was? Or was this just two friends going to a concert and street dance together. Were they even considered friends?

Of course they were. What else would he call them? Except he couldn't recall getting jumpy and nervous about going to an event with any other friend before. But this event involved a warm summer night and music and oh man...

what if she wanted to dance with him? The idea of taking Kaylee in his arms and leading her around a dance both thrilled and terrified him.

Double dang. What was this woman doing to him? And why was he still standing in her doorway getting all moony over her wearing his shirt to bed and having sappy thoughts about her looking like an adorable angel.

Her steady breathing dipped, and she let out a low snore. A grin broke across his face. Make that an adorable *snoring* angel.

Gladys whined from across the room, and he carefully pulled Kaylee's door shut and went to let the dogs outside.

He was still mooning over the woman twenty minutes later as he finished catching up on his email and emptying his first cup of coffee. He'd let Gladys back into her room, and the corgi had jumped on the bed and cuddled up to Kaylee. He'd actually caught himself feeling jealous as she sleepily threw her arm over the dog's neck and curled around her.

He needed to get out of here, needed to clear his head. He poured fresh coffee into a travel mug then scribbled a note to Kaylee about taking Max out for a ride. At the last second, he added a line about planning to leave for the Pancake Breakfast and parade at nine.

But that wasn't considered a date either. Was it?

Kaylee heard the sound of hooves and caught sight of Luke's back as he rode into the pasture as she stumbled into the kitchen for coffee fifteen minutes later.

He nudged the horse forward, and she was captivated by the vision of him galloping the huge black horse across the bright green pasture. His cowboy hat was pushed low over his forehead, and he leaned forward in the saddle as if he were trying to outrun the air behind him.

She pressed a hand to her chest as she let out a sigh. That man wasn't even in the same room with her, and he still had her heart pounding as if he'd just taken her hand. Which brought up more heart hammering as she remembered the way her hand had felt gripped in his.

They'd had such fun the day before. But she wasn't here for fun, she reminded herself. This was supposed to be work, research. Although she'd practically filled one notebook already with thoughts and ideas and bits of prompts for new scenes and settings.

And today held another array of opportunities for hand holding...er, more research. Luke had made the pancake breakfast and parade sound droll and boring, but she couldn't wait. All the events of the day sounded fun to her.

She found Luke's note and checked her watch. She'd had an idea the night before and calculated how much time she would need. Yes, she should have just enough to get ready then run into town and get back before they needed to leave.

Thirty minutes later she was pushing through the door of Milligan's Mercantile. She waved to the woman behind the register and was greeted with a warm smile. "Hi, Pearl," she called, crossing the empty store. "How's Bud doing?"

"Oh hey Kaylee," Pearl said, leaning back against the side of the counter. "He's doing real well. Almost completely back to his ornery self. Thanks for asking. Something I can help you with this morning?"

"Yes, actually there is. You know Emma Austin?"

"Of course."

"And how she's had her eye on that bicycle in the front window?"

Pearl nodded. "She's been hounding me about it all summer."

"Well Luke and I competed in this silly chicken race last night to win her the hundred-dollar gift certificate to the store, and she said that got her pretty close to having enough to actually buy it. So, I had this idea that if we knew just how much she was short, I could secretly make up the difference so that she'd be able to ride her new bike in the parade this morning."

Pearl lifted an eyebrow. "Well aren't you the sweetest?"

Kaylee's cheeks flushed as she shook her head. "No, Emma's the sweetest. She's nice to everyone she meets. So I'd really like to do something nice for her."

The older woman tapped her chin then reached for the phone. "I've got an idea." She dialed a few numbers then held the phone to her ear. "Hello, Dean? Hey, it's Pearl down at the Mercantile. Is Emma around?" She paused to listen to his response. "Yeah, he's doing fine. He's still planning to flip pancakes this morning down at the Elks Lodge. Thanks for asking."

She paused again then winked at Kaylee before turning her attention back to the phone as the young girl must have come on. "Hi, Emma. Listen honey, I wanted to call and tell you we decided to run a summer celebration sale on a few items for outdoor fun, and I'm including that bike of yours. Do you happen to know how short you are from the regular price?" She waited then a grin spread across her face. "Only fifty dollars, huh? Well for heaven's sake. That is a coincidence. Wouldn't you know that's the exact amount that silly bike has been marked down."

She held the phone away from her ear, and Kaylee could hear the squeals of excitement coming through the receiver. "Yes, I'll hold it for you. No, I double promise pinky swear I won't sell it to anyone else. In fact, we'll get it cleaned up and ready for you if you want to come down and get it this morning so you can ride it in the parade." She chuckled. "Yes, I am super-duper excited too."

She hung up the phone and grinned conspiratorially at Kaylee. "That was easier than I thought."

Kaylee passed Pearl her debit card. "I'd like to cover the remaining fifty dollars and add another fifty dollars so that she can buy a new helmet."

Pearl took the card. "You sure about that?"

"Oh yes. Just tell her it's part of the sale." She took a few steps away and grabbed a box she'd noticed on her way in. "And I'll take this too."

The phone rang as Pearl was adding up her purchases. "Go ahead and take it," Kaylee told her. "I can wait."

"Milligan's Mercantile. How can I help you?" Pearl barked into the phone. Her expression softened. "Oh, hey Luke. How are you, honey?" Pause. "Oh, he's doing fine." As Luke spoke, she looked over at Kaylee who waved her hands back-and-forth to indicate she wasn't there.

Pearl's eyes widened at whatever Luke had just said. "Oh really? That's real sweet of you, honey, to want to pay for the remainder of that bicycle for Emma. But I'm afraid somebody else had the same idea and already beat you to the punch." She paused again. "Was it Kaylee?"

She shook her head again as Pearl softly chuckled. The woman was having way too much fun with this conversation.

"I can neither confirm nor deny that accusation," Pearl told him. "But I can tell you Emma and her dad are on their way down here now, and I'm pretty dang sure she'll be riding that new bike in the parade this morning."

"Thanks for not giving me away," Kaylee said as Pearl hung up the phone.

"I'm not sure I fooled him."

Luke was working on his laptop at the kitchen counter when Kaylee's car pulled into the driveway not ten minutes after he'd hung up the phone with Pearl.

"I'll be ready in five," she said as she rushed into the house and set her bags on the counter before bending down to cuddle the two dogs begging for her attention.

He eyed the yellow bag. "Looks like you've already made a trip into Milligan's this morning. Buy anything good?" He crossed his arms over his chest. "Like a new pink and purple bicycle?"

A grin tugged at the corner of Kaylee's lips, and her cheeks flushed that adorable rosy pink color as she lifted her chin. "I can neither confirm nor deny that accusation."

He laughed. "Sounds like great minds think alike."

Ignoring his comment, she pushed the yellow bag toward him. "I bought you a present."

"Me? Why? It's not my birthday."

"It doesn't have to be your birthday. I just wanted to get you something. Like as a thank you for all your hospitality this week. I've had such a fun time."

He frowned then smiled as he pulled the box from the bag. "A new toaster."

"I couldn't stand the thought of you eating burnt toast."

He whistled as he read the description on the side. "This is about the fanciest toaster I've ever seen. But you didn't have to do this." He set the box back on the counter. "I'm sure I can get the other one to work."

Her shoulders slumped. "Oh come on. Please accept it." She pointed to the description on the side of the box. "It has a timer and different settings for how light or well-toasted you want your bread. It even has a bagel setting."

"A timer *and* a bagel setting? I didn't even know you were supposed to cook a bagel at a different setting. The last toaster I had, you just pushed the lever down and waited."

"That last toaster you had looked like it was purchased

when Reagan was in office."

He barked out a laugh as he stood up from the kitchen stool. "It probably was." He reached for her and pulled her into a hug. He wasn't sure why, but it felt like the right thing to do. "Thank you Kaylee. It's a real nice toaster. And a thoughtful gift." He leaned his cheek against the side of her forehead, the scent of her shampoo filling the air around him with wafts of honey and chamomile.

She let out a soft sigh as she wrapped her arms around his waist and melted into him. It felt so good—like this was the space where she belonged.

Losing Beth had left an empty hole inside him. But somehow this woman, with her sunny laugh and kind thoughtfulness seemed to be filling that chasm.

"I wanted to do something nice for you, but I also wanted you to have something to remember me by when I'm gone. So now you can think of me when you're eating toast."

He could tell she was trying to make light of it, but her breath hitched a little at the end, and the realization that she would be gone in a few days hit him like a punch to the gut. He wrapped his arms tighter around her and pulled her closer.

Hugging her was all he could do. He couldn't manage to say the words out loud, but he wasn't ready for her to go.

He finally pulled away, pausing for just a moment to peer down into her gorgeous blue-green eyes. And to contemplate kissing her. It would be so easy. Just lean in and press his lips to hers.

But that easy kiss would come with a lot of not-so-easy complications. The least of which being that she was leaving in a few days—a fact she'd just reminded him of.

The grandfather clock in the living room struck out a series of chimes, and Luke stepped away, the moment lost.

It was probably for the best.

He cleared his throat and clapped his hands to his front

pockets as if searching for his keys. "We'd better get to goin' if we want to make it to the breakfast before old Bud Milligan eats all the pancakes."

"I forgot to grab those books you signed," Luke said as he and Kaylee headed down the porch steps. "I'll grab them and meet you in the truck."

"Sounds good," Kaylee told him. She'd barely settled into the front seat when she heard the screen door slam and looked up to see Luke hurrying her way, Cooper and Gladys trotting happily behind him.

He opened the passenger door and gave her an apologetic shrug as he tossed the bag with the signed books on to the dashboard. "Sorry. I had to bring them. They looked so sad at being left behind. You'd better scootch over though if you don't want this guy in your lap," he said, holding the golden retriever back with his arm.

She scooted to the center of the bench seat and buckled in as Cooper then Gladys scrambled into the truck. The golden was practically in her lap anyway as he greeted her with sloppy kisses as if he hadn't seen her in years. The puppy licks and excitement distracted her from the fact that she would now be sitting right next to Luke until he climbed into the truck and started the engine.

His thigh was pressed against hers, and she could feel the heat of his shoulder through the cotton sleeve of his t-shirt. He put the truck in reverse then raised his arm over her head, resting it along the back side of the seat as he turned to look out the back window.

She wanted him to leave it there, to feel the weight of it on her shoulders as they drove to town. Except then he wouldn't be able to put the truck into first so they'd have to drive the whole way in reverse, and that didn't seem like the best idea.

His arm bumped the back of her head as he brought it back over. "Sorry," he muttered.

She ducked her head down and ran her nose right into his shoulder. "Ouch, no, I'm sorry." Lifting her hand, she pressed it to the bridge of her nose.

"Oh geez, are you okay?" Stopping the truck, he turned to face her. "Let me see." He pulled her hand gently away, and his eyes widened. "Oh crud, your nose is swollen up like a grapefruit."

"What?" She jerked her head toward the rearview mirror, trying to see her nose. But it looked perfectly normal.

He uttered a low chuckle. "That was too easy. I'm just teasing. Your nose is perfect." His voice softened as he gazed into her eyes. "Just like the rest of you."

She shook her head and started to protest, but he cut her off as he squeezed her hand and turned back to face the windshield. "They're gonna run out of pancakes if we don't hit the road." He let off the brake and the truck rumbled forward, but he didn't let go of her hand. Instead, he lowered their still joined palms to rest on top of his leg. "Because the money goes to help support the fire department, most of the town shows up. I think last year they said they served close to a thousand pancakes."

She swallowed, trying to follow what he was saying. But the only thing she could focus on was the fact that he was holding her hand as if it were the most normal thing in the world. But this wasn't normal for her. It had been so long since a man had simply held her hand. She tried to focus on breathing and calm the stomach-fluttering, roller coaster feeling inside her.

"That's a lot of pancake batter," she finally managed to squeak out.

"You're not kidding." His chest rumbled with an easy laugh. "I think Emma said her school did a whole math unit that year on what it takes to make and serve a thousand pancakes."

She made some kind of agreeable sound, or she might have mumbled a *yeah*. She wasn't sure because the feeling inside her had escalated from the pitter patter of light rain to thunderstorm to tornado as Luke's thumb moved, softly brushing her skin as he grazed it back and forth over the side of her knuckles.

She wanted to close her eyes, to savor this moment, this feeling of tingly nerves mixed with utter bliss, and she wished the drive to town was farther. Would it be weird to suggest he take a longer route? Like maybe through Wyoming?

Cooper laid his head on her leg, and she rested her other hand on his knobby head. Gladys had her front paws up on the door frame and her head poked out the window, her tail wagging with joy.

Kaylee knew the feeling. Everything about this moment filled her with happiness. The scent of freshly mown hay wafted through the window and mixed with the traces of Luke's musky aftershave. A classic country song was playing softly on the radio, and she could feel the slightest vibration in his shoulder as Luke hummed along. The sun was shining across the vast crystal blue sky and the morning air was warm but didn't yet hold the heat that would be coming later.

If she had a free hand, she might consider pinching herself. This felt so much like a dream. And one she didn't want to end.

Chapter Fifteen

THE ELKS LODGE WAS CROWDED and rang with noise and laughter as they walked through the doors. Several people waved to Luke, and Kaylee noticed a few curious stares. In a community this close-knit, there was bound to be a little talk concerning one of its most eligible bachelors.

Kaylee kind of liked the idea of being the object of curiosity—she couldn't think of a time when she had been before. Sure, she'd done some book signings where readers had shown up to meet her. But this felt different. As if their whispers were questions about if she and Luke were involved—romantically. That felt all new. And if she were honest—a little exciting.

They got in line and were handed paper plates filled with scrambled eggs, sausage links, and a short stack of pancakes. Luke's hand on her back was warm as he guided her toward an empty table.

"I'll grab us some drinks," he said, setting his plate down. "Coffee or juice?"

She set her plate next to his and took the napkins and plastic cutlery he held out. "Coffee. With—"

"I know. Two sugars and a splash of cream. I watch you make it every morning," he told her with a grin and a wink before heading toward the drinks table.

She picked up the little container of syrup and poured it on her pancakes, surprised at how delighted she felt inside that he knew how she took her coffee. It was such a simple thing, yet felt personal. Intimate—like a couple thing.

Or maybe just a good host thing. Or a friend thing.

Oh be quiet, she told her inner pessimist. Couldn't she just enjoy this moment? Even if she was deluding herself? She *was* probably making too much out of a small gesture. Luke's happy mood and a few minutes of hand-holding did not turn them into a couple. But it was fun to dream.

She'd made it halfway through her stack of lukewarm pancakes by the time Luke got back with the coffee.

"How are they?" he asked, setting the small paper cup on the table and dropping into the seat next to her.

"Best pancakes I've ever eaten."

"Wow. Either your standards are super low, or you haven't sampled many pancakes."

She shrugged and offered him a coy smile. "Maybe it's the company."

Oh my heavens. Where had that flirty flirt come from? Had she been channeling Sassy so much lately that the character's voice just popped out of her mouth? Or was that actually her?

Luke grinned back then grimaced as he shoved a bite of pancakes in his mouth. He took a sip of coffee to wash them down. "I was flattered there for a second. Now I know the flap-jack bar's been set pretty low."

Their conversation was cut off as two women walked up to their table. "Would it be okay if we sit with you?" the younger one asked as she pulled out a chair across from them.

"Course," Luke said, tipping his head to the women.

"Betty. Linda-May. How you ladies doing?"

"We're doing just fine, Luke. Thanks for asking," the older one answered absently as she sat down and scooted her chair closer to Kaylee. "I'm so honored to meet you, Miss Collins. I'm Betty Thomas, and this is my friend, Linda-May Baker. We're big fans of your books."

"Oh," Kaylee said, reaching for her coffee as she tried to swallow the bite of eggs she'd just taken. She'd assumed they sat down to talk to Luke. She wiped her mouth with a napkin. "Nice to meet you. Please call me Kaylee."

The two women smiled at each other, and Linda-May's shoulders relaxed. "We didn't want to interrupt your breakfast. We just wanted to tell you how much your books mean to us."

"I read three of them while I sat next to my husband's hospital bed last year when he was battling cancer. They really helped to give me a lovely place to escape to when things were so tough and all I could do was sit and wait while Saul slept."

"Oh, I'm so sorry to hear about your husband," Kaylee said.

"He's okay now. We just celebrated our fiftieth wedding anniversary. But for a while there, I wasn't sure we were going to make it."

Kaylee nodded. "Because of the cancer."

Betty shook her head and gave Kaylee a wry grin. "No, because the man's a cantankerous old cuss and can try my last nerve." Her smiled softened. "But I love him anyway. He may not be as romantic or as devilishly handsome as that Duke Ramsey of yours, but he does scrape the windshield of my car when it snows and rubs my shoulders while we watch television, so I guess I'll keep him around."

"Well I have to think up those romantic gestures of Duke's, but it sounds like your Saul does them all on his own," Kaylee told her. "So that's way better than my book."

Betty smiled and sat a little taller in her chair as Linda-May leaned forward. "I'm a big fan too. Although up until a few years ago, I'd never even read a romance book. Then I was scheduled to go on a trip to visit my sister in Kansas City, and I was terrified to fly. Betty stuck one of your books in my bag and made me promise to read it as soon as I got on the plane. I can remember my hands were shaking as I opened it, then I ended up reading it for the whole flight. I enjoyed it so much, and it totally took my mind off the fact that I was in a giant tin can in the sky. I've been a huge fan ever since."

"Oh goodness. That's amazing." Kaylee wasn't sure how to respond. She noticed another woman standing a few feet away who seemed to be listening to their conversation.

Betty waved the woman toward their table. "Git your fanny over here, Jean and meet this woman. She won't bite. In fact, she's real sweet." Standing up, she practically forced Jean to take her chair. "She really is one of your biggest fans," Betty told Kaylee.

"Hello," the woman said softly as she perched on the edge of Betty's vacated chair. "I'm Jean. I mean, I guess Betty already said that." Her cheeks were flushed, and she wet her dry lips.

"Nice to meet you," Kaylee said, sticking out her hand. "Please call me Kaylee."

The woman shook her hand, gripping it tightly then pressed her palm to her chest. "I think I might be having a heart attack."

"Oh no. Should we call an ambulance?" Kaylee scanned the room. "I'm sure there's a fireman around here somewhere. Can we get some water? Or something to eat?" She pushed her plate of half-eaten pancakes toward the woman. "You're welcome to share mine."

The woman shook her head and blew out a nervous laugh. "No. I'm fine. I'm not really having a heart attack. My heart is just pounding a thousand miles an hour because I'm so nervous about meeting you. I really am a huge fan. I've read all your books, and you inspired me to try my hand at writing my own romance novel."

Kaylee let out her breath, thankful the woman wasn't in cardiac arrest. "Wait. I did?"

"Yes. I saw you at a conference once. In Chicago."

Kaylee remembered. It was one of the few reader conferences she'd attended. Faye had assured her it was going to be small and signed her up to be on a panel. There had been over a hundred rabid readers there. She'd been both terrified and thrilled at meeting the ones who came up to her signing table on the second day.

"You were on a panel, and they asked you what advice you would give to new writers. You told this story about perseverance and how many times you'd been rejected, and it really moved me. You were so sincere in your encouragement, and I felt like you were talking directly to me. You gave us great advice on character development and story structure, and you gave me the courage to start writing my own book." Her voice shook as she spoke, and her eyes welled with tears.

"Oh my gosh," was all Kaylee could say.

Jean wiped an escaped tear from her cheek with the back of her hand. "I'm so sorry. I don't know why I'm crying. It just means so much to me to meet you in person and to be able to tell you how much you inspired me and my writing."

Kaylee swallowed, the emotion thick in her throat. She'd never had anyone cry when they'd met her before, and the sentiment moved her beyond words. "It's fine. I mean, you're fine. Oh, I don't know what I mean." She pressed her hand to her chest. "I'm truly honored and so pleased that something I said helped you. And I can honestly say you're the first person who's ever cried at meeting me."

Jean cringed. "I can't believe I did that. I'm such a dork.

I was just so nervous. Then I had you thinking I was having an actual heart attack. And now I've blubbered all over you."

"You think *you're* a dork? I thought you were going into cardiac arrest, and I offered you my plate of half-eaten flap jacks."

Jean snorted out a laugh and the group of women all joined in. As if the laughter had been the break in the dam, their conversation then flowed easily as they chatted about books and their favorite authors.

Luke sat leaned back in his chair, listening and watching as the women finally wound down then hugged her and scurried away. "That's really cool," he told Kaylee. "The way you and your books have made a difference in so many people's lives."

She shook her head. "Oh, I don't know. I think they were just being nice."

He put his hand over hers and gently squeezed. "Stop. Don't put yourself down. Those women read your stories and what you wrote genuinely made an impact on them. *You* did that. With your talent and your words. The credit belongs to you, so own it, and be proud of yourself."

She hadn't ever thought of it that way, hadn't really given much thought at all to the fact her books could impact anyone's life. Sitting a little taller in her chair, she turned her hand over and squeezed Luke's back.

"Kaylee! Luke!"

Luke dropped her hand as Emma's voice rang out across the hall. They both stood as the girl came running up to their table and threw her arms around Kaylee. "I did it. I got my new bike."

"You did? I thought you still didn't have enough." Kaylee's chest was full to bursting at the joy she saw radiating from Emma's face.

"I didn't. Even with the gift card. But Miss Pearl called me this morning and said they were doing some kind of summer deal. And the bike was on sale for exactly how much I had. And even included a new helmet. Isn't that amazing?"

"A helmet too?" Luke raised an amused eyebrow at Kaylee before turning back to Emma. "That *is* amazing."

"Yeah, it was quite a coincidence," Dean said, ambling up to their table after his daughter. "Imagine Pearl having a deal for the *exact* amount Emma still needed." He narrowed his eyes as he wagged his finger back and forth between them. "You two wouldn't happen to know anything about this great sale, would you?"

"Not me," Luke said, covertly pointing a finger toward Kaylee above Emma's head.

"We gotta go," Emma said, before her dad had a chance to say anything more. She gave Kaylee's waist one more squeeze. "The parade is starting in fifteen minutes, and I need to get in line. I saw Gladys and Cooper outside. Tell them I'll cuddle them later."

"Have fun," Kaylee called to her back as she was already off and running toward the door.

"Speaking of the parade," Luke said. "We should probably go claim a spot on the curb."

They cleared their table then made their way outside and joined the crowd of people lining up for the parade.

They stopped at the truck to get Gladys and Cooper. The windows were down, and the two dogs leaned their heads out the passenger side, happily greeting everyone who passed by. Kaylee put their leashes on as Luke offered them each a dry pancake and a paper cup full of water. They gobbled up the flap jacks and slopped water from the cups.

Kaylee was struck again by how close-knit they all were. Everyone in the community seemed to know Cooper by name. A few even knew Gladys's name, and the corgi ate up all the attention of extra pets and chin scratches.

Luke found an empty spot just as the parade was starting,

and he and Kaylee stood at the curb with the dogs at their feet as they watched the local Color Guard march by with the American flag and the state of Montana flag perched on their hips. Four abreast, the soldiers marched in unison, rows of metals adorning the chests of their dress blues.

Taking off his hat, Luke pressed it to his chest as they walked by. Across the street and down a little, Kaylee spotted Bear standing at the front edge of the alley. She swallowed as she watched him stand tall and raise his hand to his forehead in a salute, holding perfectly still as the flags held by the soldiers marched by.

A police car and firetruck were next in the procession, both vehicles intermittently flashing their lights and giving quick blitzes to their sirens. Firemen leaned out the windows of an old-fashioned firetruck and tossed candy to the kids lining the street. Decked out in their school colors of blue and yellow, the Bartlett High marching band filled the air with music as they trooped by.

After several floats and the Shriners driving tiny cars went by, Kaylee could finally see a group of kids on bicycles coming up the street. She tapped Luke's arm then leaned forward to search for Emma. "Here come the kids." Spotting her, Kaylee waved her arms. "There she is."

Emma sat up tall in the seat, a brand-new purple helmet perched on her head, a yellow and white daisy sticker stuck to the side. Pink and white streamers were woven through the spokes of her tires. She waved back, and the smile of joy on her face made the clandestine effort of contributing to the purchase of the bike totally worth it.

Kaylee laughed as she leaned into Luke's shoulder, raising her voice over the din of the parade noise. "She looks so happy."

Luke grinned at her. "She's not the only one. You look like you're about to bust with happiness."

"I am." She wrapped her arms around herself as if to

keep all the good happy feelings from escaping. She couldn't remember the last time she'd had such a fun day.

The fun continued through the morning and the afternoon as Kaylee and Luke went from the parade to the spaghetti luncheon the local bank put on to wandering the craft show and trade demonstrations.

"I've never been to anything like this," Kaylee said as she and Luke headed back to the farm to change for the evening's festivities. "I've had the best time. The glassblowing demonstration was my favorite. No, actually I loved the Dress Your Pig contest the most. Oh, I just loved it all." She pressed a hand to her stomach. "Although I probably should have passed up that last corn dog."

Luke chuckled. "You're gonna want to find some more room because we've still got the town barbeque tonight then they have more food vendors at the street dance."

She groaned as she adjusted the still full bag of kettle corn nestled against the bag of crafts she'd purchased. "I'll try to rally." Gladys was sprawled on the seat between them, her head and front paws slumped across Kaylee's lap, but she lifted her nose at the rustle of plastic. Cooper was already asleep on the floor of the truck. "I think we wore these two out."

Luke nodded as he pulled up to the house and cut the engine. "I could use one of those naps too." He glanced at his watch then offered her a smile. "We've got a few hours before we have to be back, if you want to grab a few winks."

She shook her head. "I could use a little couch time and a cold glass of tea, but I'm too wired to nap. My brain is buzzing with story ideas and notes, and I'm dying to jot it all down." She nodded to one of the bags in the seat. "I bought another cute notebook this afternoon because I've practically filled up the first one I brought."

His happy smile fell. "Oh yeah. Sometimes I forget you're only here to do research for your books."

"That's not the only thing..." she started to say, but Luke had already gotten out of the truck.

Chapter Sixteen

"**H**OW DO I LOOK?" KAYLEE asked Gladys, who was sprawled across her bed. She wore the cute sundress she'd bought at Milligan's the day she and Luke had covered for Pearl, and she'd paired it tonight with flats and a black cardigan.

The dress was a soft pink with lace accents and came to right above her knee. It was shorter than she normally wore, and she didn't often bare her shoulders, but the style seemed to be a popular one in the store, and Emma had assured her it was perfect.

Gladys barely lifted her head but offered a groan as her opinion. The dog had been crashed out on her bed since they got home.

"You're right," Kaylee said, looking down at herself. "Too boring." It was funny how she'd started noticing more things about her clothes and personality as she compared herself to her fictional character. She would never write Sassy into such a plain outfit, so why was she dressing herself in one?

Kicking off the flats and shucking the stuffy cardigan, she pulled on her new cowboy boots and the little jean jacket

Emma had also convinced her to buy. She'd taken extra time with her makeup and curled her hair and it fell in soft waves on her shoulders. Gazing at herself in the full-length mirror, she was surprised at the subtle changes she saw.

After spending most of the last week outside, her arms and legs had started to tan and her cheeks were a rosy pink from the day of walking around in the sun. Instead of her normal ponytail or messy bun, she'd been wearing her hair down more often and letting it dry into its naturally curly waves. She even thought her clothes felt just a tad looser and wondered if all the walking around the farm had possibly shed a few pounds.

Whether she'd actually dropped weight or not, she somehow felt lighter. Happier. And it seemed to show.

Tucking her ID, some cash, and a mint-infused lip gloss into the pockets of her jean jacket, she dropped a kiss on Gladys's nose and headed out.

Luke was waiting for her on the front porch, Cooper sacked out on the floor next to him. He stood as she pushed through the front door. "Wow. You look amazing."

"Thanks. So do you."

He wore a light blue button-up shirt, jeans, boots, and a soft grey felt Stetson instead of his normal black one. The color of his shirt brought out the ice-blue shade of his eyes, and Kaylee had a hard time dragging her gaze away from them. He'd taken a shower and the ends of his hair were still damp. The scent of his aftershave and shampoo filled the air as he walked beside her to the truck and opened the door for her.

They were leaving the dogs at home tonight, so she had no excuse for scooting into the center of the bench seat. Which meant the chances of Luke holding her hand again were slim. *Dang it.* But she still loved riding into town with him and listening to him talk about the night's festivities. The barbeque was first on the agenda then the concert and street dance. She was intrigued by the idea of a dance happening on Main Street and couldn't wait to see Chase Dalton in person.

"I'm so excited," she told Luke as he maneuvered the truck into a parking spot and cut the engine.

"I kind of am too," he said, offering her a shy smile. "I haven't cared about this festival in a long time, but I'm looking forward to attending tonight. You have a way of making everything seem more fun."

"Me? I don't think I've ever been accused of making *anything* more fun."

"Come on now," he said, his brow furrowing. "You're too hard on yourself. I've had a lot of fun with you this week, even when we were doing ordinary things that normally seem boring."

She didn't know what to say. And apparently he wasn't expecting an answer since he was already out of the truck and walking around to open her door.

"The barbeque is down by those stands." He pointed toward several rows of bleachers set up in the street. A large band stand had been erected on the lawn in front of city hall so the concert-goers could see the stage and still have a great view of the river in the background. The street between the stage and the bleachers had been closed off for the entire city block and tables and chairs filled the space.

The smoky scent of grilled meat and tangy barbeque spice filled the air, and Kaylee inhaled a deep breath as she kept pace with Luke. "It smells amazing. I can't believe I'm saying this, but it smells so good, I think I'm hungry again."

"Wait 'til you taste it." The back of Luke's hand brushed hers as they walked, his touch distracting her from the barbeque.

There were a lot of people around, and she recognized several community members as they walked toward the tables. Everyone knew Luke, and several folks waved or hollered greetings as they passed. Her hopes at him taking her hand faltered. It was one thing to do it in the truck when they were alone but holding hands in front of the whole town was much more of a statement than a simple show of affection.

"Luke! Kaylee!"

She heard someone calling their names and spotted Emma standing on a chair waving them over to the table where she, Dean, and Marnie were sitting. They zig-zagged through the crowd as they made their way toward them.

"Hey guys," Luke said, pulling out the chair next to Emma for Kaylee. "I hope you didn't already eat all the pulled pork."

Emma hugged Kaylee as she sank into the chair. "I didn't, but Dad's already had two sandwiches, so you'd better go get in line."

Kaylee started to stand back up, but Luke waved her down. "You stay and visit. I'll go grab us some sandwiches and fries. If you're good with that?"

"Yeah, sounds great. And if you can find one, I'd love a—"

He cut her off before she could finish her sentence. "Diet Coke. I know. Already on it."

"Thanks." She settled back in her seat, noting the small smile Marnie offered her. "I'm so excited for tonight. I can't believe I'm going to get to see Chase Dalton in person."

Dean chuckled. "Some people aren't quite as starstruck as you are. I heard Rita Mullins and Carol Carson were already over at his trailer this afternoon, plying him with baked goods and trying to set him up with Rita's grand-daughter."

"Oh no." Kaylee joined in their laughter. "Did it work?"

"I don't know. I heard he got so flustered over them trying to get him to choose whether he thought Rita's cream puff dessert or Carol's biscuits with strawberry jam were better that they never got around to the introductions."

"Poor guy," Marnie said.

"Poor guy?" Dean pulled his head back. "What are you feeling sorry for him for? He got to eat cream puffs and biscuits with jam."

Kaylee laughed as she settled into her seat and listened to Emma's strategy of how she was hoping to nab Chase's autograph after the concert. "It sounds like you've got a solid plan," she told her then gestured toward Marnie. "I love your shirt."

Marnie tugged at the front of her black T-shirt with the silhouette outline of Chase Dalton's face and cowboy hat on the front. "Thanks. They have a whole display set up over by the stage. I'll go over with you later to check them out, if you want."

"I'd like that."

"No need," Luke said, coming up beside her. He held two cardboard food containers in his hand, had two cans of Diet Coke tucked under his arm, and a black Chase Dalton T-shirt slung over his shoulder. He set the food and drinks down and passed Kaylee the shirt, a proud-of-himself kind of grin on his face. "I thought you needed one of your own."

She smiled up at him, her heart pounding with glee. No guy had ever bought her a souvenir t-shirt before. And as cheesy as that sounded, the idea of Luke getting her this one made her giddy. "Thank you. I love it." She stood and shimmied out of her jean jacket then pulled the t-shirt over her head. It was stiff and smelled of starch and vinyl, but she didn't care. She held out her arms. "How does it look?"

Luke's smile told her all she needed to know.

"It's great," he said with a small laugh, his gaze only on her. "You look great." He must have realized that everyone at the table was looking at him, because his smile turned to a frown as he cleared his throat and looked down, busying himself with the food as he mumbled, "Food's getting cold. We should probably eat."

"Yeah, you only have fifteen minutes before we have

to clear away these tables and get ready for the concert," Dean told them, his face still holding an amused grin at his friend's uneasiness.

Kaylee lifted the lid of the container Luke passed her way and inhaled the scent of French fries and pulled pork. "No problem," she said. "This smells so delicious, I'm planning to inhale it in five." She managed to get the sandwich into her mouth without dripping barbeque sauce onto her new shirt, a feat she was pretty proud of, and she focused on eating while Dean shared a funny story about something that happened on his ranch that afternoon.

She was glad to listen and tried to keep the goofy grin off her face while she was eating. She was just so darn happy. It was so fun to be part of a group, sharing stories and inside jokes. She'd spent so much of her time alone at her desk and had been content to be there, filling pages with adventures of her fictional characters. But now she was out in the world, taking part in her own adventures, laughing and swapping tales with real people instead of fictional ones.

It's not like she never saw people, but this felt different. Being with these people made her feel like she actually belonged. Having the people of Bartlett wave and call 'hello's' to her gave her a sense of fitting in, like she was part of the community too. Accepted.

Too bad she was only going to be here a few more days and the person they were all 'accepting' was not her, but an imitation of Sassy.

Kaylee's voice was hoarse from screaming and singing along with Emma, Marnie, and Chase Dalton for the last hour and a half. The country singer had finally wound down and after two encores, had sung his last song and headed off the stage.

"That was amazing," she told Luke as he passed them each a bottle of water. Screwing off the lid, she took a long drink and the cool liquid felt awesome on her parched throat. How did Luke always seem to know just what she needed? "Thanks. This is perfect." She tipped the bottle at him before taking another swig.

"I figured you three would need something after screaming your heads off for so long," he teased.

"That wasn't screaming," Marnie corrected him with a grin. "That was singing."

"They might have been singing," Kaylee said, jerking a thumb toward Emma and Marnie. "But yeah, I was mostly screaming. Although I was surprised at how many of the songs I knew. Or mostly knew." She laughed as she pushed her bangs off her forehead. "That was so much fun."

"I'll bet you go to a lot of concerts in Chicago," Marnie said. "I'm so jealous. There must be something fun to do every night in the city."

Kaylee shook her head. "I'm sure there is. But I never do any of it. Most of my nights are spent at home watching television with my dog. This is the first concert I've been to in years."

She ducked her head in embarrassment, but Marnie nudged her arm and leaned in to whisper conspiratorially, "Don't be embarrassed. I do the same thing. Except I have a cat." She winced then admitted, "Okay, I have *two* cats."

They laughed together, and Kaylee felt like she'd found a friend in Marnie. "I'll keep that to myself if you don't tell anyone my dog gets her own bowl of popcorn on movie night."

A mix of roadies and volunteers switched out the instruments on the stage and a local band took over, filling the air with an assortment of new and classic country songs.

Kaylee, Dean, and Marnie stood on the side of the dance floor listening to the music while Emma and Luke disappeared into the crowd. They came back ten minutes later, carrying individual bags of Bartlett's Blend, a combination of delicious caramel and kettle corn.

"You have to try this," Emma said, doling out bags to Dean and Marnie then passing one to Kaylee. "It's sooo good."

Kaylee popped a few pieces into her mouth and let out a groan. "That is good."

"It's the best when it's fresh and still warm from the kettle," Luke said, leaning against the table behind them. "It's a local family that makes it. Just another one of the many things Bartlett has to offer."

Hmm. What was that comment about? Was he trying to sell her on the town of Bartlett? She already loved it here. Before she had time to ask, Emma challenged him to a contest to see how many pieces of popcorn they could toss into their mouths.

"You're on," Luke told her. "Best out of ten wins."

Kaylee marveled at his ease—he was so good with the girl, making her laugh as he effortlessly joked around with her. Dean had told her before that Luke was Emma's godfather, and that he, Beth, and Faye had all been there for him and his daughter when his wife had left. It was obvious, just in the amount of time Kaylee had spent with them that they were like a family to each other.

She laughed along at the popcorn-tossing contest antics as she demolished her bag. She'd never thought to put the two types of popcorn together, but the sweet and salty combination was amazing. She hoped they had a website so she could order more online.

She wasn't the only one who devoured her popcorn. Dean and Emma collected the empty bags and water bottles and tossed them in the trash as she pressed a hand to her stomach. "If I keep eating like this, I'm going to gain ten pounds by the time I go back to Chicago."

"Then maybe you shouldn't go back to Chicago," Luke said, not quite under his breath.

Her pulse sped up as she blinked at him. She wasn't sure she'd heard him at all. "What?" she asked, her gaze focused on his.

He shrugged as if he hadn't said anything important. "I'm just saying, maybe you could stay awhile."

"I—" She didn't get out anything more because Marnie shrieked and grabbed her arm as the band played the notes of a new song.

"Oh I love this one," she said, already pulling Kaylee toward the dance floor. "We have to do this dance."

"Dance? What dance?" Panic bubbled in her chest.

"It's a line dance," Emma said, pulling on her other arm. "It's easy. They do it at weddings all the time. We'll teach you."

She pulled back. "Wait. I don't dance. Haven't in years. And I've *never* done a line dance."

"The steps are simple, I promise," Emma said. "Even my dad knows them." She reached for Dean's hand. "Come on, Dad. You gotta do this one with us so Kaylee sees how easy it is."

Dean frowned then shrugged at Luke. "I will if you will."

Luke's eyes widened. "Me? What do I have to do with it? I don't care if Kaylee learns the dance or not."

Emma stopped and dropped Kaylee and Dean's arms to plant her fists on her hips as she glared at her father and godfather. "Come on, you guys. We're *all* doing it. It will be fun. Now get your booties out here before the song is over."

Dean and Luke grumbled as they followed Emma and Kaylee into the street. Marnie was already in place, clapping her hands as she stamped her feet. "Stand by me, I'll show you," she told Kaylee.

She and Luke fell in line next to her, and Emma and

Dean flanked Marnie's other side. She went through the steps, shouting them out above the music. "You got it," she told Kaylee, starting another rotation.

She definitely did not feel like she 'got' anything. She was just hopping around, trying to keep up and was usually a step or two behind. But they were all laughing, and she realized Luke and Emma messed up just as many times as she did. And so did half the people in front of her. There were a few who totally had it, who made it look easy, and everyone else seemed to be trying to keep up with them.

Kaylee tried to focus on her own feet and not let them stumble over each other. She was just starting to get the hang of the sequence as the song was winding down.

Then Marnie called out, "This is the fast part. Double time."

Kaylee shrieked with laughter as the song sped back up, and they all started stomping faster and doing double claps. Trying to clap in time with the stomps was totally messing her up. Her feet tangled in each other on the last turn, and she stumbled back.

Right into Luke.

His strong arms came up around her, breaking her fall as her back landed squarely in his chest. She let out an "oof", but he didn't seem to notice.

"Whoa there, I got you," he said, lifting her back on her feet as the song came to an end.

"Well, that was embarrassing," she said. And a little exciting to be pressed that close to Luke.

"You did awesome," Emma said, patting her shoulder and completely oblivious to the fact that she'd almost biffed it and fell on the ground.

A new song started, and the tempo slowed way down. Luke's arm was still around her waist, steadying her. She looked at her feet, unable to meet his eye, so he wouldn't know how much she wanted him to ask her to slow dance.

"So," he said, his tone off-hand. "Would you want to—?"

His words were cut off as one of the guys from the line in front of them turned around and pointed a finger at Kaylee. "Hey, aren't you that famous writer?"

Caught off guard, and disappointed in the interruption, she could only mumble, "Um, well..."

"How about a dance?" Without waiting for an answer, he grabbed her hand and pulled her toward the middle of the dance floor.

Chapter Seventeen

"OH. NO," KAYLEE SAID, TRYING to pull her arm back. "Sorry. I'm not much of a dancer." Especially not with some strange guy who seemed too eager and way too over-confident in demanding she dance with him.

His face looked crestfallen, then shifted to a bit snide. "What? Are you too fancy for a lowly cowboy?"

"No, it's not that," she stammered. She was fine with cowboys. In fact, there was one right behind her who she quite enjoyed spending time with. But this guy wasn't him.

"Come on then. It's just one dance." He pulled her further out onto the dance floor then wrenched her tightly to him. *Too tight.*

She could smell the scent of garlic and beer on his breath, and she tried to pull away. Being smashed against this stranger's chest was making her totally uncomfortable. "I'm sorry. I don't even know the steps to this dance."

He seemed oblivious to her discomfort and almost lifted her off her feet as he swung her around. "No problem. I'll lead. Just follow me. It's easy."

But it wasn't easy. He pulled harder on her arm with

one hand while the other had a too-tight grip on her waist, using the pressure of his palm to turn her one way or the other. But the pressure of dancing with him was worse than the force he used on her hip, and she stumbled back then over-corrected and tried to step forward. He grimaced as she stepped on his foot. Thank goodness he was wearing cowboy boots, although it might serve him right if he weren't.

"Sorry," she mumbled as she crushed his toes. Again.

He yanked her arm back and forth. "Loosen up. This is supposed to be fun."

She wasn't loose. And she definitely wasn't having any fun. She was nervous and awkward and kept stomping on his toes. Her body was too warm and the harder she tried, the worse she was making it.

He offered her a leering grin. "You're right, you're not that great of a dancer. Do you want to just get out of here instead?"

"What? No," she said, stepping on his foot again. That time might have been on purpose.

She wasn't sure what to do. This kind of thing didn't happen to her when she stayed in the safety of her own apartment. Shame heated her neck and cheeks. Sassy would know how to handle this. Although *she* never would've let herself get dragged onto the dance floor by a Neanderthal brute in the first place.

Kaylee swallowed back the emotion rising in her throat, and she was even more embarrassed that she was about to cry.

"Ouch," the guy cringed. "Come on, baby. It's like you're not even trying." He stopped as a large hand tapped him not too softly on the shoulder.

"Mind if I cut in?" Luke asked, reaching for Kaylee's hand.

The brute yanked it out of reach. "Nah, dude. We're dancing here."

Frustration flooded her chest, and she shot a pleading

look at Luke, even as she chided herself for not just yanking her own hand away.

"Oh. Yeah," Luke countered, pulling the guy's shoulder back. "What I meant to say was, I *am* cutting in."

This time, Kaylee did manage to pull her hand free and grasped Luke's outstretched one. He folded it into his and lightly pulled her toward him.

But the other guy yanked her back. "Hey man, we're not done dancing here."

Luke fixed him with a steely glare. "I think you are."

Kaylee took a step closer to Luke, relief filling her as she pressed into the circle of his outstretched arm. She took courage from the strength of his solid embrace. "Yes, we definitely are. Thank you for the dance. Have a good night."

The brute still didn't seem to get the message. "But..."

Luke's glare went from steely to menacing. "You heard the lady. Time to take off." He didn't outright threaten the guy, but his stance conveyed the message.

"Fine," the guy huffed. "She's a terrible dancer anyway," he shot back as he stomped off the dance floor.

Luke gently pulled her to him, and she wrapped her arms around his neck and hugged him tightly. "Thank you," she whispered into his chest.

"Hey now. It's okay." He hugged her back, holding her close as he soothed a hand down her back. "Kaylee, you're shaking."

"I just feel so stupid and like a coward. Why couldn't I just tell that guy *no*?"

"Because you're a kind person who trusts that other people are kind too." He leaned his head closer to her ear. "And you did tell him no."

"Only once you showed up."

"The important thing is that you stood up to him. It doesn't matter when. And I never would have let him hurt you." He pulled back to peer down at her. "It's all okay now."

She shook her head. "No. It's not. He might have been an oafish jerk, but he was right about one thing. I *am* a terrible dancer. I don't know why I thought I could do this."

Luke lifted her chin to look at him. "You are *not* a terrible dancer. You're not a terrible *anything*."

"But I'm nothing like the rest of these people. I don't know how to smoothly glide around the dance floor."

"Most of these folks have been doing this for years. I only know how because they made us take a class in high school and another one in 4H. That's how we all learned." He tilted his head toward where Dean was circling the dance floor with Marnie.

"They make it look so easy."

"Would you like me to teach you?"

"No. Yes. I don't know. Part of me is just embarrassed and wants to go home. But the other part of me is trying to be brave and knows the only way I'm going to learn is to try." Plus she loved the feeling of being in Luke's arms and didn't want that to end.

He lifted one shoulder in a shrug. "Seems to me that everything you've done this week has been new and different. And you've thrown yourself into trying to learn all that. Why is this any different?"

"Because I wasn't running fence or mucking out stalls in front of half the town." Or with his arm wrapped securely around her waist.

He shook his head. "Oh, forget about them. Nobody's watching us anyway." He still held her chin, and he lifted his index finger and stroked it softly down her cheeks. His voice was just as soft, the deep cadence of it rumbling through her chest as he held her captured in his gaze. "All that matters is just you and me, darlin'."

"Just you and me," she repeated in a whisper.

He took her right hand in his and guided her left to his shoulder. She curled the fabric of his shirt in her fingers, somehow feeling stronger by having something to hold onto. He slid his hand under her arm and cupped her shoulder blade, completely different from the big oaf's possessive grip on her waist.

"I'm going to teach you the two-step, but we'll take it slow. There are only two basic steps to this one, two quick ones and two slow ones. And this dance is more of a glide, like our feet will just drift past each other. You barely even have to pick them up." He nodded toward Dean and Marnie again. "See how they move. The two-step is just like learning to walk to the beat of the music. Except *you* have to do it backwards."

He grinned down at her, and her stomach did a little flip. "That sounds easy enough." She took a deep breath, feeling more secure, in the dance part at least, as she watched the way the other couple moved. "Just like walking backwards. To the beat."

"You got it," he said, taking a step forward. "I'm always gonna start with my left foot and you're always gonna start with your right. You know why?"

She shook her head as she stared down at her feet, suddenly unable to remember which one was her right and which was left.

He lifted her chin to look at him again, and his lips curved into a mischievous grin. "Because the woman's always right."

She laughed and let her shoulders relax as he glided her backwards.

"It's just like walking," he reminded her. "We'll just glide first, and then we'll add the quicker step. I'll set the pace, and you just follow along."

He patiently moved her through the steps, again and again, until they felt more natural, and she only stepped on his feet a few times. But he didn't seem to care.

"Quick, quick, slowww, slowww," he said the words softly into her ear as he gracefully led her around the dance floor, his hand on her back gently guiding them around the other couples.

"We're doing it," she said.

"*You're* doing it," he told her, as the song came to an end. The band started another slow song, and he offered her an encouraging smile. "You did awesome. Do you want to go again?"

She smiled back at him, her courage blooming like a cluster of wildflowers in one of his fields. "Yes."

"Good."

This time, she felt more comfortable as she got more familiar with the steady rhythm of the steps. By midway through the song, she was really getting the hang of it and starting to enjoy herself.

Dean had switched partners and now danced with his daughter. They glided by them, and Emma let go of her dad and slipped under Luke and Kaylee's arms. "Switch partners for one go around," she called out.

And suddenly Kaylee found herself dancing with Dean as Emma stole her cowboy. "Sorry," she told him, feeling clumsy again. "I'm just learning these dance steps."

"Don't apologize. My last partner was an excited ten-year-old hopped up on soda and cotton candy," he said with a chuckle. He shrugged his shoulder underneath her hand. "We were all beginners at one time. And Luke used to be terrible. I think he used to repeat the steps—quick, quick, slow, slow—out loud throughout the whole song."

Kaylee laughed with him, not sure if Luke was still chanting the steps for her benefit, or his.

"I think he got better the more he did it, though. And Beth loved to dance. I swear, she was the life of every party. Even if there wasn't dancing happening, she'd either move the furniture and start a dance party or force us all to go somewhere with a band."

Kaylee smiled, pushing down her insecurities of knowing

she would never be considered the life of any party. She doubted her presence was usually noted at any sort of social function. That might have something to do with the fact she usually spent more time petting and chatting with the host's dog or cat than any of the guests, but still.

"I wish I could have known her."

Dean grinned. "You would have liked her. And she would have loved you. I'll bet you two would have been great friends."

Kaylee smiled back, feeling the compliment swirl then settle inside her. "Thank you," she said, but her voice was lost as the music changed tempo and the crowd let out a whoop.

By the time they made it around the dance floor, Kaylee was more at ease dancing with Dean. The partner change gave her a chance to test out the steps on her own without the added pressure of having a mad crush on her partner.

"Switch back," Emma shouted as they finished their rotation.

They laughed as their feet and hands got jumbled up switching partners again, but Kaylee loved how easily she slipped back into Luke's embrace.

"Are you having fun?" he asked her as they glided around the periphery of the dance floor.

"Yes," she told him. And meant it. "I'm having the best day. And night."

"What's been your favorite part?"

"Oh, gosh, there were so many. I think it's a tossup between..." She offered him a coy smile. "...the first bite of the Bartlett Blend *annd* this moment right now."

"Nice," he said with a chuckle. "I love that my competition for your favorite moment is caramel popcorn."

"Caramel *and* kettle corn."

"I'm honored. And a little annoyed." He sped up the steps a little as the song hit the last chorus. "Now my competitive spirit has kicked in," he said as he spun her in a twirl then dipped her slightly back. His face was inches from hers, his voice soft with a hint of flirtation. "What can I do to make *this* moment edge into first place?"

The song ended, but she was barely aware of the music, as Luke's gaze dropped to her lips.

She couldn't breathe as he bent his head closer, the anticipation of the kiss hammering like the wings of a thousand butterflies in her chest.

Closer still.

She fluttered her eyes, not quite closing them; she didn't want to miss a second of the best moment of her night. And possibly her life.

His lips were barely a breath away when a large pop sounded and a flash of color lit up the sky.

His head whipped up, his face tilting to the sky as he lifted her back to standing. She tipped her head back too. Her cheek was still close to his, and her body stayed in the cradle of his arm as they watched the sky explode into a display of colorful fireworks.

"Wow," she said, looking up at him with a grin when the fireworks ended. "Not sure how you timed that so perfectly, but you just pulled ahead for my favorite part of the night."

He laughed and leaned toward her with no hesitation this time, as if he knew that if he didn't kiss her then, he'd miss his chance. But the kiss turned into a breathless grunt as Emma plowed into them, throwing her arms around Kaylee's waist in an exuberant hug.

"Wasn't that awesome?" the girl said, wiggling between them to give Luke a hug too. "It made me feel so happy inside."

"I feel pretty happy inside right now too," Luke said, glancing up at Kaylee with a knowing smile.

She couldn't help the grin that took over her face. "Me, too."

"You all about ready to go?" Dean asked. "I think I heard

the band say they were only going to play another couple of songs. If we go now, we might have a chance at getting out of the parking lot first."

"Sure," Kaylee said, although she didn't really want the night to end. And she really didn't care if she got stuck for longer in the parking lot, because she'd still be in the truck, alone with Luke.

They started to leave, when she noticed Bear sitting in a chair off to the side of the dance floor. His foot was tapping to the music as he listened to the band.

She reached for Luke's arm. "Wait. If we have time, I need to do one more thing."

He shrugged. "Go ahead. I'm in no rush."

She crossed the dance floor and offered a little wave as she approached him. "Hi, Bear."

He nodded solemnly, his granite expression showing no signs of being happy to see her. "Kaylee," was all he said.

She swallowed, so close to leaving it at that and turning around. But she couldn't leave—she knew this was something she needed to do. "Um, so, listen I'm wondering if you'd like to dance? With me."

He peered up at her, his expression changing between a mixture of confusion and delight. "You are an odd one," he said pushing up from the chair and holding out his hand. "But you're also the best offer I've got all night."

He towered over her, but his grip was gentle as she slid her hand into his. He walked her onto the floor but kept a reasonable distance between them as he placed his hand on her shoulder blade and led them into the dance.

He kept his back straight and his chin held high as he guided her with a surprising gracefulness around the outside of the other dancers.

He glanced down at her. "I can't quite figure you out, Kaylee Collins. You don't seem particularly courageous, yet unlike most of the people in this town, you don't seem to be afraid of me."

"I'm not. Not really." She narrowed her eyes. "Should I be?"

"I don't know why."

"I'll admit, you do give off a bit of a scary vibe. But it's just because you look kind of angry most of the time, and you're...you know..." She wasn't quite sure what word to use. *Tall* didn't seem quite descriptive enough.

"A giant?" he filled in for her.

She shrugged. "A gentle giant, though."

"You sure? Most of the kids around here think I'm going to gobble them up for supper."

"*Or* take them off on a flying motorcycle to a magical school."

He shook his head as he let out a soft chuckle. "I'm not going to do either. I mainly just want to be left alone."

"If I'd left you alone, we wouldn't be having this lovely dance." Her hand seemed small in his large one, but she gave his a little squeeze. "You're quite light on your feet for a giant."

He laughed again, a deep rumbling laugh that came from his chest. It sounded a little rusty, like it hadn't been used in a while. "You are a strange creature," was all he said as his laughter died.

She lifted one shoulder in another offhand shrug. "It takes one to know one."

Another chuckle rumbled through him as the song came to an end. He released her then took a step back and leaned forward in a bow. "Thank you for the dance, Miss Collins."

She offered him a curtsy in return. "It was my pleasure, Mr...I mean, Bear."

The band announced they were starting their last song of the night, and she waved to Bear before hurrying around the floor to where Luke stood waiting for her on the other side.

He held out her jacket and another large bag of Bartlett's

Blend. "I grabbed you another bag. For the road."

A little shiver of happiness fluttered down her back. Another sweet and thoughtful thing Luke had done for her that night. "Thank you," she said, tucking the popcorn under her arm.

"But you can't eat any tonight because I don't want to take a chance on losing my standing." He teased her as they walked back toward the truck, then took her hand to help her over a rocky patch of ground at the edge of the parking lot.

She held back a sigh as he kept her hand in his all the way to the truck, only letting it go to open her door for her. She got in and considered scooting to the center, aching to sit next to him. Why was she even hesitating? They'd already danced together, *and* almost kissed, and he'd said he liked her. She scootched to the center, and her heart did a little flutter at the way he smiled as he slid in next to her.

They rode back to the ranch in companionable silence. Kaylee slumped against the seat, the excitement of the night finally starting to wear off.

As they pulled up to the house, she spotted Cooper and Gladys in the front window, their paws on the ledge as they each gave one bark to welcome her and Luke home.

"Crazy mutts," Luke muttered, as he got out and came around to her side of the truck. "I'll bet they're more excited to go outside than they are to see us."

"Speak for yourself," she said, giving him a playful nudge to the ribs. "This is the longest Gladys and I have been apart in weeks. I'm sure she missed me."

"I think Cooper only misses me if it's past his mealtime." His dog seemed to prove him wrong as he opened the front door and the golden flew out and pranced around his legs, whining and begging to be pet.

Gladys, on the other hand shot out, completely ignored Kaylee as she raced into the yard, her nose to the ground as if checking every scent to see if anything new had been there since her last patrol. Satisfied with her tour of the grass, she finally came back to Kaylee to get a cuddle. "See what I mean?" she told Luke with a laugh. "I'm obviously her first priority."

They stood on the porch for a few minutes watching the dogs race back out to romp in the front yard.

"That was a nice thing you did," Luke told her as he leaned back against the post. "Asking Bear to dance."

She shrugged. "It was more of a nice thing for *him* to do. I think I stepped on his feet three times."

"I doubt he even noticed."

"I like him. He intrigues me." She held up her hand. "But don't tell him I said so."

A smile creased Luke's face. "Your secret's safe with me."

She opened the front door as the dogs ran back up on the porch. Letting them inside, she started to follow.

"Wait," Luke said, stepping forward and reaching for her hand. "Don't go in yet."

She turned, her heart thundering in her chest as her knees felt weak.

This is it. He's finally going to kiss me.

Chapter Eighteen

KAYLEE'S PULSE RACED, AND SHE couldn't seem to catch her breath. She hoped he couldn't feel the tremble in her hands.

They were all alone with no distractions. This was the moment she'd been dreaming of.

But instead of gathering her to him, he pulled her to the edge of the porch. "I want to show you something. You can only see these every once in a while—the sky has to be super clear and all the conditions need to be just right—but they're visible tonight." He directed her attention to the sky over the far pasture. "If you thought those fireworks earlier were cool, this will blow your mind."

She sucked in a breath, thoughts of a kiss pushed aside as she gasped at the display of green and purple lights rippling through the dark sky. "What is that?"

"Those are the Northern Lights. They're God's fireworks display."

"No way. Really? I thought you could only see the aurora borealis in Alaska. And Iceland."

"You can see it better there, but you can catch glimpses

of it occasionally on some perfect nights in Montana too."

"It seems right that we'd see it tonight then," she said, squeezing his hand. "Because this is the *most* perfect night."

She stood that way with him, just holding his hand, as they watched the massive waves of color and light swell and surge across the sky.

After a while, she turned to him, feeling nervous but still knowing just what she wanted to say. "Thank you, Luke. Everything about this day and night has been amazing. And this"—she tilted her head toward the sky—"has been the perfect ending to one of the best nights of my life. So as much as I don't want it to end, I *do* want it to end *exactly* like this. I don't want anything to change or alter this perfect feeling. So I'm going to give you a hug then go right to bed and replay the whole day and night again in my dreams."

An easy smile played on his lips as he opened his arms.

She stepped into them and hugged him tight, inhaling the scent of him—the warm woodsy tone of his aftershave mixed with laundry detergent and the faint hint of caramel corn.

"You do have a way with words," he said against her ear. "And this has been an amazing night for me too."

She melted into him, memorizing every facet of the feeling of his embrace: the broadness of his chest, the strength of his arms, the tenderness of his head bent close to hers, the warmth of his breath on her neck. The joy and peace inside her that felt like, in his arms, she'd finally found a home.

Taking one more deep breath, she squeezed him again then let him go and hurried inside.

Kaylee woke the next morning to a warm nose nestled in her neck. Disoriented for a minute, she fluttered her eyes and softly uttered Luke's name. She'd been dreaming of him, of what it would be like to get married and be able to wake up every morning in his embrace.

But Luke's nose wasn't wet, and she was pretty sure his breath didn't smell like dog treats. She opened her eyes and was met with a pair of big brown ones staring at her as if she'd just hung the moon. Or maybe it was more of a *I hope you're going to feed me soon* look. Either way, it was adorable.

"Hello, Gladys," she cooed, ruffling the neck of her fur baby. "How you doing, girl? Did you sleep well?" She was pretty sure she already knew the answer to that question since the dog was in one of her favorite sleeping spots, curled up on the pillow next to her with her head in the crook of Kaylee's neck.

The dog answered anyway with an affectionate nibble of her ear.

Sunlight streamed through the window and across the bed as she laughed and sat up. She stretched her arms wide as a light knock sound on the door.

"Come in," she said, smoothing a hand over her hair.

The door opened a few inches, and Luke poked his head in. "Good morning, sunshine." He offered her a cheerful grin.

"Good morning, cowboy." She wasn't sure where that flirty tone had come from but the smile was all hers.

Cooper nudged his head in next to Luke's leg then pushed through the space and jumped on the bed, stopping to sniff at Gladys's ear before giving Kaylee's cheek a sloppy lick.

She laughed as she wiped the slobber from her face and scratched the dog's furry ears. Cooper pushed against her hand in doggy bliss. "Now that's a greeting I don't get every day."

Luke grimaced. "I do."

"Lucky."

He chuckled as he jerked a thumb behind him. "I've just finished my chores, and I wanted to tell ya I'm headed into town to run some errands for the next few hours. I need to stop by the post office and the feed store, and we're almost out of milk so I was gonna grab a few groceries. And Dean's been having trouble with a cow and wants me to stop by his place and take a look at her with him. You gonna be okay on your own this morning?"

She nodded. "Of course. I wanted to do some writing this morning anyway. There were so many things that happened last night that I'd love to use in one of my upcoming books."

He raised a knowing eyebrow. "Like discovering the Bartlett Blend?"

"Yes," she said, loving that they had an inside joke. "That, and seeing the Northern Lights, and how it felt to be at a live concert, and...oh, just so many things." She let out a happy sigh. "Listen, why don't you let me get the groceries? I plan to start packing this morning, then I wanted to run in and get a couple of things from the store anyway because I wanted to make lunch for you today."

"For me?"

"Yes you. You've been feeding me all week. I'd like to return the favor before I leave. I'm not much of a cook, so I can't promise anything too fancy, but I can *almost* assure you that it will be edible."

He frowned. "I don't know. I set a pretty high bar with those beanies and weenies the first night you were here."

She sighed again. "I can't believe that was almost a week ago. The time has gone so fast. I'm not sure I'm ready to leave."

His easy smile fell, and he took a step back. His voice took on a more formal tone. "I better get to going. See you at lunch." He whistled for the dog as he strode down the hallway.

Yeah, she wasn't super excited about the prospect of leaving, either.

Kaylee's morning flew by in a flurry of writing, packing, and running into town. She'd called Faye around ten to check in and had nonchalantly asked her about Luke's favorite meal.

"That guy will eat anything," her editor told her. "But you can't go wrong with a big pan of homemade macaroni and cheese. That's always been his favorite. If you look in the little wooden recipe box on the shelf above the sink, you'll find our Grammy's recipe. It's the one with crushed crackers on top."

"Perfect." She'd seen the box earlier and knew just where it was.

"How's the writing coming? Have you made it back on a horse yet?" Faye had said, sending Kaylee's good mood into a dive bomb.

"Not exactly," she waffled.

"Why not? Sassy is a barrel-racer. She grew up with horses and riding is a huge part of her character. To portray that, you've got to get out there and have the same experiences. I want you to know how sore your butt can feel after spending a few hours in the saddle, what the horse's tail sounds like as it swishes a fly off its backside, the feel of the reins in your hands, and what the mix of dust and horse sweat smells like."

"Um, yuck."

"Yes, some of it is yuck, but that's what makes it real. Kaylee, you've got to push yourself. And that means getting on that horse and experiencing the wind in your hair and that feeling of freedom when you're galloping across the pasture."

"Did you get a chance to read those last few chapters I sent?" she asked, trying to change the subject. She didn't want to have to admit that she'd barely walked around the corral on the horse and had come nowhere near a gallop. She'd clutched the reins and thought her heart would hammer out of her chest when the horse had just gone into a trot when it headed back to the barn.

She tried to add more excitement to her voice to move her editor toward the new topic. "The writing itself is going great. I wrote two thousand words this morning, and I swear the words just flew from my fingertips. I think being on the ranch has been so good for me. I've really felt the creative juices flow. Which totally surprises me, because I don't know if you knew that I was pretty hesitant about this idea at first."

"No. Really?" Faye said, sarcasm dripping from her words.

"Yeah, yeah. I know. You were right. Everything about my time here has been an amazing experience. I love it all— the people, the town, the animals, being on the ranch. This place is so gorgeous and quaint. I went for a walk around the pond this morning and I saw ducks, and some deer and I'm pretty sure I saw an eagle. Plus, Luke has been so great."

"Sounds like you're in love."

Kaylee had almost choked on the sip of coffee she'd just taken. "What?" she managed to croak as she set her cup down.

"I said, it sounds like you're in love. And I knew this would happen."

"You did?"

"Oh yeah. It's easy to fall in love with Montana. There something special about the Big Sky state. And I wanted you to love it, so you'll want to go back and keep experiencing it. I *did* read those chapters you sent in a couple of days ago, and I can already tell a difference in your writing. Your descriptions are richer and have more depth. And not just in the setting, but in the emotion between Sassy and Duke as well. I think the Montana air has worked magic for you."

The Montana air had been great, but it was a certain Montana cowboy who had inspired the new emotion and passion in the Duke and Sassy scenes.

"I'm anxious for you to get home, though. I've already set up a lunch with the publisher for early in the week to talk about your next contract. And I'm hoping to get this completed manuscript from you sooner rather than later."

Kaylee had hung up, feeling happy that Faye was pleased with her new work, but also sad at the thoughts of leaving the next day. She'd found something here in Montana. Even though she was a writer, she didn't know how to describe it. It was more of a feeling. A sense of.... belonging. Like maybe she'd finally found a place to call home.

Kaylee was pulling the pan of macaroni and cheese from the oven as Luke walked in the door for lunch.

"It smells amazing in here," Luke said, crossing to the sink to wash his hands. "I love mac and cheese. And that looks just like how my grandma used to make it."

"It is," she said, nodding toward the open recipe box on the counter. "I talked to Faye this morning, and she told me it was one of your favorites and where to find the recipe. I also made a chocolate cake."

"Is it the one from my grandma's recipe box too?"

"Yep." She set the warm pan of pasta on the trivet in the center of the table. "I hope that's okay."

"Of course it is. That's my favorite chocolate cake."

"I was hoping you'd be excited. I wanted to make up

for bringing you a cake with vegetables in it the first day I got here."

He laughed at the memory as he dried his hands on a towel. "I appreciate the gesture, but you didn't have to do that. That 'vegetable cake' didn't turn out to be half bad."

"You mean the part that wasn't squished against your chest?" She'd already filled the glasses with iced tea, and she leaned back to survey the table. *It didn't look half bad either*, she thought, a little pleased with herself at the cheerful table setting.

She'd found some light blue placemats with embroidered daisies on them in a drawer and had put the wildflowers she'd collected on her walk that morning in a jar in the center of the table. Her favorite things were the rosebud-shaped creations in the center of each plate she'd made from some yellow cloth napkins she'd found with the placemats.

"Wow," Luke said, nodding to the napkin roses as he dropped into the chair. "Did you do those yourself?"

She nodded. "I did. They're pretty neat, huh?"

"Yeah they are," he said, tilting his head to view them from the side. "How'd you learn to do that?"

"I'm a writer, which means I've had a lot of crazy part-time jobs, including two summers working wedding banquets at the Four Seasons."

"Cool." He dropped into a chair across from her and carefully moved the cloth rose to the side of his plate. "So how's my sister doing?" he asked as they filled their plates and dug in.

"Good. Busy. Same as always. She's already got a luncheon lined up for me as soon as I get back. She's really happy with the new chapters I sent. Well, except for..." She paused, fighting a frown.

"Except for what?"

She let out a heavy sigh. "It's just the horse thing. She thinks I'm still missing this key experience because I haven't actually ridden a horse on my own. And it bums me out, because I know it's my own fault and my own fear that's holding me back. I just really want to figure out a way to overcome this anxiety about getting on a horse."

Luke scooped up another bite, the macaroni and cheese on his plate quickly disappearing. "Seems to me, the only way you're going to get over it is to face it. And you're almost there. You've spent time with the horses, you've brushed them and helped with their tack. You just have that last step."

"Yeah, but it's a pretty big step."

"I have some time this afternoon. I could help. We could saddle up the horses and go for a ride, if you want."

She pushed back the panic that bubbled up in her chest. "I'd like that."

"It's a date."

A date?

Had he really meant a *date*? Or was that just an expression? He'd dropped the words casually enough, so he didn't seem to be making a big deal out of them. So neither should she.

"Yeah, sounds good."

"Let's do it." He eyed the cake on the counter then offered her a grin. "Right after we have some of that cake."

Luke patted Scarlett's neck as he walked Kaylee through the steps of saddling her again. This was the second time they'd done it, and he thought she was getting more comfortable with the tack.

"You're doing great," he said. "Don't forget to tighten the cinch. You don't want the saddle sliding off while you're riding."

Kaylee rolled her eyes. "That would be just my luck." She scratched the horse's neck next to Luke's hand. "She's being really patient with me."

"She's a good horse. Although she probably is wondering why we put her saddle on just to take it off then put it back on again."

"Don't tell her that I'm trying to procrastinate the part where I actually have to get into the saddle and ride her." She chewed on her bottom lip, her expression going pensive. "Speaking of procrastination, I know this might not be the best time, but I keep thinking about what you said last night. About wanting me to stay a bit longer. And I'm wondering if you really meant it."

More than I can say. He looked down at the ground where he scuffed his boot against the side of the stall, trying to figure out the best way to say what he wanted her to hear. It had been so long since he'd talked like this with a woman. Since he'd wanted to talk like this.

He let out a sigh as his gaze return to hers. "Yeah, I did."

Wow. Way to go, Montgomery. That was articulate.

She scrunched up her nose in that cute way she did when she was thinking. "Why?"

He rolled his shoulders to keep from shrugging them. He wasn't good at this mushy feelings stuff. "Because I like you, and it's been a long time since I've *liked* anyone."

"I *like* you too."

He thought she'd put the same emphasis on 'like' that he had, and his heart gave a little jolt of excitement. But he still wasn't sure he was saying enough.

"I mean I *really* like you. So much that I can't stop thinking about you. And I think we just might have something here."

"I think so too."

"You do?" His heart was doing all sorts of jolting now.

And his palms were starting to sweat.

"Well, yeah. I mean, if the something *you're* talking about is the same something *I'm* talking about."

He groaned. Yep. Clear as mud.

This was it. Time to fish or cut bait. He took her hands in his. "Kaylee, I know we haven't known each other long, and this seems really fast. But I swear I felt something for you the very first day I met you." He rubbed his thumbs over her knuckles. "And I keep feeling more every day I spend with you. I don't quite understand it myself, but maybe I don't need to. All I do know is that I'm falling for you. And the idea of you driving away tomorrow and me never seeing you again scares me to death."

Her voice was soft as she whispered in return. "Me too."

He wished she would say something more than just agree with him. Like that she was falling for him too. But at least she wasn't disagreeing with him. And maybe that's what her *me too* meant.

He took a deep breath then plunged further in. "So, what I'm saying is that I'd like you to stay. At least for a little while, just to see if this really *is* the something we think it is." He shook his head. "Dang, I feel like my mouth isn't saying the stuff right that my heart is telling it to. You're the writer, you're better at words than I am."

"I can hear what your heart is saying just fine." She smiled up at him—a smile full of promise and possibility. "You're making perfect sense to me. I've got a crazy week ahead of me, but I'll figure it out, because I'd like to stay too."

"Good." He leaned in, this time intent on *really* kissing her.

Chapter Nineteen

BZZT BZZT.

Luke's phone buzzed in his pocket. *Seriously?*

He considered ignoring it—he was *never* going to get to kiss this woman. But he didn't get a lot of phone calls. He should probably at least check to see if it was something important. If it was a call about his car's warranty, he was going to chuck the thing across the barn and finally give Kaylee the kiss he'd been dreaming about.

He sighed as he pulled it free. "It's Dean," he told her, checking the screen. "I'd better take it."

"Yes, go ahead."

He touched the screen and then held the phone to his ear. "Hey Dean."

"Hey Luke. Sorry to bug you, but I need a favor."

"Name it."

"This cow is still struggling and I'm waiting on the vet to show, but Emma's just finishing up at soccer camp. Any chance you can run into town and pick her up for me and bring her home?"

"Sure, no problem. When do you need me to pick her up?"

"About three minutes ago."

"I'm on my way," he said, already heading toward his truck. "Call her and tell her I'll be there in five."

He snapped his phone shut then turned back to Kaylee as he opened his truck door. "I've got to pick up Emma. Dean's stuck, and I don't want her waiting by herself."

"I heard. Go."

"Will you be okay?"

She waved him on. "I'll be fine. I'll stay right here and keep the horses company."

"It shouldn't take me but ten minutes to get there, drop her off and be back."

"Really. I'm fine," she assured him. "I'll stay right here. And I'll even give Scarlett a sugar cube for her patience."

He had one foot in the cab when he paused and leaned his head through the space between the truck and the open door. "Hey, Kaylee?"

"Yeah?"

"There's another reason I want you to stay."

She cocked her head to the side, the flirty move sending butterflies careening through his gut. "Yeah, what's that?"

"Because make no mistake, one of these days, I *do* plan on kissing you."

"Oh."

He slid into the truck and started the engine, grinning at the image of her standing next to the horse, her eyes wide and her mouth open in a perfect O.

Kaylee finally shut her mouth, but she couldn't stop smiling as Luke pulled out of the driveway and onto the road. "Well that was unexpected," she told the horse. "But I liked it."

Scarlett lowered her head and let out a whinny as if agreeing with her.

"And it sounds like I'm going to stay for a bit." She was sure Faye wouldn't be happy about the change of plans. Even though it had been her editor's idea to come to Montana, she was pretty sure she hadn't meant for Kaylee to want to stay.

It wasn't easy to get a lunch with her publisher, and she wasn't excited to tell Faye they'd have to reschedule. But this felt more important—like something she *had* to do.

For the first time in a long time, she let herself dream of the possibility of a future with a man. Luke had said he'd felt something for her the first day he'd met her. She felt the same way.

A spark of electricity had shot through her the minute she first saw him. Granted—that might have had something to do with the fact that he looked exactly as she pictured Duke. But then it was more than that. It was his easy smile and the way he treated the animals and his dog. And her.

Luke was the whole package, and she'd been falling harder for him every day she'd spent with him. She wasn't ready to give that up. Like Luke, she wanted to see where this thing led. She wanted to stay for another week. Or even two. Or twenty.

"He thinks we have something," she told the horse, throwing her arms around Scarlett's neck.

A faint niggling feeling crept into her happy thoughts— was Luke really falling for *her,* or was he falling for the person she was pretending to be?

And what about her? Was this all what she was really feeling, too? Or was she so embroiled in playing this character that she was experiencing what Sassy would be feeling instead of her own genuine emotions?

At times, she'd started to wonder if the two parts of her were mixing into one. She'd started to really feel more courageous and had been so proud of herself for stepping up and trying new things. But how much of that was her, and how much was the bravery she pretended to have when she was channeling her fictional character? And would this newfound courage disappear as soon as she drove away from Dusty Acres...and Luke?

Just the thought of driving away from this place, and this man, she'd grown to care so much about, was what scared her the most now. She felt like she *was* finding herself, discovering her own brand of spunkiness, but trying to figure out her feelings for Luke and finding the courage to stay was going to take all she and Sassy had combined.

She took a deep breath as she pushed back her shoulders. Actually, she didn't need Sassy to help her with that part. She *wanted* to stay, to give this thing with Luke a chance. She had the chance now to prove she was brave on her own, to face things boldly and with courage.

Things like riding this dang horse.

"You don't seem so scary," she told Scarlett as she ran her hand down her velvety cheek. "Why am I so afraid to ride you?"

The horse lowered her head and nuzzled it into Kaylee's side. She let out a laugh. It was exactly the kind of thing Gladys or Cooper would do.

She stared into Scarlett's gorgeous deep brown eyes. Isn't that what Luke had told her to do? To imagine the horse as a giant dog. Or as just a bigger version of Marigold, the mini horse. Kaylee wasn't afraid of either of them.

I can do this.

She carefully opened the gate door and stepped into the stall with Scarlett. "Hey girl. How would you feel about going for a little ride?" The horse stood still, as if patiently waiting for her to get into the saddle. She tentatively reached for the saddle horn then lifted her leg and slid her boot into the stirrup.

Wasn't this with this whole trip was about? Pushing her boundaries and getting that authentic experience?

One step at a time.

She pulled herself up and swung her leg around the back of the horse. Scarlett calmly chewed a piece of hay while she got her foot into the other stirrup and settled herself in the saddle. "Easy," she said, just as much to herself as she did to the horse. Lifting the reins, she nudged the horse with the heel of her boot. "Let's just take it nice and slow."

The horse padded out of the stall and into the center lane of the barn. Kaylee had planned to try to go a few laps around the corral but realized too late that she hadn't opened the corral gate. And apparently Scarlett had other plans anyway, since she turned and plodded out the wide front barn door.

As they crossed the driveway, Kaylee hoped the horse was planning a nice slow leisurely walk around the pond and not heading toward the steep rocky path up the side of the mountain.

She was thankful they'd taken the dogs for a walk after lunch and that they were both sacked out in the house. Two less things for her to worry about.

Trust the horse.

She could hear Luke's voice in her head, and she liked that it was louder than Sassy's. Her fictional character would have her spurring the horse on, but she chose to listen to Luke's calm, steady reassurance that she was doing fine taking it slow. She couldn't wait for him to drive up and see her sitting proudly in the saddle.

The horse stopped at the edge of the driveway and jerked Kaylee forward as she lowered her head to nibble at a patch of grass. Scrambling to stay in the saddle, she pulled the horse's head back up. "Come on, girl. Work with me. You can eat later."

She turned her head at the sound of an engine. Surely

Luke couldn't be back already. But it wasn't Luke's truck pulling into the driveway. It was a much older pickup, the faded blue paint spotted with patches of burnt orange rust.

Kaylee recognized the gentle giant squeezed in behind the wheel. But before she had time to wonder what he was doing at the ranch, the old truck backfired, letting out a loud pop.

The engine backfiring sounded like gunfire, and Kaylee screamed as the horse reared up and took off in a gallop across the pasture.

She leaned forward to clutch the horse's neck as its hooves beat thunderously against the hard ground. "Stop!" she shouted, but the horse ignored her and continued to race at the same breakneck speed.

Faye had compared the feeling of galloping across the pasture to freedom and flying, but all Kaylee felt was terror and fear.

"Whoa," she screamed as the saddle started to slide to the side. She suddenly couldn't remember if she'd tightened the cinch. But it was too late to worry about now. The horse started up the rocky path of the mountain side, then lost her footing and spooked again. Her eyes were wild as she lifted her front legs off the ground and pawed at the air, pitching Kaylee off her back.

She slammed into a branch as she fell, and pain sliced through her shoulder before she hit the ground with a hard thud and the breath rushed from her lungs. She barely had time to register the small, jagged rocks biting into her skin before another sharp jolt of pain split through her temple as her head slammed into a rock.

Then everything went black.

Chapter Twenty

K AYLEE FOUGHT THROUGH THE PAIN as she struggled to regain consciousness. She could feel herself being lifted from the ground and carried along the path of the pasture.

"Luke?" she murmured.

"I've got you, Kaylee. I'm going to get you some help." But it wasn't Luke's voice. And it wasn't Luke's arms or chest she was being held against. The man carrying her was bigger than Luke—*much* bigger.

"Bear?" she asked before slipping out of consciousness again.

She woke up again a few minutes later as Bear gently sat her in the truck and carefully pulled the seatbelt across her lap to buckle her in.

She didn't know why he bothered. She was already hurt. That thought struck her as funny, and she wanted to tell Bear the joke, but her head hurt too much.

"Stay right here," he instructed. "And keep this on your head." He lifted her hand to the wad of fabric pressed against her forehead. "It will help stop the bleeding."

"Am I bleeding?" She started to pull the wad away, but he pressed her hand back.

"I told you to keep it there," he bellowed.

"Okayyy," she answered, slumping back against the seat, too tired to argue. "Bossy-pants," she muttered as her eyes fluttered closed.

"I will be *right* back," he assured her, his voice a little softer. "That horse who dumped you off already ran back to the barn, but I've got to make sure she's secured in a stall or the corral then I'm taking you to the hospital."

He returned a few minutes later and slid into the front seat of the truck. "You okay?" he asked as he started the engine.

"I'm good." She opened her eyes and noticed that one of the sleeves of his flannel shirt was missing and looked like it had been ripped off. "What happened to your shirt?"

"You needed it more than I did." He nodded to the wad of fabric he'd instructed her to hold to her head.

She pulled it away for a second, noting the similarity of the material that hadn't been soaked with dark red blood. "Sorry."

"It's okay. It's an old shirt anyway. My wife had been pestering me to put it in the rag bin for years." He put the truck in gear then held out his hand to steady her. "Hold on now. Here we go."

She took inventory of her injuries as he drove. Beyond the cut on her head, which she assumed was the culprit of the wooziness she was feeling, she had road rash type abrasions on her elbows and lower arms and a shallow cut along the side of her shoulder. More blood soaked through a rip in the thigh of her jeans. Her leg was sore, but the cut she could see didn't seem to be as deep as the one on her head must have been. There was a heck of a lot less blood, at least. She could feel the stickiness of it covering her fingers holding the fabric to her head.

After surveying her injuries, she noticed a small blue and gold gift bag sitting on the seat, the words, "Congratulations on your Graduation" written on the side.

"Were you on your way to a graduation?" she asked, trying to think of what kind of class would be graduating in the middle of the summer. But the effort made the pain in her head worse.

He frowned as he glanced her way then noted the gift bag in the seat. "That's a gift for you."

"For me? Why? Did I graduate?"

"No," he grumbled. "If you must know, I was on my way to meet a lady-friend for coffee. I just stopped by to drop this off before you left. But there's a good chance I'm gonna be late now."

"I know I hit my head, but I'm really confused. I don't even remember taking any classes."

"There was *no* graduation. I made you something and that was the only stupid bag I could find to put it in."

"Aww. You *made* me something. Like a present? What is it? And since when do you have a lady-friend?"

"Don't worry about all that now. We're almost to the hospital."

He pulled the truck up to the door, killed the engine, then raced around to open the door and helped her out.

"Wait, my present," she said, reaching back into the truck. She pressed the bag to her chest.

"You sure you can walk?" he asked, sliding an arm around her waist.

She nodded then winced at the pain shooting through her head. "Yes, I'm fine. I can walk. I just wish the ground would stop moving."

Luke strode toward the hospital entrance, panic building in him like a pot of water ready to boil over.

He couldn't even remember how he got here. Everything was a blur after he'd gotten the call from Bear. He'd already dropped Emma off and had been heading back to the ranch when Bear called to tell him Kaylee had been in an accident.

He'd registered the words *thrown from a horse* and *probably a concussion*, but the rest was lost in the rush of noise in his ears as he whipped a U-turn on the highway and sped back to town.

He was still on autopilot as he parked and hurried across the parking lot, but once his feet hit the sidewalk, he stopped in his tracks as if he'd run into a glass door.

Memories of this exact same moment from five years before slammed into him. He'd gotten the call about Beth and raced to the hospital in the same way. He pressed his fist to his forehead, forcing the memories away. This wasn't about Beth. This was about Kaylee, and she was hurt.

Focusing on his boots, he forced his feet to take another step forward. Then another.

I can do this. It's not the same.

The automatic hospital doors opened with a whoosh and the smells hit him like a freight train, almost knocking him to his knees. The distinct scents of antiseptic and bleach, of cafeteria food and sickness. He could hear the sound of a crying infant and the hack of someone's phlegmy cough.

He swallowed the bile building in his throat as he took a step back. He *couldn't* do this.

Just the smell and the sounds of the emergency room were hitting him like a two by four to the face. What would happen when he had to walk inside and up to the desk?

Come on, Montgomery. Man up. It's Kaylee.

He pushed forward, one step at a time, through the doors and toward the receptionist, the tension-filled air of people waiting to see a doctor pressing in on him.

Thankfully he recognized the receptionist. She was an older woman who was a deaconess at his church. She smiled at him as he approached the desk then her smile turned into a concerned frown. "You okay, Luke?"

"Kaylee. Collins. She was brought in a little bit ago."

"Yes, of course. With Mr. Berenger. He said he would be calling you. She's still in the trauma center. You can go on back."

Trauma center? A bone-deep fear shot through him. Were her injuries worse than he feared?

Kaylee leaned her head back against the pillow as she waited for the ibuprofen the nurse had given her to kick in. She peered over at Bear, whose large body made the chair he was sitting in seem like a child's.

His knee bounced with impatience. "Where is that dang doctor?"

"He'll be here," she said then held out her hand. "Can I open my present while I wait?"

Bear shook his head and uttered a gruff, "Yeah." He passed the gift bag. "It's nothing special. Just something that made me think of you."

She was touched that he'd made her a gift at all. "I'm sure I'll love it." She reached into the bag and pulled out a square of cardboard. She gasped as she peered at the silver chain and pendant attached to it with scotch tape. The pendant was the "K" key of an old antique typewriter. "Oh my gosh, Bear. I do love it. It's amazing."

He shrugged but the hint of a pleased smile threatened to curve his lips. "It's no big deal. I just took one of the keys off an old typewriter I had in the basement and strung it on a chain. Some might say it's just a piece of junk. But I thought you might appreciate the significance."

"I do." She pressed the necklace to her chest. "It's wonderful." She peeled the tape from the cardboard and pulled the chain over her head, taking care to not catch it in the gauze bandage the nurse had affixed to her forehead. "It's one of the top ten best gifts I've ever received."

He frowned. "Then I'd say you don't have very good gift-givers in your life."

She laughed but the movement made her head hurt. She leaned back against the pillow as she noticed Bear check his watch for the umpteenth time. "You can go. I know you have plans, and I'm fine, really. I'm not going anywhere."

He looked from her to his watch again then pushed to his feet. "If I hadn't made plans already, I'd stay." He edged closer to the door. "And I'm not good with all this hospital stuff."

"I totally get it. And it's not like I'm going anywhere."

He reached out and awkwardly patted her hand. "Take care of yourself. It's been a pleasure meeting you."

"You too. And thanks again for my present."

"Luke should be here any minute."

"Go," she told him, waving him out of the room. "I'm fine waiting by myself." That's how she'd spent most of her adult life. Waiting by herself. But now she felt like she had a chance to have someone else in her life. Someone who would be with her when she took one of life's spills.

Except the fall off the horse had felt like a jolt back to reality and forced her to face the fact that she wasn't Sassy. She wasn't brave or coordinated or adventurous. She was boring and dull and led a humdrum life of monotony spending her days working at her desk with her dog curled at her feet. She'd given Luke this impression that she was fun and daring, but that wasn't her. That was Sassy. What would Luke do when he realized she was giving him a false sale of goods?

Luke tried to focus on the room numbers but couldn't remember if the receptionist had said Kaylee was in Room B or D.

He heard the flurry of metal rings being drawn across a rod and saw Bear step out from behind a curtain. *Thank goodness.* Kaylee must be in there.

Bear met him halfway to her room as he rushed forward. A deep scowl covered the older man's face. "It's about time you got here."

"How is she? Is she okay?"

"She will be. No thanks to you. Where were you? And what were you thinking leaving her alone with the horse like that?"

He shook his head, angry at himself for the same reasons. "It was only for a few minutes. She was supposed to wait for me."

"Well, she didn't. And now she's gonna have a mess of stitches and a sore body because she got on a horse when she wasn't ready."

Luke hung his head. "I know," he whispered.

"She's not as tough as she acts," Bear said.

"I know that too."

The older man clapped an encouraging hand on Luke's shoulder. "I gotta go, but I'll check on you all later. Take care of her."

Take care of her.

Luke nodded but the words swirled in his head. He wanted to take care of her, but obviously he was no good at taking care of anyone. He hadn't taken care of Beth, and he'd lost her. That morning, he'd asked Kaylee to stay, but now he wasn't sure he could go through this again. His heart was too broken, too damaged to try to give it away again.

And he wasn't capable of going through the pain of losing someone again. He couldn't.

His thoughts bombarded him, and he felt like he was walking through a thick fog as he took the last few steps to Kaylee's room and pulled back the curtain.

He sucked in a breath at the sight of her. She was resting, but her eyes fluttered open at the sound of the curtain rings. Her face was pale, even more so against the dark, rusty color of the dried blood streaked across her cheek and drying in her hair. A deep purple bruise peeked out of the bandage across her forehead. He winced at the abrasions on her arms and the cuts on her shoulder and leg.

The sight of the bruises and her poor battered body combined with the smell of disinfectant and the faint scent of blood did Luke in, and his knees threatened to buckle. He grabbed onto the back of the chair in front of him for support.

He could handle seeing a surgical procedure done on one of his cows and could ignore the pain of his own cuts and scrapes, but seeing Kaylee like this...hurting, and in a hospital bed was too much for him.

He'd been fooling himself the last week. For a tiny moment in time, he'd believed he might be able to find love again—had wanted to at least try. But this was too much. He couldn't put himself through the pain of caring about someone again, only to lose them. He couldn't do it. Not to himself. And not to this sweet thoughtful woman who looked at him as if he hung the moon. She deserved more. Better. Someone worthier than a broken-hearted cowboy with nothing left to give.

Any hope he'd had earlier disintegrated as she peered

up at him.

"I can't do this," he said. His throat was raw, and his voice came out gritty and rough. "Not again. Not with you."

Chapter Twenty-One

THE SMILE KAYLEE HAD BEEN bravely trying to muster fell, and her shoulders sagged against the pillow.

Her world crumbled with Luke's words and the sad resignation in his voice.

She knew this was coming, knew she couldn't keep up this charade. Falling off the horse had reminded her of who she really was and how so much of the time she'd spent with Luke had been a fantasy. As much as she wanted to fight for him, she knew winning him would be an empty victory if the victor was Sassy.

It was better to let him go and fade back into her fictional world where broken hearts happened on the page and didn't split her apart.

She pressed her lips together to keep from crying. She had to get the words out. Quick, like a Band-Aid, before she lost the courage to say them. For the last time, she summoned Sassy's mettle. "I can't do this either."

Luke winced as if her words had physically slayed him.

But she had to keep going. Had to get the truth out.

"I'm not the person you think I am. I've just been pre-

231

tending to be her."

His brows drew together in a scowl. "*Pretending*? What do you mean?"

"I'm so sorry. But this just isn't me. I'm not fun or funny or the life of any party. I'm dull and boring, and the characters in my books are way more fearless than I am. Which is why I pretended to be Sassy."

"Sassy? Who's Sassy? You mean the one in your book? I don't understand."

"I was terrified to come here, scared to spend time on the farm and hang out with you. Well, not you, not in the beginning, but with some guy I didn't know. So I thought if I pretended to be Sassy, to channel her personality and use it as my own, then I could get through this ordeal and do what I had to do to get back home."

He flinched. "Spending time with me was an 'ordeal' you were just trying to get through?"

"Well, just in the beginning. Because when I met you, you reminded me so much of Duke, you know, Sassy's hero, and you were soo good-looking and strong, and I was so intimidated, I just wanted to get back in my car and drive away. I felt like such an idiot with that stupid hat on and holding your least favorite kind of cake."

A hint of a smile tugged at the corner of his lips. "I liked that hat."

Oh gosh, his smile almost did her in. She dropped her gaze to her lap—she couldn't look at him or she'd never be able to finish. "You didn't know me—didn't know the timid awkward nerd that I normally was. And part of me liked the idea of being someone else for a while. Someone better, who was more fun and adventurous and wasn't afraid of her own shadow. So, I took on the persona of my fictional character and pretended to be her."

She lifted her shoulders as she picked at a spot of dried mud on her hand. "When you asked me to muck out stalls and run fence, instead of shying away like Kaylee would do, I channeled Sassy and jumped in with a shovel. But now it's gone too far, and I feel like I've misled you."

He took a step back, his expression pained as if her words had slapped him in the face, any hint of a smile gone. "So all this time we were together, that was all just pretend for you?"

"No, of course not."

"Because *my* feelings were real."

"My feelings were real too. *Are* real. But *my* feelings don't matter. What matters is that you think you fell for someone who *isn't* real."

"You *are* real. This doesn't make sense to me. I've spent an entire week with you. I do know you."

A sob threatened to break from her. She wanted so much to take back everything she'd said, for things to go back to the way they were this morning, but now that the truth was out, she couldn't undo it. "You don't know *me*. You know the person I was pretending to be."

He took another step back. Another step *away* from her. Every step he took broke off another piece of her shattered heart. "I guess I did. And I bought it all, hook, line, and sinker. I thought we really had something."

"I know." She sucked in a breath, swallowing at the pain in her throat. "I did too, but I can't start something with you that is based on a lie. I tried to be Sassy, but I'm not her. I don't know how to do this."

"I don't even know what to say."

"I do. I'm leaving. Today. I'll start back or find a hotel." She pointed to the bandage on her head. "As soon as they stitch me up and discharge me, I'll get Gladys and the rest of my things from the ranch and leave."

He slowly nodded as if mulling the idea over. "I think that's probably best." He turned to leave then stopped and looked back at her. "I thought I was strong enough to do this, to care about someone again, but I'm just not. This is too hard. Too painful. My heart broke when I lost Beth, and I just don't know how to grow another one." He took a deep breath. "I'll send Dean back to pick you up. Goodbye Kaylee."

She tried to tell him goodbye, but the word came out as a sob as the curtain dropped behind him, and she could hear his boot heels walking away.

Luke thought his heart had already been broken, but it shattered anew as he walked into the farmhouse and felt Kaylee's presence all around him. Her sweater was draped over the arm of the sofa and one of her notebooks and silly purple pens was on the coffee table. The scent of her perfume mixed with chocolate cake hung in the air.

He heard a thump from her bedroom as Gladys jumped off the bed then her toenails tapped on the hardwood as she came running out to greet him. It hadn't been that long, but he'd already fallen in love with the silly mutt and was used to having her around. He swallowed as it hit him again that she and Kaylee were really going to be gone.

Cooper had been asleep on the sofa, and he stretched and yawned before getting off the couch and coming toward him.

Luke bent down and gave them each a scratch before heading down the hallway and into Kaylee's room. The scent of her was even stronger in here. Her suitcase was on the bed, and his flannel shirt was folded and lay across the side of it, as if she couldn't decide if she could take it or not. He picked it up and held it to his cheek. He could smell her shampoo and that plumeria-scented lotion she used.

Her laptop was on the desk and another notebook was

open in here, just waiting for her to come back and fill it with her words and ideas.

How could she have been pretending with him this whole time? It didn't make sense.

He didn't know what to believe or what was real anymore. Except for the sharp, aching pain in his chest. That was real. He'd thought his heart had been so broken after Beth died that he'd never feel anything in it again, but he was wrong.

He pushed the suitcase aside and sank down on the bed. Gladys and Cooper jumped up on the other side and barreled into him, their tails wagging into each other's as they crowded around him. He turned and hugged the corgi's neck. The dogs must have sensed his sadness, because Gladys licked his cheek and Cooper leaned into him, trying to nudge his nose in between Luke's chest and the corgi.

"I can't do this," he muttered into the dog's fur. "I'm not strong enough. It's gonna kill me to watch you two drive away."

He needed to get out of here. If she wanted to leave and walk away, he wouldn't stop her, but he dang sure wasn't going to be here when she left.

"Goodbye girl. Take care of Kaylee for me," he told the corgi as he gave her one more hug then patted his leg for Cooper to follow. "Come on boy. We're going for a ride."

Kaylee felt numb as she followed Dean out to his truck. He opened the passenger door and helped her inside. He'd been nothing but kind and patient as he waited for her to be discharged. He'd even helped her get cleaned up at the sink and wash some of the blood out of her hair.

"I hate being such a bother," she told him. "I know you

have a sick cow to take care of."

"You're not a bother. This is what friends do. And my cow is doing better. She was bloated, but the vet checked her out, and he thinks she just ate something bad. We gave her some baking soda, and now we just have to wait."

"Baking soda?"

"Yeah, it sounds like a weird remedy, but it works. And my farm hand finally showed up, so he's keeping an eye on her." He pushed the door shut and hurried around to the other side.

"I wish baking soda would remedy my problems," she muttered as she laid her head back on the seat.

"Hey, you okay?" Dean asked as he slid into the driver's seat.

She shook her head, the movement making her brain hurt. "No, I'm not okay. Not at all."

"What hurts? Do you want me to take you back in?" He passed her an empty fast-food bag from the floor of the truck. "Are you gonna throw up?"

"No, I'm not gonna throw up. And I don't need to go back in. The ibuprofen they gave me is managing the pain—or at least the pain from the fall." She offered him a weak smile as she folded the paper bag and set it in the seat. "I'll bet you're a really great dad."

"I try. It hasn't been easy on my own. I've had to learn to accept help from my friends too."

"I've never been to a place like Bartlett where the whole community is like a big family. I've really had the best time here and loved meeting all of you."

"Then why are you leaving so soon? Luke told me he was going to ask you to stay."

"He did. And I was going to, but I can't now."

"I don't get it. Things seemed to be going so well for you two. I haven't seen him so happy since before Beth died."

"That's just it. I'm not Beth. I'm not the life of the party or the fun one everyone wants to be around."

He raised an eyebrow. "First of all, no one's asking you to be Beth or the life of the party. You have your own great things that we all like about you. And you didn't see Luke the way he was before you got here. It's like he's been a different man since you showed up. Honestly, I think he might already be in love with you."

His words were like a stab to her heart. "That's what makes this so awful. Because he doesn't even know me. He fell for the person I was pretending to be."

"Pretending?"

She pressed her fingers to her eyes as if pushing the tears back that were trying to fall. "I don't expect you to understand, but I was terrified of coming here. I'm normally completely awkward and nervous in new situations, and I tried to turn around several times as I was driving here. But Faye told me I had to come, for my career, and she suggested that every time I wanted to crawl into my shell and hide, that I channel my spitfire heroine in my books and force myself to do what Sassy would do instead."

"Okay. That sounds like good advice."

"Maybe. But I think I took it too far. I tried to take Sassy's personality and make it my own. All the times I was with Luke when I was fun or witty or trying something new, like learning the two-step, that was all me trying to act like Sassy. So that's who Luke fell in love with—not the real me, but this fake persona that I've been trying to be."

"I don't believe it. You all have been together all day every day. You couldn't have been acting the whole time."

"No, but during the most important times."

"I doubt that. I have a feeling he fell for you in the times when you were the most you."

"But that's a problem too. Because now I've spent so much time acting like Sassy, I'm not sure where the real me ends and the fake her begins."

"But Kaylee, she's *all* you. If you were acting like one of your fictional characters, she's still one of *your* characters. You made her up. So she comes from *your* feelings and emotions."

What Dean was saying made sense, and Kaylee wondered if she hadn't acted too soon in pushing Luke away. "I want to believe you. But it's hard. And non-writers don't understand the way these characters can become almost real in our heads. The way they talk to us." She lowered her chin to her chest. "I must sound like a crazy person."

He huffed out a laugh. "Believe me, I know all about characters coming alive in your head. And I also know firsthand, that writers put pieces of themselves into their characters all the time. That's why I'm sure Sassy is made up of pieces of you."

Either something Dean had said or the way he'd said it stopped the rebuttal she'd been ready to give him. "Wait. What do you mean by *firsthand*?"

He pulled the truck to a stop at the town's only traffic light. Gripping the steering wheel, he took a deep breath then turned to her, his normal easy-going expression now humorless and severe. "If I tell you something, you have to swear that it stays in the confines of this truck."

The intensity of his voice told her he was serious, and her writer-brain curiosity was piqued. "Okay."

"I mean it. Not keeping your word could hurt Emma."

"I would never do that. I promise. I won't tell anyone."

The light changed, and he eased up on the brake and drove toward the highway. "I know firsthand about all this stuff, because I'm a writer too."

"Oh," she said, feeling a little letdown after that big buildup. Half the people she knew claimed they were writers. Almost everyone wanted to write a book at some point in their life. "I mean, really? Have you written a novel? Or tried to get something published?"

"Yes, and yes. I've written several novels, and a bunch of them have been published. But I write under a pen name to protect the innocent."

Several novels? Protect the innocent? Okay. He had her hooked again. "That's amazing. Would I have heard your pen name, do you think?"

"You might have. I write thrillers," he paused again, "Under the name JD Hawk."

Kaylee's mouth fell open. "*You're* JD Hawk?"

He nodded again, a sheepish grin on his face.

"Oh my gosh. I can't believe this. I'm a huge fan. Like one of your *biggest* fans. I've read every single one of your books." A flush heated her cheeks. "Well, that's embarrassing that I just told you that. I'm totally fan-girling right now. But I mean, come on. Dean, you're like *really* famous."

He laughed. "This is kind of fun. I don't get to meet fans in person. And I never get to tell anyone who I am."

"I'm in shock. Faye was just using you and the research you do for your books to convince me to come to Montana." She narrowed her eyes. "Did you really spend two weeks camping out alone in grizzly bear country when you were writing *Mountain Justice*?"

Dean chuckled. "No, but Emma and I did spend two *hours* at the Grizzly and Wolf Discovery Center in West Yellowstone. And we also spent time with the grizzlies at Zoo Montana in Billings."

"Zoo Montana?"

"Yeah, but maybe we should keep that between us. I'm not sure who exaggerated that research experience more— me or Faye." His eyes sparkled with amusement.

She tried to frown at her editor's embellishment but couldn't do it and ended up laughing with him. "I'm sure it was Faye. But I don't get it. Why don't you go public? Your books are amazing. If I were you, I'd tell everyone."

"I can't. And you promised you wouldn't either."

She nodded. "Your secret's safe with me. But why?"

"At first, it was to protect Emma. I write thrillers and murder mysteries and they sometimes get a little gruesome, so I didn't want her reading the books. But then I made a little money, and it was more about …well…still protecting her, I guess. Her mom left when she was a baby because she wanted out of the small-town life and being a mom. She wanted nice clothes and fancy cars, and she'd always cared more about money and success than she had about us. And now the only time I hear from her is when she's just broken up with her husband-of-the-month or is on the brink of bankruptcy and needs money. If she got even a whiff of my success, she would want a part of it."

"That makes sense."

"I'm doing this because I love it, but also *for* Emma. I've put most of the money away to secure a future for her—college savings and all that."

"Does Luke know?"

"Yeah. He's the one who encouraged me to write the first book. You know we've been friends since grade school and we were farm kids, so I was always making up stupid stories and telling them to him while we did chores. Then later, after my wife left, I got pretty depressed, and one night, he took me out for a beer and I told him this crazy idea I had for a book. And he told me to write it. Then he read it. Then he practically forced me to pitch the idea to Faye, who ended up buying it and she's been my editor for every book since then."

She shook her head. "I can't believe it."

"I know. It's pretty crazy. I'm trusting you with an important secret—because I owe Luke. And I believe you'll keep my secret identity."

"You make it sound like you're a superhero."

"I am, in a way." He held up his arm and flexed his bicep. "Writing is my superpower. And it's yours too." He dropped his arm. "Look Kaylee, I'm telling you this because I'm someone who knows. You and your character are one and the same. The thoughts you give what's-her-name? Sassy?"

She nodded.

"The thoughts you give Sassy are *your* thoughts. And if you have been acting like her, you're really just acting like another version of yourself. You haven't been *tricking* Luke. We've all used techniques or forced ourselves to step out of our boxes and try new things. Most people don't like public speaking, but they make themselves do it if they have to. How many times do we make ourselves go out or to an event when we'd rather stay home?"

What he was saying made sense. "I guess you're right."

"I'm a dad. I know I'm right." He grinned at his own joke. "We all try to be our best selves, especially when we like someone, and we want them to like us back. But I'm sure in all that time you and Luke spent together, he saw the real you too."

She thought about the first time she'd met him and how she'd shrieked and launched herself at him to get away from the dragon-goose. And when he'd found her in the storeroom at the church and she'd beaned him with a roll of paper towels. And how nervous she'd been dancing with that other guy at the summer celebration.

"Yeah, he has seen the real me at times. Unfortunately, those were the times I was embarrassed or angry or afraid."

"But that's what makes Luke's feelings for you real. If he's seen you at what you think are your worst times, and he still fell for you, then that should prove he likes the authentic you."

She nodded slowly as his words sunk in, soothing her aching heart. "You're right. He has seen the real me. But it's too late, I've screwed everything up and already pushed him away."

"Do you love the guy?"

She nodded again. "Oh yes." Of all the craziness and doubt swirling around her that day, that was one thing she knew for sure to be true. She was in love with Luke Montgomery.

"Then what are you going to do about it?"

"I don't know. This is where I would normally default to 'what would Sassy do to fix this?'"

"Forget about Sassy," he said as he pulled into Dusty Acres. "What would *Kaylee* do to fix this?"

She chewed her bottom lip as she considered her options, for the first time feeling hope for her and Luke's future. She thought about how she would write the scene in a book but this time she made *herself* the heroine. "She would find Luke and throw herself into his arms as she apologized and confessed her love for him. Then she would tell him she wanted to stay and try to make him fall in love with her again—the *real* her."

Dean smiled. "A little dramatic, but it works. And it sounds to me like you, not Sassy, has known what to do all along."

Luke leaned back against his 'thinking' bench and gazed out across the sky. He hadn't even told Max where they were going. He'd saddled him up on autopilot, and the horse had just known where to head.

Tied to a tree, Max was now munching on a nearby patch of sweet grass as Luke contemplated his life. Or lack thereof.

Cooper had crawled up on the stone bench with him and had been steadily inching closer and closer until the golden retriever was now sprawled across Luke's lap with his blocky head resting on his chest. Luke stroked the dog's soft furry ears as Cooper looked adoringly up at him with big brown eyes. He only wished he could *be* the person his dog thought he was.

"I get it, boy. I'm going to miss them too. You and I are both gonna lose our girls today," he told the dog. Cooper huffed out a sigh and licked Luke's chin. He sighed back. "I just don't get it. How could she have been *pretending* to be someone else? It doesn't make sense that she could keep that up for a whole week."

He thought about how quick she was to smile and offer a kind word and about the time they'd sat on this very bench and laughed so hard at their bad date stories. He thought about the feel of her hand in his and the soft, shy way she'd let him teach her to dance. Which led his mind to remembering how they'd almost kissed that night and then about *all* the times they'd almost kissed. And what about that hard, tight hug she'd given him on the porch the night before?

There was no way all of that was fake. He didn't believe it.

There had to be parts of her genuine personality in there somewhere—she had to have shown him her real self.

Cooper scootched another inch higher and nestled his nose into Luke's neck.

"You're right," Luke told him. "It's not like I knew everything about her anyway. And how will I *get* to know her better if she's gone?" He scrubbed his hand across his neck. "Why did I agree to let her leave today?"

Cooper stared up at him as if he were agreeing with Luke's every word.

"Right? How are we supposed to figure out if we really have something if she's gone?" He buried his face in the dog's neck. He knew the answer—knew why he'd agreed to let her go. Because he'd let himself hope for a future with her. And the idea of that future either working out or *not* working out scared him to death.

He hadn't been afraid when he'd fallen in love with Beth. He'd jumped in with both feet. But then he'd felt the bone-deep grief of losing her—and the fear of ever feeling that pain again became his constant companion. That's why he hadn't dated again or let himself get close to anyone new.

Then Kaylee had, thanks to a protective mother goose, quite literally fallen into his arms and his life. Then he'd fallen too.

"When did I become such a chicken?" he asked the dog.

Cooper pressed his feet into Luke's chest and let out a bark.

He nodded. "Yeah, I know. I do love her."

So why was he sitting up here on this mountain having a conversation with his dog? He should be down there, stopping her from packing her pudgy pup in the car and driving away.

"Come on boy," he told the dog, sliding out from under him and pushing up from the bench. "Let's go get our girls."

Cooper jumped down from the bench and raced around Luke's legs before tearing off toward the trailhead.

"Okay, I'm coming," Luke called, untying the reins and swinging up onto Max's back. He nudged the horse with his legs, and it followed the dog down the trail.

Luke leaned back in the saddle, letting the horse do the work as they made their way down the rocky trail. His thoughts were occupied with rehearsing what he was going to say to Kaylee and how he was going to apologize and convince her to stay.

She thought she was a dull and boring and not worth the trouble. He needed to tell her, to show her, she was worth fighting for.

If he wouldn't have been so focused on Kaylee and been paying better attention to the mountain and the trail, he would have noticed the fresh claw marks in the sides of the ponderosa pines and the faint musky odor in the air.

But he didn't catch any of that. It wasn't until they were right on top of it, and his horse whinnied and reared back that Luke noticed the bear.

The animal was standing next to the path, working his way through a huckleberry bush, as they came around the corner of an outcropping of rocks. They must've startled him as much as he startled them, because he raised up on his hind legs and let out a grunting huff as he pawed the air.

Max was a big horse, and he didn't get spooked by much. But he hated cougars, rattlers...and bears. The horse took a few steps back, and his hind foot slipped in some loose shale on the steep trail. The sound of the scraping rocks and the motion of slipping must've freaked him out even more, because he reared up, striking the air with his hooves, his eyes wild, as he let out a frightened neigh.

Another mistake of not paying better attention—Luke had only a loose grip on the reins and not enough control of the horse.

He fought to stay in the saddle as the bear let out another angry huff and the horse reared back again, trying to turn around and head back up the trail.

"Whoa, Max," Luke called, trying to calm the horse as he pulled back on the reins. But instead of calming, the frightened horse bucked, kicking his legs back as if to fend off the bear and pitching Luke off his back.

He landed with a hard thud, his body sideways across the path.

The whole time the horse had been freaking out, the dog had been barking and growling at the black bear, as if trying to scare it away.

Between the horse's wild bucking, the dog's growling, and Luke's loud cursing as he fell, they must have made enough of a commotion to frighten the bear. It took off up the side of the mountain, lumbering through the brush, and then its paws knocked loose a fallen tree.

The tree crashed down, tearing up brush and foliage as it plummeted toward him.

Luke scrambled out of the way—clawing at the dirt path as he tried to gain purchase. But he wasn't quick enough, and the tree rolled down the hill and right over his leg, tearing a gash through his calf and pinning him to the path.

He shouted in pain and frustration as he tried to pull his leg free. But it was no use. He was good and stuck. Patting his pockets, he searched for his phone to call for help.

But his pockets were empty.

Crud. Had he lost his phone in the fall?

Well this is just flipping great, he thought as he surveyed his surroundings, looking for the lost phone and something to use to help free his leg.

Max had taken off down the mountain, crashing down the path almost as loudly as the fallen tree had. But Cooper came over and laid down next to Luke, pressing his body close to offer comfort.

"It looks like we're on our own here, boy," Luke told the dog, ruffing the fur around his neck.

He let out an infuriated growl. Now instead of racing down to stop the woman he loved from leaving, he was trapped on the side of the mountain with no phone and no way to get help.

At least the bear had run away.

For now.

Chapter Twenty-Two

KAYLEE DECLINED DEAN'S OFFER TO help her into the house. She just wanted to find Luke and straighten out this whole mess. She prayed he'd forgive her and want to start again as she hurried up the porch steps, ignoring the pain in her cut leg. Thankfully she hadn't needed stitches for it too. The bandage pulled and tugged on the skin with each step, but nothing would deter her from getting to Luke.

The sound of Dean's truck driving away barely registered as she pulled open the front door and rushed inside. Gladys came running from her bedroom and pranced at her feet as she searched the house, calling out as she moved from the living room down the hall. "Luke, I'm back. I'm sorry. I was wrong. I was just afraid."

But Luke wasn't there. The house was empty.

Crestfallen, she trudged into her room and sank down onto the edge of the bed. All her fantasies of rushing into the house and him taking her into his arms evaporated. Just like him.

"Luke, where are you?" she called out into the empty rooms.

Gladys jumped on the bed and tried to crawl into her

lap and lick the bandage on her head. "I'm okay girl," she assured the dog as she pulled her phone from her pocket and tried to call Luke.

Bzzt. Bzzt.

She felt the vibration behind her as the phone rang in her ear. Turning around, she spotted Luke's phone tucked in next to her pillow. What the heck? What was it doing in here?

She picked it up and held it to her chest. He'd been in her room, and it must have fallen out of his pocket while he was sitting on the bed. That seemed like a good sign, right?

She hadn't been paying much attention when Dean had dropped her off, but now she remembered seeing Luke's truck parked by the barn when they'd driven in. That's what had made her think he was home. He must be out in the barn, probably feeding the cows or doing something with the horses.

Catching a look at herself in the mirror above the dresser, she cringed as she pushed to her feet. Dried blood was crusted across the shoulder and neck of her shirt. Mascara smudges were under her eyes, and her hair had dried in a frizzy tangle where she'd tried to wash it in the sink at the hospital.

As much as she wanted to see him, it was worth taking a few minutes to clean up and change clothes—she wanted to win him back, not scare him away. She hurried into the bathroom and washed her face and dragged a brush through her hair. Smoothing it back, she gathered it into a ponytail then pulled on a clean shirt, joggers, and tennis shoes.

Tucking both their phones in her pockets, she headed for the front door. "I'll be back in a few minutes," she told the corgi as she tossed her a treat. "Wish me luck that Luke will forgive me and still want me to stay."

Gladys let out a tiny yip before gobbling down her treat, which Kaylee took as the dog's blessing.

Except the corgi's wish didn't matter because the barn was empty too. As was Max's stall and the spot where Luke's saddle usually sat. He must have taken the horse for a ride. She had a feeling he'd taken the horse and the dog up to his thinking spot.

Now all she could do was wait. Scarlett was in her stall, and the horse plodded over and leaned her head over the gate. Luke must have taken her saddle and bridle off and put them away. "No hard feelings, huh?" she told the horse as she fed her a sugar cube. Scarlett nestled her head into Kaylee's side.

Kaylee left the barn and walked toward the pond. Maybe she could meet Luke as he came down the mountain. She gazed up at the imposing peak then around the farm at its base. It was so beautiful here. She could hear the whisper of grasses as the breeze spread across the bright green pastures, the pattern of crops and fields reminding her of a patchwork quilt.

She could smell the earthy scent of freshly turned dirt and the hint of pine from the trees marching up the side of the mountain. The sun dappled off the gentle lapping water of the pond, and Kaylee couldn't help but smile as she watched the mother goose swimming across it, her fuzzy goslings paddling happily along behind her.

Her musings were interrupted by the thunder of hooves and crashing of branches. She took a step back as a black horse came charging out of the trees and galloped toward her.

Max.

As frightened as she was of the galloping horse, she was more terrified of his empty saddle. *What happened to Luke?*

"Whoa," she called, raising her hands as she took a step closer. The horse slowed but his eyes were wild, and he seemed in obvious distress. "It's okay, boy." She spoke softly, trying to soothe the frightened horse as she reached for the reins hanging loose around his neck.

He seemed to settle as she ran her hands gently over his neck. "What happened? Where's Luke?"

She jerked her head up as she heard frantic barking, and Cooper shot out of the trees in the same place the horse had. He raced to her, his barking ramping up even more. The dog circled around her legs then ran back toward the mountain, stopping once to look back at her as if to make sure she was following.

She might not always know how to talk or act around people, but she understood dogs perfectly. And this one was definitely giving her a message. Something had happened to Luke—she was sure of it.

Every instinct told her to run after the dog. But she'd been up that path, and she knew how rocky and steep it was. It would take her forever to try to run up it. And that was if she could remember exactly where it was.

She turned to Max and looked him in the eye. Her heart hammered at the thought of getting on the huge horse—she'd just left the emergency room after getting bucked off the last one she'd gotten on. But she had to do this. For Luke.

Her mind automatically reached out for Sassy's courage. *No.* Not this time.

Sassy and I are one and the same. She reminded herself of Dean's words. She didn't need to channel the fictional character's bravery, she just had to dig deep for her own.

She leaned her head against the horse's neck as she reached for the saddle-horn. "I don't want to do this any more than you do, but I need you to take me to Luke." Taking a deep breath, she put her foot in the stirrup and hauled herself up into the saddle.

The horse stamped his feet, and Kaylee let out a yelp as she leaned forward and clutched his neck. But he didn't rear back or try to buck her off. Her hands were shaking as she pushed herself up and gathered the reins.

"I can do this." Her voice also shook as she spoke the

words out loud. She couldn't quite reach Luke's stirrups with her feet, so she turned the horse around and nudged him with her legs. "Come on boy. Let's go find Luke."

Cooper barked again and raced back through the trees and up the path. Max broke into a trot as he followed the dog.

"Please God, let Luke be okay," she whispered as she clung to the saddle horn. "And as much as I want to meet you someday, please Lord, don't let it be today."

Kaylee leaned forward, alternately searching the ground among the trees for Luke's body and the path ahead as she prayed she'd see him walking down it.

"Luke!" she called out, but the breeze rippling the leaves of the trees was the only sound she heard in reply.

Cooper's barking got louder as they neared an outcropping of rocks ahead, and she thought she saw a spot of color near the base of the boulders.

Then she nearly wept as she heard his voice. "It's about time you came back, you jerks. Thanks for leaving me. I hope you brought back a pizza. Or a phone. Or at least something to help with this stupid tree."

"Luke," she cried, urging the horse forward with her legs.

"Kaylee?" His head popped up over some bushes up ahead of her—he must have been lying down before. He stared at her as if she were a mirage. "Kaylee? Is that really you?"

"Yes, it's me." The horse stopped when it got closer, and she could see that Luke's leg was pinned under a fallen tree. "I'm coming to help. Oh my gosh, Luke. Are you okay?"

He stared up at her. "Are you riding my horse?"

Okay, that was an odd question, since he could clearly

see her sitting in the saddle. "Did you hit your head? Are you delirious?" she asked as she slid sideways until her foot found the stirrup, then swung her leg over and dropped less than gracefully to the ground.

"Maybe," he said, holding back the dog who was desperately trying to lick the smudge of whiskers off his face. "Because I can't quite imagine how the woman who was afraid to get on a small mare this morning just rode up the side of a mountain on *my* horse."

"I seem to be braver than I thought I was." Stumbling forward, she got her legs under her and hurried toward him. Dropping to her knees, she threw her arms around him in a hug. "Are you really okay?"

He squeezed her tightly to him. "Define okay."

She let out a relieved laugh against his chest then pulled back to search his face. "Are you hurt?"

He shook his head. "It's hard to tell. My leg might be busted up under that log. But it's nothing compared to the ache in my chest at the thought of you leaving and me not being able to stop you."

Her gaze had been traveling over the damage of his leg under the fallen tree, but she froze then returned it to his. "*Stop* me?"

"Yeah. Why do you think I'm stuck up on here on this mountain? I was racing down to tell you that I didn't want you to leave. But the bear and my horse had other plans."

"The *bear*?" Her head jerked up, and she wildly searched the trees around them. "What bear? Is it still here?"

"Nah, don't worry. It's long gone. And really, it's my own fault I'm in this mess. If I would have been paying attention, I could have warned it we were coming and not snuck up on it. I can't blame the bear—we startled him, and he was just trying to protect his food source." He nodded to a nearby set of bushes. "He was working his way through those huckleberries. Which, by the way, I was planning to eat to save myself if you left and I had to spend the winter up here trapped under this log."

She eyed the bush. "It doesn't look like there's very many berries left, so I guess it's a good thing I didn't leave."

He took her hand. "It's a really good thing."

A warmth spread through her that felt a lot like hope. She squeezed his hand. "Let's move this log off your leg and get you home." She stood, trying to focus on the task and praying she still had a chance at making a home with him, as she peered around at what she had to work with. "There," she said, pointing to a large, downed branch. "That oughta do it."

Cooper ran with her and bit into an errant bough, pulling alongside her as she dragged the tree branch over and wedged it under the log. "Good dog," she told him, scratching his ears. It seemed like he was really trying to help, but it was also possible he thought she was starting a game of fetch with a giant-sized stick.

"Good thinking," Luke said, leaning forward and trying to shove the branch into a better position. "Did you learn how to do this for one of your books?"

"No," she said, tossing him a grin over her shoulder. "I saw it on an old episode of *MacGyver*."

"Nice." He tried to grab the top of the branch to help pull it down, but he couldn't reach it. "Dang it. I'm no help." He held up his hand. "Not that I'm doubting you're strong enough to push it down on your own. Pretty much nothing you could do right now would surprise me."

"Oh, I'm not going to use my muscles," she said, turning around to face him. "I'm going to use my brain." She perched on the edge of the branch then gingerly sat down. Her body weight was enough to lower the branch and leverage the log up several inches.

It wasn't a lot, but it was enough for Luke to pull his leg free before she shifted her weight and let the log drop back down.

"You did it," Luke said, examining his ankle.

She knelt next to him, her victory short-lived with worrying over his injury. "Are you okay? Can you walk?"

"I don't know. But I'm gonna try."

She got an arm under his and helped him to stand. He gingerly tested his weight on his ankle.

"It's a little sore," he said with a wince. "But it's not bad. And I don't think it's broken."

"Are *we*?" she asked quietly, peering up at him. "Broken, I mean."

He shook his head. "I don't think so."

"I'm so sorry, Luke. All that stuff I told you before. I realize now that only part of it was true. I said I was channeling my inner Sassy, but she's still a part of me. So many of my actions this week were my own, or mine with just *a hint* of her. But all the feelings I have for you are definitely from me."

"I know."

"You do?"

"Yeah. You were wrong before. I *do* know the real you. I've seen her plenty of times this week. And I just saw her right now. She's the woman who cared so much about another person that she pushed her fear aside to get on a horse she was terrified of and then used her smarts to get me out of a treacherous situation."

She shrugged, but his words sent warmth to her cheeks. "Anyone would have done that."

He shook his head. "No, they wouldn't have. You keep saying you were pretending to be someone else, but I think you were just giving your real self the freedom to be you. It might have taken more guts than you normally have to join the Dusty Acres Chicken Chasers team or to face down a Cheez-It-eating axe murderer, but the place you pulled that courage out of wasn't from some fictional character, it was from inside you."

She laughed at the memories of the chicken chase and the raccoon. "I know that now. I wasn't living a lie. I think I was finally living my true self. But the reason I was able to do that was because during all those times I was scared, you still made me feel safe. You gave me a place where I felt I belonged. Being here, in this place, with you, I feel like I've finally found a home. And I don't want to leave."

"Then don't. Don't leave. Stay here. With me."

"Really?"

"Yes, I want you to stay. For a week, a month...for forever." He swept his arm around her waist and pulled her to him. Lifting his hand, he touched her cheek with the back of his fingers, the expression on his face so tender it made Kaylee want to cry.

"I didn't fall for the woman who cheerily mucked out some stalls—although she *was* pretty great. I fell for the woman who choked down beanies and weenies like they were a gourmet meal and who anonymously donated money so a little girl could get a bicycle. And who took the scary town grump a piece of cake then later asked him to dance with her. You weren't pretending to be someone else when you did all those things. You were being you, and that's the woman I fell in love with."

She froze as her breath caught in her throat. "What did you just say?"

His lips curved into a flirty grin. "You heard me, darlin'."

"Say it again."

He drew her closer. "This is how I know it's really you. Sassy would have given a flip of her hair and said 'I know' when I told her I loved her. You just asked me to repeat it."

She smiled up at him, her heart bursting with happiness.

He turned his hand over and cupped her cheek as his gaze shifted from her eyes to her mouth. He leaned in, then stopped, his lips a half and inch from hers. "I love you, Kaylee Collins."

"I love you too, Luke Montgomery." Her words came out in a rush of air as her heart pounded against her chest. But this time, her heart was pounding and her pulse was racing not from fear, but from excitement. "I'm tired of being afraid," she whispered.

"Me too."

"I don't think it was Sassy who made me feel brave, I think it was you."

He bent the slightest bit closer, and his lips grazed hers. The softest touch.

As she felt that barest caress, Kaylee knew she didn't need Sassy anymore. She was strong enough on her own. And with that, she didn't wait for Luke to finally kiss her— she leaned in and kissed him.

The kiss wasn't like in her books—it wasn't fictional. It was real. And it was amazing. In all its toe-curling swoony glory. She melted into him, and everything else fell away.

Until Cooper jumped up on them, trying to get in on the affection.

They laughed as they both reached to rub the dog's head at the same time. Luke took her hand in his. "You ready to go home?"

She nodded. *Home.* It was only one word, but it meant so much.

"I know you're the writer," Luke said, putting his arm around her shoulder and drawing her to him. "But I say we curl up on the couch with Cooper and Gladys and some of that chocolate cake and make our own story-book ending."

She grinned. "You, our dogs *and* cake? That sounds like a happily ever after to me."

The End...
And just the beginning...

Extra Delicious Carrot Cake

In *Cowboy Ever After*, Luke declares his distaste for carrot cake...not realizing that's exactly the kind of cake Kaylee brought him. Later on, though, she finds him enjoying a piece! This recipe plays off the best part of a carrot cake and takes the carrots into the sweet end of the food spectrum. Combine them with pineapple and macadamia nuts for an extra delicious cake!

For the optional topping of candied carrots: grate several carrots, boil simple syrup (equal parts sugar and water) for 30 minutes or until translucent, cool and sprinkle or toss in sugar to coat. Will hold in an airtight container 2 weeks.

- **Prep Time:** 15 minutes
- **Cook Time:** 45 minutes

Ingredients

CAKE
- 3 cups grated carrot
- 1 cup chopped macadamia nuts
- 1 ¼ cup vegetable oil
- 1 teaspoon salt
- 4 eggs
- 1 teaspoon ginger
- 2 cups flour
- 2 teaspoons baking powder
- 2 cups sugar

FROSTING
- 2 8-oz. packs of cream cheese
- 4 cups of powdered sugar
- 2 teaspoons pineapple extract
- 1 teaspoon vanilla extract

Preparation

CAKE
1. Preheat oven to 350°F. Grease two 9" round cake pans.
2. Finely grate 3 cups worth of carrots and set aside.
3. Chop 1 cup macadamia nuts and set aside.
4. In a mixing bowl, combine vegetable oil, eggs, ginger and sugar, mix until well-integrated.
5. Combine flour, salt and baking powder, and add to the mixing bowl.
6. Add grated carrots 1 cup at a time, mixing between each cup.
7. Add macadamia nuts and mix until well-integrated.

8. Once well mixed, pour batter evenly between the two cake pans, each should be approximately half full.
9. Bake 40 to 45 minutes, or until a tester inserted into the center comes out clean. Allow to cool before frosting.

FROSTING

1. In a mixing bowl, soften the cream cheese and slowly add in powdered sugar. Continue adding powdered sugar and mix on high until it is light and peaks. Add pineapple extract and vanilla extract. Mix for an additional two minutes.
2. Refrigerate covered until the cake is ready to frost.
3. Top with Candied Carrots (optional).

Thanks so much for reading *Cowboy Ever After*.
We hope you enjoyed it!

You might like these other books from Hallmark
Publishing:

Rescuing Harmony Ranch
Country Hearts
Country Wedding
A Down Home Christmas

For information about our new releases and exclusive
offers, sign up for our free newsletter at
hallmarkchannel.com/hallmarkpublishing-newsletter

You can also connect with us here:

Facebook.com/HallmarkPublishing

Twitter.com/HallmarkPublish

Acknowledgments

This book was so much fun to write. I loved living in the world of Bartlett, Montana and staying on the Dusty Acres Ranch with Kaylee and Luke.

First and foremost, I have to thank my husband Todd, who not only supports every aspect of my writing career, and never stops believing in me, but has also shown me what a real-life romantic hero is supposed to be like. We learned the two-step together, have eaten our share of beanies and weenies, and lived in the wonderful small town that inspired Bartlett.

If you've ever been to Fort Benton, Montana, you'll recognize where the inspiration for Bartlett came from. A small town down in a valley off the highway that sits on the banks of a river and has a Summer Celebration every year. After college, my husband and I lived there for several years, and that's where I first saw the northern lights and learned about street dances and made some of the best friends of our lives. In the book, Kaylee learns there is something special about Montana, and it's so true. The town and the people of Fort Benton will always be special to my heart.

A huge shout out goes to my sister, Teri Rand, for reading my books and for being the inspiration for the scene where the cows run after Kaylee in the field when she's carrying an empty feed bag. I still crack-up when I remember Teri running across that field with a whole parade of cows trotting after her—and I've got it all on video. Love you, Sis!

Thanks goes out to my dad and stepmom, Dr. William and Gracie Bryant, for letting me use their Dine for a Dime night that they participate in at their church. My family has helped out on a night they've hosted, and it went pretty much the same way it did in the book—good food, good fellowship, and always just enough in the can to cover the night's expenses.

Big thanks to my family for your support and encouragement. To my mom, who loves everything Hallmark and never doubted I would get a Hallmark deal.

I have to thank my plotting partner, Anne Eliot, for the hours we spend on the phone, laughing and talking about plot ideas, small towns, character motivations, and hunky heroes. You are the best, Annie, and I'm so thankful to have you in my life.

Enormous thanks goes out to my editor, Stacey Donovan, whose favorite cake actually is vegetable (carrot) cake. Thank you for your belief in this story and for your invaluable help with this manuscript. Thanks also to Eunice Shin and to the whole Hallmark staff who worked to make this book so perfect, especially the cover artist who created this amazingly gorgeous cover.

Huge shout out thanks to my agent, Nicole Resciniti at The Seymour Agency, for your advice and your guidance. You are my rock, and I'm so blessed to have you in my corner.

Special acknowledgement goes out to the women who walk this writing journey with me every single day. The ones who make me laugh, who encourage and support, who offer great advice, plotting help, marathon sprinting runs, and sometimes just listen. Thank you to my writer besties: Michelle Major, Lana Williams, Anne Eliot, and Ginger Scott. XO

Big thanks goes out to my street team, Jennie's Page Turners, and for all of my readers: the people who have been with me from the start, my loyal readers, my dedicated fans, the ones who have read my stories, who have laughed and cried with me, who have fallen in love with my heroes and have clamored for more! Whether you have been with me since the first book or just discovered me with this book, know that I write these stories for you, and I can't thank you enough for reading them. Sending love, laughter, and big Colorado hugs to you all!

About the Author

Jennie Marts is the USA TODAY bestselling author of award-winning books filled with love, laughter, and always a happily ever after. She is living her own happily ever after in the mountains of Colorado with her husband, two dogs, and a parakeet who loves to tweet to the oldies. She's addicted to Diet Coke, adores Cheetos, and believes you can't have too many books, shoes, or friends.

Jennie loves to hear from readers. Follow her on Facebook at Jennie Marts Books, or Twitter at @JennieMarts. Visit her at www.jenniemarts.com and sign up for her newsletter to keep up with the latest news and releases.